WHAT YOU SOW

Also by Wallace Ford

The Pride

Published by Dafina Books

WHAT YOU SOW

WALLACE FORD

Kensington Publishing Corp.
http://www.kensingtonbooks.com

DAFINA BOOKS are published by

Kensington Publishing Corp.
850 Third Avenue
New York, NY 10022

All Kensington Titles, Imprints, and Distributed Lines are available at special quantity discounts for bulk purchases for sales promotions, premiums, fund-raising, and educational or institutional use. Special book excerpts or customized printings can also be created to fit specific needs. For details, write or phone the office of the Kensington special sales manager: Kensington Publishing Corp., 850 Third Avenue, New York, NY 10022, attn: Special Sales Department, Phone: 1-800-221-2647.

Dafina and the Dafina logo Reg. U.S. Pat. & TM Off.

ISBN-13: 978-0-7582-0955-9
ISBN-10: 0-7582-0955-X

First trade paperback printing: November 2006
First mass market printing: April 2012

10 9 8 7 6 5 4 3 2 1

Printed in the United States of America

To my mother, Carmen Ford
(1926–   )

ROCK WITH ME

I can't even remember a time
When loving you
Was not a part of my every day
And my every tomorrow
And I cannot wait to feel the rhythm of your heartbeat
Turning on the syncopation of my heart
And I know that our souls will continue
To dance
For
Ever

—WF

ACKNOWLEDGMENTS

I wanted to avoid clichés in writing every aspect of this book, including the acknowledgments. But some things simply cannot be avoided. And I really must thank my friends, family and colleagues for their support and inspiration.

I want to especially acknowledge my son, Wallace III, who is only nine years old as this book is going to press. It will be a few years before he will be reading this and understanding what the great hopes and promises that are a part of his present and his future really mean.

It is a simple truth that children are our future. But children are also our present and the evolution of our past. This book is about hopes and excellence and dreams that don't come true and some dreams that actually do become reality.

So it is only fitting that I acknowledge my son, who is a dream come true and his cousins: Amina, T.J., and Brian; Wallace's friends—his peers—who have blessed the reality that is the planet Earth: Adonay and Hanna and J.J. and Zoë and Chad and Dejanee and Amanda and Graham and Jared and Justin and Julian and Gibran and Zara and Laila and Emily and Nico and Alex and Miles and Brandon and Max and Danielle, and all the other little dreamers who have already made this world a better place and who will do even more as they make their own dreams come true.

Of course this book would not have been written without the support of my agent, Marie Brown, and the patience of my editors at Kensington Publishing, Karen Thomas and Stacey Barney. To each of them I offer my eternal gratitude.

IF

If you can keep your head when all about you
Are losing theirs and blaming it on you;
If you can trust yourself when all men doubt you,
But make allowance for their doubting too;
If you can wait and not be tired by waiting,
Or, being lied about, don't deal in lies,
Or, being hated, don't give way to hating,
And yet don't look too good, nor talk too wise;

If you can dream—and not make dreams your
    master;
If you can think—and not make thoughts your
    aim;
If you can meet with triumph and disaster
And treat those two impostors just the same;
If you can bear to hear the truth you've spoken
Twisted by knaves to make a trap for fools,
Or watch the things you gave your life to broken,
And stoop and build 'em up with wornout tools;

If you can make one heap of all your winnings
And risk it on one turn of pitch-and-toss,
And lose, and start again at your beginnings
And never breathe a word about your loss;
If you can force your heart and nerve and sinew
To serve your turn long after they are gone,
And so hold on when there is nothing in you
Except the Will which says to them: "Hold on";

If you can talk with crowds and keep your virtue,
Or walk with kings—nor lose the common touch;
If neither foes nor loving friends can hurt you;
If all men count with you, but none too much;
If you can fill the unforgiving minute
With sixty seconds' worth of distance run—
Yours is the Earth and everything that's in it,
And—which is more—you'll be a Man, my son!

—Rudyard Kipling

CHAPTER I

Gordon

Come See About Me

I guess that this must be a pretty close approximation of what hell is going to be like. I don't remember a whole lot about what I have taken to calling the Battle of New Orleans. As best as I can tell, it was about four years ago when I passed out in a hotel room in New Orleans while sampling cocaine, champagne and four of the freakiest bitches that New Orleans had to offer.

I have had a lot of time to think. In fact, all I have had is time to think. My newfound friend Ray Beard was in the hotel room with me, and I'll be damned if I know what happened after I felt something like an elephant kick me in the chest before I fell face first into the carpet. I do remember Ray making what sounded like a bubbling, gurgling-type noise before he collapsed and fell down next to me.

I could not move a muscle, but out of the corner of my eye, I could see Ray mumbling and drooling with his eyes rolling around in his head like jet-propelled pinballs. I also remember hearing glasses breaking, champagne buckets being knocked over and the unmistakable hiss of cocaine being snorted and scraped into various bags and other highly mobile receptacles. And I will never forget seeing two of those bitches arguing over the contents of my wallet: probably four or five thousand dollars and a few credit cards.

It was one hell of a way for a celebration to come to an end. After all, Ray and I were on top of the world. He had helped me engineer the sweet, sweet, sweetest, sweet double-cross of Diedre Douglas, Jerome Hardaway and Paul Taylor. Smart-ass Paul had encouraged Diedre, Jerome and me to merge our firms and start up something called Morningstar Financial Services. One of the first projects that my new partners and I were to announce to the public was our support of the incumbent mayor of New Orleans, Prince Lodrig, in his quest for reelection.

But Diedre, Jerome and Paul hadn't counted on the sweet backdoor move that I engineered, with a little bit of help from Jerome's former protégé, Ray Beard. We secretly supported the challenger, a manipulating, pliant and totally corrupt knucklehead by the name of Percy Broussard. By raising money through Ray's new firm and getting some outright lies about Lodrig published in the *Times-*

Picayune, New Orleans's leading newspaper, Broussard won the primary in an upset.

I sometimes spend entire days thinking about what Paul's face must have looked like when he saw Ray and me standing behind Broussard on the stage at the victory celebration that night. I bet his eyes popped out like they do in the cartoons—replete with springs and that "boing" sound effect.

I thought that I had thought of everything. I had moved funds from my former firm, G.S. Perkins, out of the reach of my Morningstar "partners." I also made sure that there was no way that my scheming bitch of a wife, Kenitra, would be able to get anywhere near the Bahamian bank where my funds were located—at least, where I had put a good amount of my money. I never have believed in having just one backup plan.

But that night, in the Presidential Suite of the Windsor Court Hotel in New Orleans, Ray Beard and I decided we owed ourselves a private party of epic proportions. So I arranged for the cocaine and the champagne and the women. Actually, Ray had to be persuaded to join in, and I remember wondering if his hesitancy was due to guilt—he had recently married a New York City television reporter, Monique Jefferson—or to an aversion to being around too many women, or women at all.

Frankly, I could care less, but lying in a hospital bed for God knows how long gives a person time to think about damn near everything. Like I think about the fact that I can see and hear everything going on around me, but I cannot speak or move a muscle. I feel like I have been suspended in amber.

And because I must seem like I am in some type of goddamn coma, people walk and talk around me like I am just a piece of furniture. Nobody looks at me except as some kind of clinical experiment. I have tubes and wires stuck into every part of me, and every day, someone comes in and washes me, changes my bed linen and moves my arms and legs so that my muscles don't atrophy completely. I have to say that the care is pretty good. The staff here even lifts me up and moves me around so that I don't get bedsores or infections.

I pay special attention when the doctors come in the room, trying to listen for a clue, a hint, a shred of information, that will let me know when I am going to get back to being myself. I have heard words like "catatonic" and "long-term coma" and "suspended animation," but I have not heard a syllable that lets me know when I can get up out of this bed and start kicking some ass again. And there are some asses that will be kicked, that's for sure.

I just can't wait to get started. I have a lot of plans and bright ideas that I am only too happy to share with all of my so-called friends and my lovely, faithful, loyal wife, Kenitra.

CHAPTER 2

Sture

Standing in the Shadows of Love

Since I came to America, romance has been a somewhat elusive element in my life. I have had my fun, flings—amorous adventures that make me smile as hints of their memories cross the horizon of my mind. It's pretty hard to be young and single and not have fun in New York City. When you are involved with running a place like Dorothy's By the Sea, it's almost impossible to avoid having fun.

But romance . . . that has been more elusive. I have thought that I have fallen in love on more than one occasion. But I have always found that the woman that I loved was not the person who I thought she was, and reality has come crashing over my head like some persistent, eternal wave that has been intent on beating some sense into my head.

This state of affairs—no pun intended—has not had a melancholy effect on me. I have seen too many good people do too many bad things in the name of love. While I have been curious about immersing myself in the experience of true romance, true life has made me something of a cynic when it comes to the sometimes-opposing axes of love and happiness.

Of course, the reason that I mention any of this is that I am now officially, truly and absolutely in love. I tried to deny it to myself. I tried to deny it to Kenitra. And we tried to deny it to each other. But I now know what those love songs are all talking about—the power of love is an undeniable power, and I am loving every minute of it. I am particularly enjoying the delicious improbability of it all.

After all, I had seen Kenitra with Gordon, and with Gordon's driver Alex, over the past few years, and I was witness to the misery and the contrived passion that seemed to form an imprisoning web that she no longer tried to escape. It would be hard to miss the signs of degradation of her body and spirit, and it was hard to believe that she could ever find her way back to herself.

After all, Kenitra Perkins used to be Kenitra, the media star, supermodel, fashion icon and internationally adored personality. Born Kenitra Simpson in a middle-class neighborhood in Chicago, she combined beauty, ambition and a disarming personality into a formidable arsenal that left men helpless and women growling with envy. She became famous, wealthy and worshipped. She also became one of those one-name icons like Madonna and Michael and Cher and Naomi and

Aretha. You would be foolish to inquire as to her last name.

I just cannot begin to remember when I fell in love with Kenitra. But I know that during one of her infrequent visits to check on Gordon, she stopped at Dorothy's and asked me to sit with her, as she didn't want to drink alone.

Like it was yesterday, I can remember when I sat down on the banquette where she was sitting, delicately sipping from a flute of champagne and then licking her lips like some kind of impossibly beautiful fairy whore. Working at Dorothy's, I was used to maintaining my composure in all kinds of impossibly bizarre situations. But there was something about Kenitra's subtle but obvious tongue, flicking its tip my way, that turned my mind in the direction of twisted, sweaty sheets and moans that echoed into the universe. And up to that point, she had not said a word.

"How have you been, Mrs. Perkins?"

"Sture, please, call me Kenitra. And I'm fine."

It was amazing how a few innocuous words could hold such power and inference that they carried my very soul to the far corners of the universe of passion and longing. What was even more amazing was that I had seen and spoken to Kenitra Perkins for years and had never felt even a tremor of desire or passion.

But when she focused her golden eyes of love on me, I was simply helpless. From that moment, I was putty in her hands. I was her slave for life. A sledgehammer would have been less subtle.

I tried to pretend that I still had some control over the situation—and myself. Of course, I didn't.

I remember wondering what it was about Gordon Perkins that he could so totally dominate a woman who seemed to have the power to control any being on the planet that she chose for her own. It was a mystery then, and it remains a mystery to this very day.

"You look lovely, as always. How long are you in town this time?"

"How long would you like for me to stay in New York, Sture? And please, be honest."

Before I could think, my heart overruled my head. And then I spoke. But it was as if this wondrous world of love and lust beckoned me, and her words and her eyes and her tongue extended to me a very special one-time-only invitation to go to heaven.

"If you could stay for one week, Kenitra, and I saw you for one hour, it would be the most wonderful week of my life."

She smiled. I thought I might have blushed. I certainly had shocked myself.

"In that case, Sture, I will stay for a week. But you have to make me a promise."

"A promise?"

"Promise me that you will let me be your friend and your lover for one week. After that . . . we'll see."

"It's an offer I can't refuse . . . Kenitra." I had such a collision of feelings and emotions that I could barely choke out the words. In my dreams, I might have been desired by Kenitra Perkins, but not in my life, not in my lifetime. And now, here she was, wanting to be my friend and lover.

"What time are you finished at Dorothy's tonight, Sture?"

"One o'clock."

"I'm at the Waldorf. Can I expect you to knock on the door of room thirty-two thirty-two at one-thirty?"

"The hounds of hell couldn't stop me" was the best riposte I could offer. After all, my heart was alternately threatening to stop and to burst out of my chest. My hands were sweating, and my loins—well, let's just say that my loin area was just about out of control.

And so, she left Dorothy's a few minutes later and I started to count the milliseconds until it was one o'clock. In the story of my life, the best, and the worst, was yet to come.

CHAPTER 3

Jerome

Just Ask the Lonely

After my wife Charmaine died, it amazed me how lonely a person could be in a city of eight million people. And, I personally knew thousands of those millions, and thousands more of those millions knew me.

Yet, when Charmaine passed away, it was like I was cast into a personal dungeon of loneliness. Nothing was the same without her. The movies, the cafés, the restaurants, the plays, the concerts, the very streets of the city—they all reminded me of the times that we had spent together, the moments that we had shared. And those reminders just plunged me into depths of depression and loneliness that made me feel as if some primordial monster was sitting on my chest, making my every breath an ordeal.

Every step, every breath, every moment, everything, reminded me of Charmaine, and everything ripped open the wounds in my very soul. She and I had been together for so long that I had stopped imagining being without her. And now, I was incomplete. I was off balance, all the time.

A thousand times a day, I turned expecting to see her smile. A thousand times, I heard the phone ring and expected to hear her voice. A thousand times, I reached for her hand and grasped nothing but air. And it seemed as if a thousand times a day, tears came to my eyes for no reason except that she was gone from my life.

Our sons needed me, now more than ever. Morningstar and my partners depended on me, now more than ever. And so, after Charmaine's death, after her funeral, after placing an urn with her ashes on a special shelf in our living room, I knew that life had to go on. But knowing it and doing it were two entirely different things. And I found myself suffering more than I ever did when I knew that she was dying.

I thought of myself as living in a special kind of hell. A hell that I didn't deserve. A hell that would last forever. A hell from which there was no escape. I wished for relief from this awful misery. I prayed for relief from this awful misery. And there was no relief, no answer to my prayers. Or so it seemed at the time.

CHAPTER 4

Sture

Nowhere to Run, Nowhere to Hide

It occurs to me that it might be a good idea for me to let everyone know who's who in this story. My name is Sture Jorgensen, I was born in Norway and came to New York City to find a better life than what I knew in Bergen, and, like those of many immigrants to America, so many of my dreams have come true.

I started out living in Queens on the couch of my sister, Ilse, washing so many dishes in so many restaurants that I lost count of both a long, long time ago. And then I got my big break.

While working at the Water Club, one of the great restaurants in New York City, I filled in for a waiter friend who had a date with a double-jointed contortionist that just couldn't wait. I guess I impressed the owner, Buzzy O'Keefe, and from that night on, my life was different.

I became a full-time waiter, and then a host and maitre d' of the entire restaurant. During this dizzying rise to the heights of the restaurant universe, I met Paul Taylor, and in the process, I was introduced to a fascinating part of New York City and America, The Pride.

Paul is a tall, elegant and profoundly brilliant black attorney who is a part of this informal grouping called The Pride. He is a graduate of Dartmouth College and Harvard Law School, but you would be hard-pressed to ever remember him telling anybody about his many credentials.

Paul has worked pretty much his entire professional life as an attorney, managing an eclectic practice that has included movie stars, investment banks and countries in the Caribbean and Africa. He has lived a life that most of us only dream about, traveling the world, dining in the best restaurants and staying in the best hotels on the planet. Loving and being loved by some of the most beautiful women on the planet as well.

But even with Paul Hiawatha Taylor, all is not what it seems. Along with all the glamour and pleasure and outright opulence, he has his private pain. A few years before we met, his father died suddenly in the hospital after a "routine surgery" was botched in some unfathomable, unknowable manner. A few months later, his younger brother died in a hang gliding accident in the mountains of Northern California.

And then, the woman whom I heard Paul describe as the love of his life, the beautiful lounge singer Samantha Gideon, died of throat cancer a few years after he and I met. It was an awful event that was simultaneously devastating and transforming for Paul.

After Samantha's death, Paul seemed to be more serious about his work than he had ever been. Most of us didn't think Paul could be more driven or obsessed with work . . . and we were wrong. He was the driving force behind the Morningstar deal that merged the firms owned by Diedre, Jerome and Gordon. And after Gordon's sabotage fiasco in New Orleans, Paul was the one who kept everyone on course so that the firm was able to become the successful enterprise that he had envisioned in the first place.

As interestingly, he reunited with his ex-wife, Diedre, and soon after the Morningstar deal was closed and the firm had recovered from Gordon's broadside, they remarried, and now they have a young son. Paul calls their son, Paul Jr. or P.J., the Last Gasp of the Baby Boom. Paul always has had a talent for truly surprising his friends and adversaries, and this was just one more example of this quirky talent of his.

Paul had been a regular patron of the Water Club when we first became acquaintances, then friends and finally partners in the restaurant-club, Dorothy's By the Sea, that Paul, Jerome Hardaway and Diedre Douglas now own—in which I am a very minority partner, no pun intended.

In retrospect, it would seem that I knew about The Pride before I learned about it. After all, Paul Taylor was not the first or only black patron of the

Water Club. However, since there were so few
blacks that were customers of the restaurant, I
would always notice them. And since far fewer
were anything like regular customers, it was hard
not to remember the repeat visitors. And in any
event, it would have been almost impossible to forget Paul Taylor.

Working at the Water Club was an education for
me in many ways. I learned, for example, that
clowns and idiots come in any and all colors, that
there are as many black idiots and clowns as white
idiots and clowns. There are the kind that are too
loud, too ostentatious, too ready to treat waiters
and restaurant staff as their own personal servants,
or worse.

But Paul is the person who introduced me to
The Pride. I can still remember his exact words:

> *"The Pride" is the term that I have used to refer
> to the black men and women, lions and lionesses
> actually, who have risen to prominence on Wall
> Street, in corporate America and in the canyons of
> its law firms, accounting firms and management
> consulting agglomerations. Being in New York, I
> am, of course, speaking of the New York version of
> The Pride. But The Pride is in Atlanta, Detroit,
> Chicago, Houston, Dallas, Philadelphia, Wash-
> ington, Miami, New Orleans, Oakland, San
> Francisco, Denver, St. Louis and Los Angeles. Ac-
> tually, The Pride is to be found all over America.*
>
> *As a charter member of The Pride, I know that
> we are the beneficiaries of the seismic changes that
> hit America in the sixties and seventies. It was a
> change that allowed some black men and women*

to actually achieve on the basis of their ability and some limited opportunity.

The Pride consists of some of the most interesting, talented, intelligent, bizarre, insufferable, heroic, treacherous and memorable people that I can ever hope to know. I don't kid myself: whatever I see in The Pride—the good and the bad—is in me too.

Many of them I genuinely like and some I love like brothers and sisters. Others are just too grasping, self-centered and opportunistic to suit my tastes. However, these are character traits that have virtually insured their success in these United States of America.

Paul has been my mentor when it comes to The Pride, New York City, America and just life on this planet. He has been more than a partner and a business colleague. He has been a friend, and he is one of the people whom I admire most on this planet.

And then there is Jerome Hardaway. Jerome is one of the principals of Morningstar Financial Services, the financial services firm that was Paul's brainchild and involved the merger of Jerome's firm with those of Diedre Douglas and Gordon Perkins.

Jerome is a graduate of Yale University and Columbia's School of Business, and he has, from the very beginning of his career, been one of the rising stars of Wall Street. His firm, the Hardaway Group, was one of the great success stories of the financial world when he joined in the merger that Paul had proposed.

But there is a lot more to Jerome's story. For starters, this tall, elegant, articulate and remarkably controlled investment banker used to be a gangbanger in Philadelphia. With both feet on the highway to the penitentiary or the cemetery, he was plucked away from those bleak prospects by the Star Search Foundation, which, along with the National Scholarship Service for Negro Students and the A Better Chance Foundation, changed the lives of so many bright young black men and women in the 1960s and thereby changed America.

And so, Jerome went from the hard streets of Philly to the ivy-covered halls of Yale and Columbia, and then to Wall Street, to overwhelming financial and professional success. He also married Charmaine Cumberbatch, the lovely and loyal and incredibly supportive woman from Shaker Heights and Mount Holyoke who completed Jerome. They had two sons, a wonderful home, a wonderful life, and then multiple sclerosis struck her.

And that was when the whole world saw what Charmaine and their sons already knew: Jerome never wavered in his dedication to Charmaine. Despite his tremendous responsibilities running the Hardaway Group and then, as co-chair, Morningstar, he was with her for every doctor's appointment, every treatment, every health episode.

Although he could afford all of the home-care personnel that they might have needed, he still attended to her, and the boys, constantly and without complaint or pause. He took the pledge of loyalty "through sickness and in health" literally, and he showed his love of Charmaine, with devotion and without complaint, to her dying day.

As fate would have it, multiple sclerosis was not what killed Charmaine. No one could have anticipated the breast cancer that struck her so suddenly and killed her with terrible swiftness. And when she died, it seemed to all of us—friends, family and colleagues—that the cancer almost killed Jerome too.

He survived, but sometimes, it seems just barely. I have read about the phenomenon of twins and how close they can be—so close that when one of them dies, the other one is psychically and spiritually and physically diminished. Even though Jerome and Charmaine were not biological twins, they were clearly that most unique of couples: true soul mates. And it was painful watching Jerome summon the courage and energy to try to cope with the astounding blow that life had dealt him.

And now, a few words about Gordon Perkins. Gordon was perhaps the most malevolent and dangerous person that I have ever had the misfortune to know. And I am sure that there are hundreds, if not thousands, of acquaintances of Gordon who feel the same way.

Born in New Rochelle, New York, to a middle-class family, Gordon displayed nothing in his early years to indicate that he would become a latter-day version of a cross between Gordon Gekko and Ras the Destroyer. To put it simply, he has always been an awful man.

Whether in his personal life or in business, he was not to be trusted. Correction: In all the years I have known him, and known of him, Gordon could always be trusted to do the wrong thing, the worst thing, in any situation—any time, anywhere.

It was common knowledge that Gordon borrowed money from his first father-in-law to start his investment-banking firm. What is not-so-commonly known is that when the company was assured of success, he sent his wife the check to pay off her father in full with divorce papers attached to the check.

Many members of The Pride, and others, thought they knew about the abuse and cruelty that Gordon visited upon his second wife, Kenitra Perkins. But Kenitra is the only one who knows the entire truth, and she has never told me the entire story. But I sense that it is too grisly and twisted to be recounted without the teller and the listener both recoiling in horror.

I would guess you could say that he is a little more trustworthy at the moment, since he has been laid up in the Critical Intensive Care Unit at New York Hospital for the past four years, trapped in a coma. More about how he got that way in a minute. But with Gordon, you can never really know.

I know that I still don't trust Gordon, and I do know that Kenitra believes that the coma is all part of some bizarre and insane plot that Gordon has hatched to wreak more havoc in her life and to extract a few more triple-distilled ounces of pain and misery from her. I know that it sounds crazy. And I can't say that I blame her in the least.

You just would have to know Gordon Perkins to know what I mean.

CHAPTER 5

Kenitra

My Favorite Things

From the first time I saw him lying in that hospital bed, intubated, wired and monitored like some kind of monstrous experiment gone awry, I couldn't banish the thought that I was looking at some kind of malevolent creature that was simply at rest. He reminded me of a somnolent cobra: sleeping, but always dangerous, always vicious, and always to be avoided at all costs.

From the very first time that I saw Gordon in the hospital, I never stood close to his bed. When the doctors suggested that speaking to him might stimulate some kind of neural response that would bring his brain out of hibernation, I simply went mute. The thought of Gordon awake and alive made my flesh crawl.

I remember that September day when Paul Taylor called to tell me the news of the New Orleans debacle. I was still living in our Park Avenue apartment at the time, the site of so many degrading scenarios that I never felt completely clean when I walked across the threshold.

I also remember that there was nothing that Paul told me that surprised me. Certainly, the cocaine binge was not a shock to me. Gordon had used the seemingly satanic power of coke to control my body and my mind, and to abuse both, to an extent I never would have believed if I hadn't lived it all for myself.

The hookers, the involvement of Jerome's former protégé, Ray Beard, certainly were not surprises. For Gordon, screwing women was not a sexual experience; it was a power experience. And he was addicted to power.

Gordon was also addicted to corruption; he enjoyed corrupting other people—men, women, it made little difference to him. He always enjoyed exerting his power by bringing people down, by making them confront their frailties, in the cruelest and most undeniable ways possible. So it was no surprise to me that Raymond Russell Beard III, who seemed to me a sycophantic wannabe, would come under Gordon's spell—and be doomed like some pedestrian house fly caught in a kaleidoscopic web from which there was no escape.

Ray is lucky that he didn't die. I guess. Although, I hear that after spending a couple of years in a rehabilitation home trying to recover from the near-fatal stroke and heart attack that he suffered during the New Orleans Fiasco, he was trying to get Jerome to put in a good word for him at Morningstar, as he wanted to get back into the finance business. And through it all, his wife, Monique Jefferson, the news reporter that he married just before his near-death experience in New Orleans, has stayed with him.

I had lunch with Monique during a few of my infrequent visits to New York, and she told me how she practically held his hand during the seemingly eternal rehabilitation process—helping him learn how to read, how to speak, how to walk, how to care for himself. And she was the one who went to Jerome to beg him to give Ray another chance. Paul told me that he, Diedre and Jerome were thinking about it.

I am still in awe of Monique. Her loyalty to Ray, in spite of his obvious weakness and very public betrayal of her, is based in either true love or true stupidity. But, to be kind and to be honest, having gotten to know Monique, I am certain that it is a matter of true love. And who am I to question someone's choice of lovers? After all, I married Gordon Perkins.

But that September evening, I remember that I hoped and prayed that Gordon would die, all the time knowing that fate would not be that kind to me or to the world. And I remember Paul telling me that he would help me out of the terrible place in which I found myself even as it seemed that his grand plan for Morningstar was collapsing around his ears. And I will always be grateful to Paul for his kindness during my moment of need even though he himself was facing disaster at the very same time.

Well, Paul may not be a magician, but he could

have given Merlin and David Copperfield runs for their money over those next few weeks. While somehow managing to repair the damage that Gordon had visited upon the Morningstar joint venture—and upon his partners, Jerome and Diedre—he also found the time to trace some ten million dollars that Gordon had put in a Bahamian account in my name, thinking he would hide this money from his new partners—and from me.

Paul told me that he routed the money through a bank in Geneva, then to a bank in the Isle of Man and finally to a bank in Vanuatu to which only he and I had access. He also helped me purchase a modestly palatial condominium with three bedrooms and a gorgeous view of the Pacific Ocean in Venice Beach, California. His thinking, with which I agreed, was that Venice Beach was far enough off the beaten path that very few members of The Pride would be poking into my business. And since I lived practically next to LAX (Los Angeles International Airport), I could still get to New York to check on Gordon and my other business matters from time to time.

It was during that time, that I began to see Sture—and that was when my life changed again.

CHAPTER 6

Gordon

Bitches' Brew

During all the time before my "accident," I could always count on one friend. The Dark Lord. He seemed to be the only one who cared about the same things that mattered to me. While he never shared any of the cocaine that I would offer him, he always seemed to come around when I had a few lines or grams or ounces around. Sometimes he would bring the coke to me.

And it was the Dark Lord who always seemed to have the right idea at the right time. Whether it was tying up Kenitra and beating her and abusing her in the most creative ways or devising the best way to subvert the Morningstar merger, it was the Dark Lord who was there at my side.

But during my hospital confinement, for many months I found that I was fully conscious twenty-four hours a day but unable to move or speak or respond to any external stimuli. At first, I thought that I had simply lost my motherfucking mind and that I was imprisoned in my own body for the rest of my life. And the strangest thing was that all the while that I felt fully conscious, I also don't think that I ever actually went to sleep.

And the worst part was that the Dark Lord was nowhere to be found. At least at first.

And then, just like that, one night, it seemed like I had fallen asleep. But in the middle of the night, I could see the Dark Lord walk past the sleeping orderlies and nurses, like an assassin slipping past dozing sentries. And then he was at my side. And then he was reminding me of all the good times that we had had together and how I had to get my shit together so that we could go out and have some real fun—get some blow, hook up with some bitches, kick some ass, just like in the old days, which were not that long ago.

"How the fuck am I going to go anywhere? You see all these tubes and wires and shit?"

The Dark Lord didn't say a word. He just started yanking and pulling—tubes, monitors, catheters, wires—removing all of those biotethers one by one, until I lay there on the bed free for the first time in at least two years. I thought that I was going to die at that very moment, but instead, I felt fine. It was like a miracle.

"That's great, but how am I going to go anywhere? All I have is this damn diaper and hospital gown. I don't even have a pair of fucking shoes!"

Up to that moment, I had not noticed that my only friend had a gym-bag-sized black leather satchel in his hand. He put it on the bed, opened it up and started pulling items out. There was a pair of jeans that seemed too big for me, and I am a pretty big guy. There was a checkered flannel shirt, a white T-shirt, some Timberland shoes, an oversized denim jacket, a pair of blue striped boxer shorts, a Los Angeles Lakers baseball cap, a pair of Gucci sunglasses and some gold necklaces and bracelets.

I didn't have to be told twice. I put on the clothes and checked myself out in the mirror. I would have fit in on just about any street corner in Harlem, South Central LA or the South Side of Chicago, or on just about any rap video playing on BET.

It was already after midnight and I had sense enough to know that I needed to have my ass back in that hospital bed by the time those assholes on the night shift woke up. So I followed the Dark Lord past the sleeping nurses and orderlies and went downstairs to the hospital lobby and out into the street. Nobody seemed to notice us; it almost seemed as if we were invisible to everyone in the hospital.

As we got into the taxicab that magically materialized at the curbside of the circular driveway in front of New York Hospital, the Dark Lord passed me a small piece of foil brimming with cocaine and a small plastic spoon. As I gratefully snorted the first clouds of coke that I had had in what seemed like years, I heard the Dark Lord tell me that during our adventure in the evening, I would be known as G-Perk.

And then our adventure began.

CHAPTER 7

Paul

In My Solitude

As I sat in my admittedly nondescript offices on West 57th Street, in the heart of Manhattan, I was in my normal state of being nearly over-whelmed by work, work and more work. There was the memo that I needed to get to the minister of trade and industry in the West African country of Benin. There was the Broadway actress who wanted to negotiate a new deal with one of the largest talent-management companies in the United States. There were the paperwork and rituals of business related to Dorothy's By the Sea, even though Sture does most of the heavy lifting. And then there was Morningstar.

During the seven days of the week, a day never goes by that I am not working on some aspect of the investment banking firm that I helped to organize by getting Gordon Perkins, Jerome Hardaway and my then-ex-wife and now-wife, Diedre Douglas, to merge their respective firms. Morningstar Financial Services survived its spectacular betrayal by Gordon, and in the three years since the now-infamous New Orleans Fiasco, Morningstar had become one of the most successful boutique investment banking firms in the United States.

As counsel to Morningstar, I have been involved in the firm's every deal, every corporate transaction, and every aspect of organization. Morningstar has been involved in deals all over the United States. As time and success ensued, Jerome and Diedre started making noises about using the London base of operations as a jumping-off point to start doing business in Africa, particularly in South Africa.

And, of course, every move that is made by Morningstar means more work for me and the few new associates that I have had to hire to handle all of the paperwork that accompanies this activity. And, given that Morningstar is my best client by far, I am not complaining. But lots of fees mean a lot of work, which means a lot of stress. All the time.

And through it all, I have been trying to reconcile all of the work that I do with all of the work that Diedre has to do in her position as co-chair of Morningstar, as well as with the work both of us have to do for our marriage and our son. Trying to do all of these things simultaneously brings to mind the image of a clown juggling roaring chainsaws while riding a unicycle across the Grand

Canyon on a rapidly fraying filament of a tight-rope.

When my fiancée Samantha Gideon died in the middle of the Morningstar merger negotiations, Diedre and I suddenly moved from being friends, business colleagues and reasonably adjusted ex-spouses to passionate lovers and then husband and wife. And then we became father and mother to our wonderful son, Paul Jr. And it all made sense at the time.

And, at the time, all of our friends and colleagues thought that our story was kind of a modern-day fairy tale, where love prevails over everything. And for a while, fantasy and reality accommodated each other quite nicely. But at some point, dawn arrives.

When Samantha died, Diedre was caring and compassionate and loving. When I needed some-one to be on my side, she was there for me. And I can never forget how kind and wonderful she can be. Which makes the current state of affairs more puzzling and perplexing.

You might think that by working together on Morningstar every day that we could grow closer. The opposite has been the case, however. Diedre is so very busy. I am so very busy.

It seems that rarely a week goes by that one of us is not out of town for at least two or three days. Whatever time we do spend together is involved with raising our son and trying to find the right schools, arranging playdates and his attendance at birthday parties, and doing all of the things that go with trying to raise one of the last heirs of the Baby Boom in New York City.

Somehow, amazingly, perversely, all the things that we have shared and that we do together seem to have drawn us apart. Romance is barely a memory, and the passion that used to flow between us like some lavalike river of emotion became a memory that was more and more difficult to revive.

I had not given up hope, however, and I continued to believe that the love that we had between us would revive the most important part of our relationship. I became afraid that our friendship was at risk. In the meantime, while hoping, I absolutely welcomed the chance to assume the loving duties of fatherhood every day. The loving duties of being a husband—became something of a challenge.

There was also the bittersweet story of Jerome and his loss of Charmaine. Jerome and I always had a friendly relationship, although I would not describe us as bosom buddies. Ours was more of a relationship based on respect and affinity and appreciation. Our work together was always professionally enjoyable, although we both are sufficiently committed to our work that we have had very little time for anything but business during these early years of Morningstar Financial Services. And then Charmaine died.

When Charmaine died, Jerome joined the sad secret society of those who have been nearly devastated by the loss of a truly loved and treasured someone. I had been thrice initiated into this remorseless tribe—by the sudden and unexpected deaths of my father and brother and by the expected but nevertheless sudden death of Samantha. And now, Jerome had joined the club.

A word about this unwanted membership that he and I share. It is a part of the human condition to experience death, and billions of us through the history of this planet have learned to deal with death through the rituals of funerals and eulogies and wakes and memorials and burials and cremations.

But it is one thing to lose an elderly parent who has lived a full life and seen his or her children grow to adulthood and pursue their own lives and adventures. It is one thing to lose one of your work colleagues or fraternity brothers or college classmates that you might have known and loved.

It is quite another thing to lose that someone (and there are never that many special people in anyone's life) who was a part of the foundation of your every day and your life experience. It is quite another thing to start the day or the week or the year expecting that this person would continue to be a part of your life just like your arm or your heart. And it is quite another thing when, through disease or accident or just pure capricious, random and ferocious fate, that person is suddenly gone one day. Never to return.

That is how I felt when my father died. That is how I felt when my brother died. That is how I felt when Samantha died. And I know that is how Jerome has felt ever since Charmaine died over a year ago.

He has told me how he has to stop himself from calling her a dozen times every day. And I know, I still think that when the phone rings, I will find Samantha or my father or brother on the line.

Jerome has talked about hearing her voice calling his name as he walked through a crowd in Grand Central Station or in the American Airlines lounge for first-class passengers at Kennedy Airport. I know, I have seen my brother's face through the window of a subway car leaving the station a hundred times.

And, Jerome has told me about the ultimate phase of initiation, an experience that he and I also share. About three months after she died, Charmaine appeared in a dream. She was healthy, radiant, no longer in a wheelchair. Her multiple sclerosis had been banished and she was no longer ravaged by cancer and chemotherapy—these were all in her past life.

Jerome said that she smiled and laughed and teased and comforted him. She told him that she was fine and that she would always be there for the boys and him; they just had to look for her.

His encounter with Charmaine was so real, so vivid, that he said he leaped out of bed and searched the house looking for her, swearing that she was alive and that the real, live Charmaine had been in the bedroom with him. And then he knew. He knew that she was gone. And he knew that she would always be with him.

And it is that sadness and that priceless nugget of happiness that all members of the sad secret society carry for the rest of their lives.

CHAPTER 8

Jerome

Blame It on My Youth

During the past two years, surviving the loss of Charmaine has been a daily battle. Work has helped—being busy kind of takes my mind off things for a few seconds every now and then. Raising the boys is the remaining treasure of my life, and everything that I do with them keeps her memory alive for all of us.

I will be eternally grateful for Paul's special friendship during these darkest of days. I know he understands that expressions of commiseration, while well intentioned, cannot begin to find someone trapped in the quicksand of grief and pain and loss. Nevertheless, knowing that someone has been there for me has meant a lot.

Diedre, Paul and I have been working like

beasts over these past few years getting Morning-star in a position to recover from Gordon's New Orleans Fiasco. Since then, there has also been the matter of building the firm that resulted from the merger of our three operations, and trying to make that new firm successful. And, just as Paul had predicted at the luncheon at the Water Club, what seems like a million years ago, our combined forces have created a formidable synergy that was starting to make some real progress in the world of finance known as Wall Street.

And then one afternoon, it occurred to me that the sadness and the manic nature of business and the constant themes of grief and loss needed to be put in their proper places. It was a Wednesday in September, the afternoons were getting darker earlier, and I had a couple of business meetings in Los Angeles on Thursday and Friday.

On the spur of the moment, I called Paul. He didn't know it when he picked up the phone, but we were going to California. I didn't think that Paul would offer too much resistance.

"Paul, it's Jerome. Are you trying to work your way into a mental institution as usual?"

"Jerome, you would have to be about the last person to lecture someone on being crazy about their work. I figure that they have already fitted you for a three-piece, pinstriped straitjacket . . . although I do think the asylum attendants will have some problem buckling it once they get a look at your face."

"Paul, I am so glad that you are a lawyer."

"And why is that, my brother?"

"Because if you were a comedian, you would be

starving to death and begging me and everybody
else for money."

"If that was a compliment, Jerome, it was a very
subtle one. And, you know, subtlety was never your
strong suit."

"Well, let me get right to the point, intergalactic
soul brother. We are going to Los Angeles tomorrow afternoon and coming back on Sunday. And
before you start yammering on and on about your
precious schedule and all the eight million ap-
pointments that you have and cannot possibly
reschedule, a couple of points.

"First, it's on Morningstar business, and that has
got to trump just about anything else that you have
to do. Second, since it is on Morningstar business,
Diedre is not going to give you too much static
about going. Third, since you are going with me,
she probably will trust your sorry ass not to get
into too much trouble. And finally, I have already
had my assistant, Berta, make the arrangements.
We have two seats reserved on an American Express corporate jet that a buddy of mine was kind
enough to offer when I mentioned that you and I
were going to LA."

"Well, I am glad that you were kind enough to
let my sorry ass know where I was going to be for
the next few days."

"Paul, on the flight back to New York, you will
be thanking me."

"Where have I heard that before?"

"Don't play hard to get, Paul. You and I both
need a break. So just let Diedre know that you
have to go to LA with me for a few days. Or should
I get permission for you?"

"Jerome, I think between the two of us, you might be the comedian."

"I don't hear you laughing, Paul."

"And you don't hear me saying no either. When you are right, you are right. Let's go to the left coast!"

"I knew there was a reason why I thought you were a smart guy. Berta will call you later today to let you know what time we have to get to Teterboro Airport in New Jersey to get on the Amex jet. We can ride together, and we will be in Hollywierd by tomorrow night."

"Jerome, I have never thought of you as a particularly spontaneous brother . . . but this is a great idea. Count me in!"

"Count yourself in, Paul. I will call you later tonight about our Friday meetings, but you can give me some thoughts as to how we can spend Friday night and Saturday."

"I'll see what I can come up with, Jerome."

"See you tomorrow."

When I hung up from my conversation with Paul, I thought about how my bright idea to roadtrip with Paul had started. There actually were several very important meetings that I had to attend regarding some entertainment and technology deals that were on the Morningstar radar screen. Having our esteemed counsel in the room would certainly up the ante in terms of expressing how serious we were about trying to get a deal done.

And then there were the thoughts that were born out of my solitude, out of my prison of loneliness. I knew I could not keep my sanity without finding some relief from this awful misery, as King Pleasure might have said many years ago.

But how did a trip to California come to mind? Interestingly enough, I was having a drink—by myself—at Dorothy's By the Sea when I happened to run into the Unholy Trio, Trini Satterfield, Ralph Watson and Jerry James. Trini, Ralph and Jerry were fixtures at Dorothy's, and while they each were a story in their own right, together they were something of a cross between a carnival and an asylum.

Trini was a somewhat legendary advertising executive and world-class jokester. I guess you could call him one of the original members of The Pride. Trini knew just about everyone worth knowing and to hear him tell it, he also knew just about everything.

And there was Ralph Watson. He was a third-generation Harlem undertaker with an MBA from Stanford. Ralph fancied himself as the quintessential *bon vivant* who, because of his family wealth, led a life of pleasure, luxury, ease and indulgence.

And then there was Jerry James. Jerry, who was a convicted felon as a teenager on a direct road to nowhere, somehow found his way to getting a high school diploma and college degree as a prison inmate. After being released from prison and obtaining his Master's of Public Administration from Columbia University's School of International and Public Affairs, he worked in senior positions for New York State governors Carey and Cuomo, as well as for New York City mayors Beame, Koch and Dinkins. He was now a management executive for a new foundation founded by one of the new dot-com billionaires that seemed to bloom by the dozens in the last decade of the twentieth century.

Jerry was loud, profane and amazingly hilarious. His propensity for drugs and alcohol was legendary. His sexual adventures were the stuff of myths and legends that would be told around campfires deep into the future.

But on this particular night last week, as I was enjoying my second (or was it my third?) Myer's Rum and tonic (with a wedge of lime), I heard Trini pontificating about California. For some unknown, godforsaken reason, the conversation intrigued me and I listened. And I learned.

CHAPTER 9

Jerome

Tracks of My Tears

As fate would have it, I already was thinking about making a trip to Los Angeles. There was a medium-sized film production company that was looking to raise capital to finance the creation of a television series based on the real lives of a famous politician, business executive, female sports figure and television personality.

The creative executives of this production company called it reality television. I had never heard of such a term at the time, and I figured that it might make some sense to learn a little bit more about this coming phenomenon in the broadcast industry.

There was also a quirky biotech project in Tarzana, east of LA, involving a Nobel Prize–winning biologist who was working on the technology that would allow doctors to "grow" organs—livers, hearts and lungs—on demand. It was a natural progression in the entire concept of cloning, and if it worked, it would change the world of medicine. Indeed, it would change the world.

As I was contemplating these weighty issues, I heard one of the Unholy Trio of Ralph, Jerry and Trini laugh more loudly than usual. This normally would not have gotten my attention, but then I heard Trini talking about California.

"Everybody knows, or should know, that of the forty-four people who founded the City of Los Angeles, twenty-six were black."

"Man, you are so full of shit!"

That would have been Jerry James. You could always count on him for sober and insightful commentary, no matter what the subject. Trini was implacable, however, and he pressed on with his peroration.

"Listen, my waterhead friend, and you just might learn something. Although I really doubt that it is possible, given your advanced age and diminishing brainpower."

"You can kiss my diminishing ass is what you can do."

"As I was saying, what is even more amazing is that the majority of the founders of San Francisco, San Jose and San Diego were of African descent. And, Orange County, Beverly Hills and Malibu were once owned by people of African descent."

I have to confess that at this point, I had to put my drink down. Either Trini was revealing some fable born of too many vodka cocktails and magnums of champagne, or there was some real un-

known history that I was learning for the very first
time. And now it was Ralph Watson's turn to
speak.

"Trini, you better not be making this shit up."

"The truth shall set you free, Ralph. Just finish
your drink and listen. The Picos, black Spanish-
speaking brothers named Pio and Andres—and,
by the way, Pio was twice governor of California—
owned San Fernando Valley, Whittier and the area
that we now know as Camp Pendleton."

"What in God's name possessed you to tell us all
of this shit, Trini? We are in fucking New York.
What the fuck do I care about California anyway?"

"Well, Jerry, I am going to try and be patient
with your sorry ass. The fact is that California is in
the media every day. What is more amazing to me
is that most of us know nothing about the fact that
the state is named after a black woman queen."

My jaw dropped involuntarily, the exact same
way that most jaws drop. It was now Ralph Watson's turn to put in his two cents.

"You mean to sit there and tell me that California was named after a black woman? A black
queen? You better explain some more or you will
have us thinking that you have gone back to the
glue-sniffing days of your youth."

"The name of the state of California begins with
a story read by the Spanish explorer Hernando
Cortés. That's right, the same Cortés who con-
quered Mexico and demolished the Aztec empire
before entering Baja California, continuing his
search for even more gold."

Trini's story had the ring of truth. Everyone at
the bar at Dorothy's went silent, or at least they be-

came less noisy, as he continued. He was clearly on a roll. A friend of mine has used the expression, "Coincidence is God's way of staying anonymous."

Perhaps it was a coincidence that I was thinking about going to Los Angeles just before Trini started in with his story about California. And perhaps it was a coincidence that Trini started to spin a tale about the black origins of the state of California that pretty much sealed the deal as far as my making the trip was concerned.

Even as Trini was speaking, I was looking forward to being in California and looking at the place with new eyes born of the historical perspective that I was hearing. Trini took a sip of his ever-present scotch on the rocks and continued.

"Actually, Cortés read the seventeenth-century best-selling adventure story written by a Spaniard named Garcia Ordonez de Montalvo. The name of the book was *The Exploits of Esplandian,* and it was published in Seville in 1510. It was written as a sequel to a popular Portuguese poem, 'Amadis de Guala.'"

By now, crazy-ass Trini Satterfield had not only managed to capture the attention of everyone at the bar at Dorothy's By the Sea, everyone within earshot was lending an ear. Relishing the attention, he reached into his jacket pocket and pulled out a few sheets of paper with something of a flourish.

"I have been reading about this whole black-California story on the Internet, and I printed out some background because I knew that there would be some nonbelieving, white-man-glorifying fools in the house. There's always one." Trini stared meaningfully at Jerry. Jerry looked up from his drink and gave him the finger, smiling all the while. Trini continued reading.

"Here is an excerpt from the book that gave rise to this black-California story that featured a nation composed entirely of fierce, powerful, wealthy black women:

"Know ye that at the right hand of the Indies there is an island named California, very close to that part of the terrestrial Paradise, which was inhabited by black women, without a single man among them, and that they lived in the manner of Amazons. They were robust of body, with strong and passionate hearts and great virtues. The island itself is one of the wildest in the world on account of the bold and craggy rocks. Their weapons were all made of gold. The island everywhere abounds with gold and precious stones, and upon it no other metal was found. The commanding Queen Califia ruled this mythical island.

"An island of fierce, powerful and wealthy black women? Hell, that sounds like right here in Manhattan to me!"

We all had to laugh at Ralph Watson's smart-ass remark. But Trini was on a roll, and he was not finished. So we continued to listen.

"I did some more research and found out more about this mythical island of California. It turns out that there were four black governors of California when it was a part of Mexico, but in the mythical California, which was an island on which gold was the only metal and pearls were as common as rocks, the women were considered to be most powerful, and they had beasts that were half men, half birds."

Reading with a dramatic flair that surprised us all, Trini continued. His enthusiasm was readily apparent and infectious. I actually wanted to know more about this myth.

"Get this: After mating with a man, the women would feed him to these beasts, called griffins."

"Sounds like a girl in the Bronx that I dated about two months ago."

You had to hand it to Jerry James. If nothing else, he was irrepressible.

"Now, when Cortés arrived in California searching for this mythical queen, he found her influence on him to be so profound that he paid tribute to this powerful black woman, Queen Califia, by naming the state after her. I could not believe it when I did some further digging and found out that a painting of this Queen Califia can be found in the California State Senate chamber in Sacramento, the state capital. There is a mural painted in 1926 by Maynard Dixon and Frank von Sloun in the Hall of the Dons at the Intercontinental Mark Hopkins Hotel in San Francisco. And, believe it or not, there is a large painting of Queen Califia on a wall of the Golden Dreams building at Disney's California Adventure in Orange County."

I thought about my early days as an investment banker. That was when I worked on municipal finance deals, a number of them based in the state of California. I tried to recall the stationery from California state officials. Trini seemed to be reading my mind as he went on.

"Unfortunately, on the Great Seal of the State of California, you will see the Greek goddess Minerva instead of Queen Califia because Minerva was more acceptable to the Europeans who settled in the state. None of this matters, though. At the end of the day, after all the historians and anthropologists attempt to spin this story in another direction, the truth will still be the truth: California was named for the black woman Queen Califia."

"Well, I'll be damned."

"Yes, Jerry, you will be damned. In fact, you already are damned."

The rest of the bar at Dorothy's laughed at Trini's rejoinder. But the story stuck in my head for some unknown reason. And I am glad that it did. It was because of that story that I did something that I know Charmaine would have wanted me to do: take a break and breathe the fresh air of relaxation and pleasure. As Trini ended his story, I knew one thing: I was on my way to California.

CHAPTER 10

Diedre

A Day in the Life

I will never forget that September morning when I first heard the news of Gordon's New Orleans Fiasco. The fact that he had almost killed Ray Beard and himself messing around with cocaine and prostitutes was not surprising, and frankly, it was always difficult to summon up anything approximating sympathy for that lousy son of a bitch.

But the fact that he had betrayed Jerome, Paul and me was something that I don't think I will ever be able to forgive. I had put all of my money and all of my dreams into my asset management company, DBD Financial Advisors. When I merged my firm into Morningstar Financial Services along with Jerome and Gordon, I wasn't only investing my money and my dreams, I was also investing my future and my life.

When I found out that Gordon had damned near killed himself while celebrating his betrayal of Morningstar, I experienced a feeling of pure hatred that I had never known before. I know that I have a very bad temper and that I struggle daily to control it and to master it, to make that negative energy serve me instead of making me its servant. But for a few moments that day, all I wanted was to be able to visit severe and vicious and interminable vengeance upon Gordon's nappy head.

Paul and I will probably always have our differences, but that morning, as we lay in his bed listening to CNN in disbelief and shock, he was the one to come to his senses first. While I was flailing and cursing and plotting all manner of pain and suffering for Gordon, Paul almost immediately got on the phone to call Jerome to begin to find a way to salvage the Morningstar venture.

And he did more than salvage the venture. With Jerome, Paul and me working together, we were able to get our company back on track, and we have been even more successful than Paul had predicted when he first suggested a merger of three of the top black investment banking firms on Wall Street.

We have greatly expanded our asset management business by focusing on union pension funds across the country. And Jerome has turned out to be a virtual genius when it comes to identifying great corporate opportunities way ahead of anyone else on the Street.

And through it all, Paul has been the perfect counselor. He has not just been making sure that the firm complies with the legal requirements attendant to the business these days. He has also been the advisor, the steady hand and the one person who never seems to ever get overwhelmed by the relentless pressure of Morningstar or the rest of his practice.

And then there is the added detail: Paul and I used to be married. Paul and I divorced many years ago. Paul and I remarried after the New Orleans Fiasco. Paul and I now have a two-year-old son, Paul Jr.

Several years after our divorce, Paul and I were able to establish an uneasy truce, and that eventually evolved into a comfortable friendship. And it was on this basis that we coexisted for a number of years. And it was pretty remarkable considering the conflagration of passion that consumed the end of our first marriage.

It's still difficult for me to recall exactly why we came to a parting of the ways. We met soon after we graduated—Paul from Harvard Law School, me from Columbia's School of Business. We were full of dreams. Paul was going to change the world through his work as a public interest lawyer, and I was going to found a community development bank that would change America, neighborhood by neighborhood.

We both found that neither the world nor America changed that easily. And it may be that the frustration of encountering the brick wall of harsh reality turned our union of idealism into a steel-cage match. To put it simply, we took our frustrations out on each other, and in the end, neither of us could take it anymore and we both moved on.

Paul became the suave, sophisticated and eminently successful corporate lawyer whose greatest asset seemed to be a network of contacts and relationships all over the United States and throughout much of the world. Whatever a client needed, Paul seemed to have a contact, colleague, friend or old classmate who could be of assistance.

I went on to climb the corporate ladder at Citibank. I think that it is fair to say that I was one of the rising stars at the bank. And then one day, literally one day, I was summoned to the executive suite and fired on the spot. I had less than three hours to get out of the building, and after my forced sunny sabbatical on the beaches of Anguilla, I came back to New York and founded DBD Financial Advisors, building it into one of the most successful asset management firms in the country.

Paul and I continued to build on our comfortable friendship after he proposed that Gordon, Jerome and I merge our firms. There might have been something more to it as time progressed, but I still don't think that any word but "friendship" would describe our relationship.

As the merger progressed, however, Paul's fiancée, Samantha Gideon, died of throat cancer. Her decline was sudden and certainly unexpected, and it seemed to devastate Paul in a way that I would not have thought possible. After all, Paul was always the rock; he was always there for everyone else. Indeed, Paul was the one who always made sure that everyone else was all right.

I had seen Paul endure the death of his father and his brother, but when Samantha passed away, it was something entirely different. He seemed to have absorbed a psychic beating that left him just going through the motions of life.

I don't think that most people would consider me to be a compassionate person. I will never be the soft, cuddly type. But Paul's pain almost broke my heart and I did reach out to him because, after all the years, I really did care.

And somehow, in reaching out to him, we both found that there was something special about each other that we never had been able to appreciate. And to put it simply, we fell in love, just like silly teenagers in some Norman Rockwell setting.

But it felt good and it made sense. And we got married and, even though we were both getting to that "certain age," we went ahead and had a son. And even though the stress and strain of every day has made every day a little more difficult, our getting married made it possible for our wonderful, beautiful, lovely son to come into this world. And whatever maddening differences there have been between Paul and me, I can only be grateful for the blessing of that little boy in our lives. And I keep hoping that the blessing of Paul Jr. will be enough to keep our classic little nuclear family together.

CHAPTER II

Sture

Cloud Nine

After Kenitra left Dorothy's that evening, I found myself counting the moments until one o'clock like a child waiting for Santa Claus to come down the chimney. Except I knew exactly what my present was and where it was located: not under a tree, but in a suite at the Waldorf-Astoria Hotel.

And so, after Kenitra left me savoring the delicious invitation to spend a week as her friend and lover, I tried to concentrate on my work as the manager of Dorothy's By the Sea—with very little success. I tried to keep an eye on the bartenders and waiters, but all I could think about was Kenitra's lips and that serpent of a tongue that darted out between them in the most sensual fashion. I tried to make sure that the waiters and waitresses were being polite and courteous and hospitable, but thoughts of Kenitra's breasts and thighs kept clouding my vision.

I should have been thinking about the obvious streak of madness that possessed this woman to stay with a maniac like Gordon Perkins for the years before he met his comeuppance in New Orleans. I should have been thinking about the danger of cavorting with Gordon's wife while he was still alive. Instead, I just thought about those long, lovely thighs as being a highway to a heaven that I just had to visit that night or that might be lost to me forever.

And finally, one o'clock came and it was time to start closing the restaurant. Trini Satterfield, Jerry James and Ralph Watson were always among the last to leave, and this night was no different. Mercifully, they had exhausted their hoary hoard of stories and lies and legends, and they trudged off to whatever adventures the remainder of the night had in store for them. I waved good-night to them as they headed out the door. I don't remember if any of the Unholy Trio even grunted a response that night. They might have, but my mind was already on an elevator in the Waldorf, and I wanted to make sure that my body wasn't too far behind.

As always happens when you want to hurry, a hundred thousand little items demanded my attention before I could finally say goodnight to the night manager and get into the car-service car that I had already called. Kenitra had given me her cell phone number with instructions to call only when I was in a car and on my way. I absentmindedly noted that it was a California area code that I called as the driver headed north and then east. Thankfully, there was no traffic to speak of at two o'clock in the morning.

"Good evening, Kenitra." I was truly at a loss for words. I hardly felt like the sophisticated manager and part owner of a big-time New York City nightspot.

"Good morning, Sture. I was starting to think that you might have gotten a better offer tonight and that I would have to play all by myself. Actually, I have already started. Playing—with myself, that is."

Her laugh was soft and enchanting. It was the kind of laugh that promised pleasure and passion. I wished that I were driving the car so that I could just push the gas pedal to the floor. In retrospect, it's a good thing I was in the backseat.

"Well, Kenitra, if it's too late . . ."

"Sture, you really are a madman, aren't you? Please get your Norwegian ass over to room thirty-two thirty-two right now. I have two chilled champagne glasses and a bottle of Veuve Clicquot that I need you to open . . . and I may need for you to open something else, too."

"The next sound you hear will be me knocking at your door."

"*Ciao*, Sture."

I never knew that the sound of words could feel like velvet—on my ears and all over my body. I felt myself shuddering in anticipation.

The way she said my name made my palms sweat and my heart beat like I had just crossed the finish line of a footrace. There was no force of logic or power of reflection that could have kept me from room thirty-two thirty-two at the Waldorf that night.

Within a few minutes, I was in the ornate lobby of the Waldorf. Since it was past two in the morning, the place was practically deserted with the exception of some security and maintenance staff. And, since I was a well-dressed, blond, blue-eyed, white man, no one even suggested an inquiry in my direction as I made my way toward the elevators. A few moments later, I was in front of room thirty-two thirty-two.

I have to confess that I hesitated a moment before knocking on Kenitra's door. Maybe it's the same thing that prey experiences when it knows it is just about to be captured by the hunter. But my hesitation did not matter. As I took a breath to contemplate what it would mean to begin any kind of relationship with Kenitra Perkins, the door opened. She must have been looking through the peephole in anticipation of my arrival.

I remember that she was holding two chilled champagne flutes in one hand and an icy bottle of Veuve Clicquot in the other. She was wearing . . . well, she was wearing almost nothing. The "almost" consisted of a sheer black camisole with a matching pair of panties and the most impossible five-inch high-heeled shoes that I had ever seen. I entered, and I remember that Brenda Russell was playing on the sound system that she had in her room. I don't remember too much else.

"You certainly believe in making a girl wait, don't you?" Kenitra virtually slinked across the room like some wonderful sexual feline.

"Sorry to be so late, Kenitra. . . ." I could not believe that I was feeling so shy and nervous, like a teenager in a wet dream.

"Don't be sorry, Sture. You can start making up for it by opening this bottle, and then one more thing."

Looking at her smile was like staring into a galaxy of never-ending starbursts.

"Sure." I felt like my tongue was tied into a million-million knots. It was then I knew what was meant by "bewitched, bothered and bewildered."

I quickly and expertly opened the bottle of champagne, the cork escaping silently, like the sigh of a controlled woman, and then poured until the two flutes were full. We toasted and sipped. The champagne was excellent, although it could have been flat ginger ale that night, for all that I cared. Kenitra was simply intoxicating. And now, being alone with her, in the hotel room, with her dressed like some sex fantasy come to life, I hardly knew where to begin.

"You mentioned something about one more thing?"

"Yes, I did, Sture. Yes, I did. Tell me, where would you like for me to kiss you first?"

Clearly, this entire evening was some kind of dream come true. So I told Kenitra, and she kissed me where I asked, over and over, and I kissed her where she asked, over and over. And she introduced me to a universe of pleasure that I never knew existed and never wanted to leave.

CHAPTER 12

Jerome

In My Solitude

I hung up from my conversation with Paul feeling pretty satisfied with myself. I had been battling the demons of loneliness and sadness and simple misery ever since Charmaine had died, and I had finally attacked those demons by taking the initiative to do something that would be enjoyable, pleasant . . . fun. For a moment, I thought I might have turned the corner for which grieving survivors search with desperation and limitless hope. Or so I thought.

Missing Charmaine has always been more than a matter of grief; it was more than sadness and it was more than simple misery. I truly felt that a part of me was just missing. I had always been in control of my surroundings and myself. I have prided myself on being able to handle any challenge, any adversity, and any crisis. But it has always been more than pride. It has been the way that I have chosen to define myself.

I have never wanted anything more than an opportunity to be myself. Whether it was in the mean streets of Philadelphia, the ivy-covered halls of Yale, the urban intellectual boot camp of Columbia's business school or the cutthroat, tailored-suit, hand-to-hand combat that is Wall Street, I have never known fear and I have never doubted that I would prevail.

Much good fortune has come my way, that's for sure. But I have always believed that good fortune is only good if you recognize the opportunity and use it to your advantage. I have had friends and enemies, and Gordon Perkins has taught me everything I ever want to know about betrayal. But there are no sad songs that I need to sing.

I guess the best way to put it is that I have always been comfortable in my own skin. That is, until Charmaine died. Since then, I felt like I have been in a constant struggle to stay behind. And the tomorrow that everyone writes songs and poems about never seems to come for me.

After his girlfriend Samantha Gideon died, Paul would come and visit Charmaine and me for company and consolation. The few times that he did come by the house, it was for dinner and casual conversation. Paul certainly didn't want to be alone and he didn't want to be with his usual rotation of alternate beauties who seemed to characterize so much of his past lifestyle.

But I remember one evening after dinner when Charmaine had excused herself and Paul told me how Samantha's loss had affected him. His words haunt me these days.

He told me how he would be all right through most of the day, but when evening fell, he was helpless to avoid the waves of sadness that would crash against his very soul, over and over. It was almost as if he was suffering from some kind of photophobic disorder. He was fine during the daylight, but when the sun set, he felt like he was just going to pieces.

He did mention that he felt he had some kind of "closure" after Samantha started appearing in his dreams from time to time. He said that she would try to comfort him and encourage him to live life and to enjoy it.

About a year after Charmaine died, some friends suggested that dating might help—that sitting around being sad was just not the way to live the rest of my life. And I do recall having drinks with Trini Satterfield, Ralph Watson and Jerry James, and being advised that the best cure for my continuing malaise was to go out and get a woman, any woman, preferably several. They were adamant in their belief that frequent, rambunctious, sweaty sex was the cure for me. They even offered to "make a few calls and hook me up."

I have never thought of myself as any kind of monk or prude. If the truth were told, even with her illnesses, Charmaine and I had a loving and intense relationship that carried into the bedroom. And despite her illness, Charmaine was actually a ravenous lover, until her life started to ebb away. And feeling her loving arms, her willing body, her knowing hands, her voracious mouth, was just something else that had been missing from my life.

But from the time that Charmaine was too ill to even think about sex to the time she died and then to this very moment, almost two years, I had not had sex. And while I truly missed having a physical relationship with a woman, I had not met a single woman with whom I wanted to go to bed. It had gotten really strange.

I certainly felt the need. I was a healthy human. I wanted to be with a woman. There just was no woman that I wanted to be with. It was a mysterious condition in which I found myself. Things got so bad, I actually thought about taking up Trini, Ralph and Jerry on their offer. But then I figured that at that point in my life, some meaningless fling would just make things worse.

And after hanging up from my conversation with Paul, I noticed that it was after six, and since it was September, it was going to get dark soon, and that meant another losing battle with sadness. And I hoped, I really hoped, that this night would be different.

But I could almost hear the footfalls of heartache and the desolate winds of inconsolable loss as if they were just around the corner, and I knew that this night would be just like all the others. And already I was sure that going to Los Angeles, or the moon, wasn't going to change anything. At that moment, I almost called Paul back to change our plans.

But something told me to at least wait until the

next morning. So I waited for the next morning, and I waited for Charmaine to finally visit me in the middle of the night to let me know that everything was going to be all right. And I waited for someone to remind me what it felt like to be embraced with passion, if not with love.

CHAPTER 13

Gordon

'Round Midnight

It's hard to explain, but at some point, I started to be able to relax in that hospital, even with all of the tubes and monitors and wires and nurses and doctors. And it's hard to explain, but even though I am sure that I didn't go to sleep, once I started to relax the Dark Lord would pay me a visit. He would always have my new G-Perk wardrobe with him, and after he disengaged me from my wires and tubes, I would get dressed in my gear and simply stroll out of the hospital. As I look back, I am amazed that the nurses, doctors and orderlies seemed to be asleep or just unaware of my departure from and then return to what was supposed to be one of the most exclusive wings of New York–Presbyterian Hospital. But that was simply of no concern to me.

The Dark Lord and I always had a few runs to make, starting with picking up some excellent cocaine from one of my old suppliers in East Harlem and then on to my new hangout on 125th Street, the Purple Dragon, a bar and lounge just west of the elevated commuter train tracks on Park Avenue. I had my reasons for going to the Dragon: I was putting together a crew to take care of some of my new business operations, even though my new crew couldn't spell "Wall Street," much less find it.

After getting my personal ration of coke on East 112th Street and immediately snorting up almost a gram of what I thought was close to pure Colombian product, we flagged a livery cab to go up to the Dragon. With my denims and Timberland boots and shades and baseball cap, my G-Perk persona was absolutely complete and in keeping with my new ventures. I was also glad that the Dark Lord had come up with a nine-millimeter Glock pistol someplace along the line. It was equipment that would come in handy.

When we got out of the livery cab on 125th Street, it must have been close to one A.M. on a Wednesday night. Clearly, there were a number of late-working motherfuckers or a gang of niggers who never heard of a job because the Purple Dragon was very busy. It was a dingy, worn-out joint that had seen its best days decades ago. At some point, it might have been a slightly respectable joint, but now it was just a dive, and as the Dark Lord and I walked in the door, all I could see were pimps, whores, faggots, fences, undercover cops, hustlers, boosters, gangsters, snitches, knuckleheads and a few squares hoping to score some drugs or some pussy or both. The squares had no way of knowing that they might as well have been wearing bull's-eyes on their foreheads, since everyone else in the Dragon had them down as pure, grade-A marks, ready and begging to be taken.

"What's happening, Ernie? Busy night, I see. Give me the usual."

Ernie Argentina (no one knew his real name) was the bartender, and he knew enough to start pouring my Rémy Martin straight up as I came in the door.

"Another quiet night in Dodge City, G-Perk." Ernie was a big guy, with a baseball bat and a shotgun under the counter. It made no sense to mess with him, and it was only the rare pure fool who did.

Since most people didn't notice the Dark Lord when we hung out, I needed a seat for only one at the bar. As I moved toward the one empty seat that I saw at the middle of the bar, a hand attached to a wrist dripping with half-ass bling jewelry was thrust out to block my way.

"Excuse me, brother, I'm just going to have a seat."

"Not in this seat, motherfucker. It's saved."

This turned out to be one of those pivotal moments that passes for a test of manhood in the Dragon and in similar joints in similar 'hoods across the country. Even though no one stopped talking and the jukebox kept playing yet another Luther Vandross tune, I knew that all eyes were upon me and that the people behind those eyes wanted to see what G-Perk was going to do.

I took a better look at the Gatekeeper to the Bar Stool. Although he was seated, he was at least six feet tall and had to weigh well over two hundred pounds, in the fashion of the knucklehead overweight "big boys" who proliferated throughout the surrounding neighborhood. He had on the mandatory denim outfit with shades and baseball cap (his proclaiming the supremacy of the Boston Red Sox). In the moments that I had, I also noticed that he had a keloidal scar that snaked around his throat like some kind of fleshy necklace. The tattoos creeping up from under the collar of his jacket told me that he had probably been in some gang in prison, and probably not that long ago.

What to do, what to do? If I backed off from the Gatekeeper to the Bar Stool, I would be marked as a punk and a pussy, not only at the Purple Dragon, but far and wide. If I got into a fight with this knucklehead, it could get messy, and Ernie Argentina might end up kicking everybody's ass, including mine. That was when the Dark Lord whispered some strategic advice into my ear. I am still amazed that neither the Gatekeeper nor Ernie Argentina nor anyone else in the Purple Dragon noticed him, but that was their problem, not mine.

I knew that I had only moments to make a move. So I did. I grabbed the Gatekeeper by the back of his neck and slammed his face onto the bar, at the same time taking the Glock pistol out of my waistband and shoving it into his mouth as far as it would go. Those two moves pretty much took all of the fight out of the Gatekeeper.

"Motherfucker, why do you want to fuck with G-Perk? All I want to do is sit my ass down and have my Rémy, and you want to fuck with me? I should make you eat this pistol . . . or maybe just shoot your stupid ass."

The Gatekeeper's eyes were bugging out of his head. If he could have spoken, I imagine begging for mercy would have been one of his first priorities.

"Now get the fuck out of here right fucking now and let me drink my motherfucking Rémy. And the next time you come to this place, motherfucker, or to any place else where you might see my ass, just remember to leave G-Perk the fuck alone. Got that, motherfucker?"

I removed the pistol from his mouth and placed it squarely between his eyes. I could see in the mirror that Ernie Argentina was eyeing his shotgun, but since the situation seemed to be under control, at least in the universe of the Purple Dragon terms, he didn't see the need to blow me to kingdom come.

"Now tell me, nigger, are we straight? Are we clear?"

The Gatekeeper nodded a vigorous assent while picking up his shades off the floor and skittering out the door. And from that point on, word spread quickly that it was not a good idea to fuck with G-Perk.

And after having a few glasses of Rémy, I took a livery cab back to New York Hospital later that night. I had picked up a couple of miscellaneous bitches on my way out of the Dragon, and they accompanied the Dark Lord and me back to the hospital. It's amazing what those bitches did for a couple grams of coke and two hundred dollars.

The Dark Lord took care of securing my G-Perk gear and getting me hooked back up to all the tubes and wires and monitors. The nurses and orderlies and doctors just never seemed to notice a fucking thing.

And after my late night excursion, I relaxed and got myself some much-needed rest. I knew that G-Perk would be going up to the Purple Dragon again real soon.

CHAPTER 14

Kenitra

But Not for Me

My affair with Sture was meant to be nothing more than one more fling. It was meant to be a fulfillment of passion and fantasy for the moment and nothing more. And that first night at the Waldorf, I thought I was going to be the one to rock Sture's world, and I certainly did my very best to do just that.

But whatever they feed the boys in Norway turned Sture into a treasure and a pleasure. Once he got over being nervous (I guess he thought Gordon was going to come into the suite and tap him on the shoulder), he proved to be so skillful and fantastic with his lips, fingers and tongue that when he finally entered me, first on the couch, then on the carpeted floor, and then, finally and wondrously, on the king-sized bed, he ended up feeding hungers that I had suppressed for much too long.

After that first night at the Waldorf, I just couldn't get enough of my Scandinavian Snow Cone, which was my nickname for Sture. It was a nickname he hated until I spelled S-C-A-N-D-I-N-A-V-I-A-N S-N-O-W C-O-N-E all over his body with my tongue, again and again. After that, just whispering "Snow Cone" into his ear would arouse Sture, no matter how cool, calm and collected he tried to be.

I had planned to be back in Venice Beach communing with the wonders of my Pacific Ocean panorama after just one week in New York. My spontaneous fling with Sture was meant to be an adjunct to shopping, taking in some Broadway shows and more shopping. But it was the Sture part of my little plan that changed everything.

In addition to letting me be a total sex beast, in addition to satisfying me in a way no man or woman ever had, Sture Jorgensen was gentle, kind and, most of all, lots of fun.

Sture opened the doors to passion, sexual freedom and mirth. And it was the mirth that meant the most to me . . . and it was being able to smile freely again that made me extend my stay in New York City for another two weeks.

During those three weeks, we were apart only during his hours at Dorothy's By the Sea. The rest of the time, day and night, we were together. We dined together, bathed together, slept together and found new ways to pleasure each other together, and those three weeks seemed like three hours. And then it was time for me to go back to Venice Beach.

Ever since the night of the New Orleans Fiasco, when Gordon damned near killed himself—and Ray Beard—I had not spent more than seven days in New York City. As soon as Paul Taylor was able to assure my sole access to the ten million dollars that Gordon had put into a Bahamian bank account in my name, my sense of survival told me that I needed to be as far away as possible from Gordon's evil ass for the rest of my life.

My well-honed survival instincts told me not to be fooled by Gordon's coma or seeming helplessness. Gordon was evil incarnate. Gordon was the devil. Gordon was hell come to life in a human form. I needed to be away from Gordon forever.

From the moment I decided to stay in New York longer than my planned one week, I had this sneaking feeling that I was placing myself in jeopardy because I was within two miles of Gordon. And, his comatose state notwithstanding, Gordon was my mortal enemy as long as he was alive.

But being with Sture was just so much fun. And I hadn't had fun in years. The laughter, the loving, the liberation, were too much to leave behind. So I stayed for two extra weeks. And then it was time for me to go. Sture couldn't just get up and leave Dorothy's, but he planned to come to California in two weeks. So we spent our last night together in my suite in the Waldorf trying to find a way to make up for the two weeks of lovemaking that we would be missing. It was fun. And it was wonderful.

At some point, we took a (short) break from the kissing and licking and sucking and loving and moaning and sweating and writhing and loving. The sheets were soaked and twisted all around our bodies, and our bodies were intertwined in such a fashion that it seemed like we would never part again. And that would have been just fine with me.

"Kenitra?" All Sture had to do was whisper my name across the pillow and all I wanted was for him to be inside me again and again.

"Yes, Snow Cone?" My hand had been resting on his stomach, but now it started on a slow, sure journey south of the equator.

"Do you know how happy you have made me these past three weeks?" Sture managed to be a man and a boy at the same time. One more reason that I couldn't admit even to myself that I was falling in love with him.

"I don't know about that, Sture. But I do know how hard I have made you in the past few weeks."

We both laughed and cuddled and snuggled and waited for the next wave of passion to overtake us. We both knew that it wouldn't be long before we were happily drowning in ecstasy.

"You know that I don't want to leave." I don't even remember where those words came from. As I look back, I guess they came from my heart. Sture made me feel so free that for a few moments, I forgot to be careful. For a few moments, I started to believe that anything was possible for me, that anything was possible for us.

"You don't have to say that, Kenitra . . . unless you mean it."

"Of course I mean it, you crazy Snow Cone! Why do you think I said it?" We laughed and giggled and tickled and kissed and hugged and groped like teenagers who had snuck away to a no-tell

motel for the very first time. I knew that I had forgotten how wonderful happiness could be.

And then my cell phone rang. I had set my
phone to ring a special tune when it was New York
Hospital calling about Gordon. The call tune was
the dirgelike "Song of The Volga Boatmen."

I grudgingly disengaged a leg and an arm from
the tangle of arms and legs that was Sture and me
so that I could pick up the phone.

It was the hospital. It was about Gordon. And to
this day, it amazes me how the my universe could
change just because of a forty-second phone call.

CHAPTER 15

Paul

My Funny Valentine

Things moved pretty fast right after the New Orleans Fiasco. My two priorities were to make sure that Morningstar survived Gordon's treachery and that Kenitra could use the occasion of Gordon's demise to get free of her personal demon once and for all.

Working with Jerome and Diedre, it was a fairly direct project to get the Morningstar ship back on even keel. It was a matter of connecting the dots in terms of shoring up corporate and municipal business opportunities and making certain that the assets of the firm were not looted by some other predatory strategy.

Of course, Jerome and Diedre were not exactly rookies in the world of finance and corporate intrigue, so the three of us worked together as a team in protecting Morningstar and ensuring that the opportunities for future success remained a reality. As a result, within less than three years, Morningstar was exceeding even the most sanguine projections that had accompanied the formation of the firm in the first place.

Kenitra was a different story. It goes without saying that no one was really that close to her. Gordon treated her like a prized slave. He wrapped her in furs and diamonds and pain. And he kept her away from her friends, his friends and the world at large. To say that she was on a short leash would be the definition of understatement.

Of course, she was *seen* in public every time Gordon had to make some kind of appearance. She was the quintessential trophy bride, except this trophy had barely visible scars and bruises and this trophy had an eternal air of sadness and loss about her.

And I guess there was something about her misery that made me want to help. But helping Kenitra would mean going to war with Gordon. It was not physical fear that kept me from helping her, but the knowledge that it meant having Gordon as an enemy for life.

So when Gordon went into a cocaine-induced coma in New Orleans, there arose a perfect opportunity to get Kenitra free from Gordon, who unwittingly had provided her with the keys to her freedom. By putting ten million dollars in her name in a Bahamian bank account, thinking that Kenitra would never dream of touching that money even if she knew about it, Gordon meant to sequester some funds for some unforeseen rainy day.

But, once he went into a coma, it was a pretty easy matter to discover the funds and move them into an offshore account—in Vanuatu—that only Kenitra and I knew about and to which only she had access. And thanks to my good fortune in having a Dartmouth College classmate who was a real estate broker in California, I was able to arrange for Kenitra to purchase a condo in Venice Beach.

Kenitra decided to keep the Park Avenue apartment, but she moved almost all of her belongings to California, virtually shuttering the scene of some of Gordon's most abusive and horrific behavior. Even when she came to New York for periodic shopping sprees and to consult with Gordon's doctors, she never set foot in the apartment. It was as if there were some kind of force field surrounding the place and she was simply incapable of going through the doors of what had to be one of the most expensive and rarely used pieds-à-terre in all of New York City.

But there was one other task that arose out of the New Orleans Fiasco, and that concerned what to do about Gordon Perkins. Even though he had been in critical condition from the moment he fell face first onto the carpeted floor of the hotel suite in New Orleans, moving him by air ambulance to New York City a few days later did not endanger or worsen his condition. Acting at Kenitra's request, I arranged for Gordon to be placed into the Special Intensive Care Unit at New York Hospital, one of the best medical facilities in the world.

Kenitra visited Gordon once before leaving for California, and she asked me to accompany her. I think she wanted to make sure that the devil was truly caged, and I think seeing him intubated with a swarm of tubes and wires and monitors snaking over his body convinced her that he was truly powerless. The doctors told her that his chances of recovering from the coma were virtually nil. But she was not fully convinced.

And I could understand why. Throughout the entire time that Kenitra and I stood by his hospital bed, his eyes never moved. They never showed recognition. They never responded to light. They never responded to movement. They never closed.

It was beyond bizarre. It was spooky. And for Kenitra, it was absolutely terrifying. There was no way to convince her that Gordon was not consciously plotting his next move right there on the hospital bed. And there was no way that I could be sure that she wasn't right.

But thoughts of Gordon were in the backrooms of my mind late that evening. I was packing for my three-day trip to Los Angeles with Jerome. While I was somewhat skeptical about going when he first made the suggestion, after thinking about it, I was actually looking forward to making that West Coast run with him. That's when the phone rang.

Gordon's doctors were under instructions to call both Kenitra and me if there was any significant change in his condition.

I picked up the phone and listened. There had been some kind of significant change in Gordon's condition. I was needed at the hospital. Right away.

CHAPTER 16

Jerome

Don't Worry About Me

After getting Paul to agree to make the trip to Los Angeles with me, I spent the rest of my workday trying to get enough done so that when I was getting ready to leave for the airport the next afternoon, I wouldn't be running around like a bat out of hell. It was always more than a notion to get out of town, and this trip would be no different.

I could almost tell when memories of Charmaine would start to come out of the darkening skies. But at the moment, I was relatively at peace. I had made arrangements for the housekeeper to stay with my sons while I was gone over the next few days—and they were more than happy to be going on playdates and sleepovers for the weekend. I was happy that they were happy.

I was just about ready to call myself finished for the evening when Diedre came down the hall from her office at the other end of our suite of offices. She usually left a little earlier than me, but it was certainly no surprise to see her at work late in the evening.

She had an expression on her face that I could not quite interpret. And for a fleeting moment, I thought that her visit had something to do with Paul going to Los Angeles with me on such short notice—or at all.

"Jerome, do you have a couple of minutes?" Diedre continued walking into my office, correctly assuming that as partners, we had to be able to speak with each other about anything at any time.

She sat down in the chair right next to my desk with a style that was both alluring and professional. Diedre had always been a good-looking woman, and years of corporate warfare and motherhood had done absolutely nothing to diminish her look of quality and demure appeal.

She also was the consummate professional who was always focused on success. In that regard, she could be somewhat cold-blooded in her pursuit of what she wanted. And since we had come to know each other better in our Morningstar adventure, I had become ever-more grateful that we were on the same side.

But she still had that look on her face. It would have been hard for me to believe that she wanted to sit and talk about Paul taking a trip with me. Paul, Diedre and I were friends and we were business associates. And we were scrupulous about keeping our personal and business lives separate.

Sometimes, the crossing-over couldn't be helped. Like during the entire New Orleans Fiasco. Or when Charmaine had died. Or when Paul and Diedre got married. But on a day-to-day basis, business was business and our personal lives were left usually at the door when we went to work.

So, what was the look on her face all about? It was not Diedre's habit to beat around the bush, and her hesitation in getting to the point was kind of surprising.

"I had an interesting call today, Jerome. Actually, it was one of several interesting calls that I have been getting recently. They were all from Monique Jefferson." Her voice was flat, almost monotone, but her eyes were searching my face for a reaction.

At the mention of the name of Ray Beard's wife, memories cascaded through my brain like one of those sudden flash floods in the desert when all hope is lost for anyone or anything unlucky enough to be in the wrong arroyo at the wrong time. Ray Beard had been the most trusted member of my firm along with my longtime assistant, Berta Colon. I even had the conceit to consider him a kind of protégé, and I was grooming him for further success until he eventually became my full partner.

And then, when the Morningstar merger that Paul proposed and outlined started to gain momentum, in my view, Ray just got stupid.

One moment, he was a brilliant, attractive avatar of success on the ascent. And then, when he felt slighted by not being a principal player in the merger negotiations, he became surly, vainglorious and just another problem in my life. And then he left my firm right in the middle of the Morningstar merger negotiations. And he left by means of a letter, which he had delivered to my home in Sag Harbor. It's one piece of correspondence that I am sure I will never forget. I remember reading it not like it was yesterday, but more like it was a half hour ago.

It was sent to my home by Express Mail, and it was on the most expensive paper I had ever seen and printed in a script that looked like it came straight from the palace at Versailles.

Jerome:

By the time you read this letter, the Wall Street Journal *will have received a press release announcing my resignation from your firm, effective yesterday. I really would have preferred to tell you this in person, but time and circumstances simply did not permit me to do it that way. I did not, however, think that it would be right for you to hear this from anyone else. Not after all that we have been through.*

An opportunity has arisen, and just as you have taught me, and would have done yourself, I had to take that opportunity. The release to which I referred will announce the formation of R.R. Beard & Company, a venture capital and asset management firm. My partner for domestic work will be Merrill Lynch. Merrill is providing me with much of my start-up capital as well as the initial infrastructure resources. I will be the majority shareholder.

You should also know that five members of your

asset management group and three members of
your firm's financial advisory group will be joining me, along with five secretaries. I have attached
a list of their names.

I truly wish that things could have turned out
differently. I have learned so much in working
with you. The most important lesson that I have
learned is that business is business and every opportunity must be seized at the right time. I think
that is exactly what I am doing right now.

I truly hope that we can maintain our friendship, although I know that you might not feel that
is appropriate right now. But I am sure that you
would have done the same thing . . . indeed, your
new venture with Gordon and Diedre is proof of
just that. In your new partnership, I just don't see
a place or a future for me. As we have worked together, I always expected that my future would in-
volve our continuing to work together. Obviously,
you have chosen another alternative. And just as
I have had to understand, I hope that you will
understand, too.

Just for the record, I did not seek out this opportunity. Merrill initially approached me, and initially I turned them down. And then I thought
about what you would do, and I called them back.
There was no way that I could tell you about any
of this, and there was no way that I could turn
down the opportunity when our negotiations were
finalized.

I could go on, but it is probably best that I close
for now. My new office manager (you will recall
my secretary Lucretia) will call Berta on Wednesday to work out an orderly transfer of papers, be-

*longings, etc., of all the people who are leaving
you and joining me.*

   Please give my love to Charmaine and the boys.
                                             Ray

P.S. The New York Times *will be publishing an
announcement that Monique and I will be getting
married in June of next year. I want to extend the
first invitation to the wedding to you and Charmaine. The two of you will always be like family
to me.*

                                             RRB

One of the things that I will never forget is that
when Charmaine read the letter, it was one of the
few times that I ever heard her curse. And I don't
mean a few "goddamns" and "bullshits." She let
loose with a stream of obscenities that would have
made a Madagascar sailor blush. And I remember
promising myself that I would never let Raymond
Russell Beard III ever have the satisfaction of
knowing that his betrayal had hurt me—a lot.

As it turned out, Ray's initial betrayal was just a
head fake. He eventually partnered with Gordon
Perkins in an effort to disembowel Morningstar in
one cruel masterstroke. If Ray and Gordon had
pulled off the theft of the New Orleans mayoral
election and wound up with the mayor of a major
U.S. city in their pocket, the two of them would
have had a bargaining chip that they could have
parlayed into a miniempire, first in the world of
municipal finance and ultimately in the rarified
air of corporate finance.

And if it hadn't been for a bit too much cocaine

and a little bit of bad luck, they might have pulled it off. And if they had been successful in their gambit, Diedre, Paul and I—along with Morningstar— would have been left high and dry.

I knew the basics of Ray's condition in the aftermath of the fiasco. He and Gordon were both in a comatose state when the emergency medical staff found them in their hotel suite—facedown on the floor, wearing only their underwear, with vials of cocaine and empty champagne bottles strewn about the room. The fact that the room was locked from the inside was only one of the unsolved mysteries of the New Orleans Fiasco.

It was my understanding that Ray had had a massive stroke that left him blind in one eye and partially paralyzed on his left side.

He had spent most of the past year in a rehabilitation facility in New Jersey. Amazingly, because in my view the son of a bitch deserved no mercy, his Monique, a rising star of a TV news anchor in New York City by way of Memphis, had stayed by his side throughout his entire ordeal as they had been secretly married in a private ceremony right after he sent that fateful letter.

I knew that Diedre had not come to chat about Ray's condition, so I was puzzled as to why she felt a need to tell me about her communication with Ray's wife. And I imagine that after the flood of emotions and memories raced through my brain, the expression on my face that Diedre saw was one of puzzlement. I am sure that all she saw was pure bewilderment.

"I hope Mrs. Beard is in good health." That was about the only decent thing that I would trust myself to say with the memory of Ray Beard lurking in my consciousness. I wanted his half-blind, paralyzed ass to live forever so that he could suffer the consequences of betraying me. But, of course, I just would not allow myself to say such a thing to Diedre.

"Monique is fine, Jerome, but Ray wants to meet with you." She spoke evenly and coolly, knowing that she was treading on ice so thin, she could see the fish swimming below. But she wasn't finished. And it was just as well. My brain was reeling and I was in hand-to-hand combat with my emotions.

"Ray wants to meet with you, Jerome, because he wants a second chance. He regrets that you feel he betrayed you and, Lord knows, he has paid for it. He is a broken man, Jerome, and he feels that he has made a huge mistake, the consequences of which he will have to live with for the rest of his life."

"What do *you* want to do about this, Diedre? I know we both took a big hit when Ray and Gordon tried to pull their little scam, but for me, Ray's play was personal. It's not for me to forgive. I am not God. I am not a priest. I have sinned far too many times to sit in judgment of anyone else. But what do *you* think *we* should do about giving Ray a second chance?"

"Well, Jerome, the truth is that Wall Street and corporate finance is all that Ray Beard knows. And the truth is that after his stunt with Gordon in New Orleans, he couldn't get a job as a window washer with any firm except ours."

"So, what should we *do,* Diedre? I'm asking you

because I can't possibly make a rational decision on my own."

"Jerome, you know I know how you feel. After New Orleans, I was ready to kill Ray. You ask Paul. I seriously considered trying to put a contract out on that fool. But I figured that there was a lot of downside to that move, like a hit man with a big mouth." With that, a smile started to insinuate itself on the corners of her mouth, and I could have sworn I saw a twinkle in her eye.

I had to stifle a laugh because I knew how she felt. Hell, I felt the same way. But because we were partners, and because I have always respected Diedre's judgment, I continued to listen.

"I am not going to tell you that we should hire Ray. But I have been talking to Monique a lot over the past few months. Jerome, despite everything that has happened to him, she has stayed with Ray and has been by his side. And there is something to be said for loyalty and—dare I say it?—love in these days and times.

"Frankly, if it was just about Ray Beard, I might be fresh out of mercy myself. But I came to see you as a favor to Monique. She didn't just fall off the truck last week; she's no ingenue. She's a big girl, and she believes in Ray because she loves him and she's not prepared to put that love on the shelf just yet.

"It took a lot of heart for her to come to see me on Ray's behalf. I have to imagine that she had to swallow a whole bucketful of pride to even try and help him this way. And I respect that, and maybe we should give her request some thought—just because of that, if nothing else." Now she looked me dead in the eyes and had my attention riveted to her next words.

"So, Mr. Hardaway. It really is up to you. If you are asking me what you should do, I think that you should take Ray's call and meet with him. I am with you either way. If you think we should pass on hiring Ray, I will tell Monique and she will just have to go to plan B. After all, they aren't hurting for money—she is still a star news anchorwoman in New York City." And then she slid the stiletto right between my ribs.

"Of course, if you can find it in your heart to rise above the past and give Ray a chance, I will be behind you one hundred percent as well. After all, isn't life about second chances, Jerome?" And, with that, she sat back in her chair and tried to appraise my reaction and predict my response.

"I don't want to meet with Ray." I said my words slowly, and they took on an air of unarguable finality.

"Okay, Jerome. If that's the way you want it, I understand and I am with you. Our partnership, our friendship and Morningstar are more important than one thousand Raymond Russell Beards." She started to get out of her chair. Her face was impassive, and I could not tell what she was thinking, except that she had to be disappointed if that was all that I had to say. But it wasn't.

"Diedre, please sit down. I haven't finished. I don't want to meet with Ray because there is no need for me to do so. If you think we should hire him and give him a second chance, I am with you one hundred and ten percent. You are right about second chances; Lord knows I have had mine. We will just have to see how Ray Beard handles his last second chance."

I could see Diedre's eyes light up, and in that moment, I knew that I was making the right decision. At least, it felt like the right decision at the time.

"Jerome, however things turn out, I know we are making the right decision. We are making history at Morningstar every day. Maybe we can make a little more history by being uncharacteristically compassionate." She said this with a smile on her face, and when she got up to leave my office, I was glad that she had helped me to rise above my baser instincts. Of course, instincts are part of the survival mechanism, so it would remain to be seen whether or not we had made the right decision.

"Good-night, Diedre."

"Good-night, Jerome. And, Jerome? Have a safe trip to Los Angeles, and try not to get my husband in too much trouble." An interesting throwaway line that I had to believe was meant in jest. But, of course, the truth is many times spoken in jest.

In any event, after all of this, I was home packing and trying to unwind and trying not to think about what I was going to say to Ray Beard the next time I saw him. And that was when the phone rang.

It was Paul. He and Diedre were on their way to meet Kenitra at New York Hospital. Something had happened with Gordon. It sounded serious.

I hung up and decided that it was best for me to go to the hospital as well. I got dressed and got moving.

CHAPTER 17

Sture

Green Dolphin Street

There are, of course, many moments that change our lives. But it is rare when we recognize those moments at the precise point in time that they occur. The moment that Kenitra hung up her cell phone and told me that she had to go to the hospital to see about Gordon, I knew that our lives had changed.

I also knew that I was going to go with her. And in making that decision, I moved our relationship from a fling to something that mattered. There wasn't time to think through all of the ramifications of what my coming with her meant. But Kenitra wanted me with her, even though she didn't say so. And I wanted to be with her.

And so, we both showered quickly and dressed in silence. Our laughter and passion and frivolity and fun of just a few moments ago seemed to be centuries away, and we felt as forlorn as the twisted, sweaty sheets knotted at the foot of the bed.

I called a car service, and within thirty minutes of that fateful call, Kenitra and I were in the Waldorf elevator on our way down to the lobby. We both stared at the elevator doors as if we were expecting some kind of revelation. Kenitra spoke in a low, tense voice. I had to strain to hear her words.

"Thank you." The near-silent motor of the elevator was louder than she was. It took me a moment to even realize that she was speaking.

"You are welcome, Kenitra. This is not the time for you to be alone."

"I can handle it, Sture. I have been alone for a long time." Her eyes never wavered from the elevator doors. It was like she was trying to stare a hole through them.

When it came to Kenitra, I always knew that there was steel under the velvet. I also knew that I needed to make sure that I was offering more than my sympathy or my courteous assistance.

"I know you can handle it, Kenitra. And I know you have been alone. I guess I'm saying that I don't want you to have to be alone anymore. I am here for you—for as long as you need me to be here."

I was looking at her as I said this, searching her face for some sign of a response. She continued to stare straight ahead, but the tension around her eyes seemed to move away, if only for a moment.

And then the elevator doors opened to the

lobby. We headed for the Park Avenue side of the
ornate, old hotel. During the busy parts of the day,
the limousines and black cars of the rich and powerful Masters of the Universe would be lined up
and double-parked, waiting to take their liege
lords to their next appointed destinations. But it
was almost three o'clock in the morning and the
boulevard in front of the hotel's beflagged entrance was virtually deserted, except for the car
service that I had requested, which was posting a
lonely vigil. When we got in the car, I directed the
driver to New York Hospital, and as we started up
Park Avenue, Kenitra spoke again.

"Thank you, Snow Cone. I really mean it. Thank
you for being you. And thank you for coming with
me. I would never want to be alone in the same
room with that son of a bitch. And, to tell the
truth, I don't want to be alone at all anymore."

As I came to know Kenitra better, I realized that
she would have preferred gargling razor blades to
making that admission on the way from the Waldorf that night. That night, I was just glad to be
with her and glad that she wanted me there with
her in a place other than bed.

As the car headed from the Waldorf to the
Upper East Side of Manhattan, I reflected upon
our destination. New York Hospital was one of the
most famous and prestigious health facilities in
the world. Located on the ultimate aspects of the
Upper East Side of Manhattan, it was cocooned in
a sanctuary of wealth, luxury and indolent repose.
It had, on its ground floor, the psychiatric institute
where Marilyn Monroe had spent more than a few
days. And this hospital had been the site of the re-

covery or demise of countless sheiks, dukes, princesses, queens and charlatans.

It was only fitting that this hospital would be the base of operations for Gordon Stallworth Perkins. Gordon had been the most successful black investment banker in the history of corporate finance on the planet. He had managed to be brilliant and scurrilous and masterful and craven—a genius and a demon—simultaneously. Prior to the Morningstar merger, he had already fulfilled the dreams of half a hundred Harvard MBAs. And he was just hitting his stride when he teamed up with Jerome and Diedre.

Even given the possibility of vengeful exaggeration on the part of Kenitra, Gordon was a beast in person. The way that he beat, raped, tortured, abused and degraded her was the fodder for a whole libraryful of psychiatric tomes. After she told me about some of her misadventures, ordeals and outright suffering as Gordon's prisoner–trophy bride, I was amazed that he had managed not to kill her. And I was similarly amazed that she had never killed him. I was even more amazed that she had never even tried.

The circular driveway off of the main avenue, the manicured lawns, the cobblestone walkway, all gave New York Hospital the air of a privileged retreat.

When the air ambulance landed at Teterboro Airport in northern New Jersey, Gordon's doctor never considered a choice other than New York Hospital for his most-favored patient. Upon his arrival, Gordon was installed in the (Very) Special Intensive Care Unit, and that is where he had resided for almost three years. Festooned with wires and tubes and monitors, he had been under constant medical supervision during this time and had never moved from the bed or shown even the slightest signs of consciousness.

Since Kenitra had not divorced Gordon during those three years, she was technically and legally his next of kin. Consequently, all medical personnel associated with his case reported to her. And she received weekly briefings about his condition and, of course, she was the first person to be contacted in the event of an emergency or any serious change in his condition.

The late-night call from the hospital had to mean that something important had occurred, but the nurse on duty would not discuss the details over the phone. Given Paul's role as her counsel and advisor, she had directed that he be contacted as well in the event of an emergency.

And that is how I found myself in the backseat of a car service limousine with Kenitra Perkins at three in the morning on the way to New York Hospital. And I had this not-very-pleasant feeling that things were about to really get interesting—and not in a good way.

CHAPTER 18

Kenitra

You Keep Me Hanging On

I leaned back in the car as we headed through the nighttime streets of Manhattan. I put my hand in Sture's and he squeezed it gently. And I was glad he was there.

"Sture . . . thank you, baby. I had no idea how much I needed you to be with me right now. But I do. So thank you."

"You don't have to thank me, Kenitra. I should be the one to thank you because I am so glad that you want me to be with you."

"You do know how to make a girl feel special."

And then my mind and my mood took a terrible turn into a hate-filled morass that was my life with Gordon.

"I hope that God will forgive me, but I don't care if I go to hell. I hope that I am going to see the motherfucker die tonight. I was too scared to kill him while we were together, although I constantly dreamed about him dying and I fantasized about killing him every day—slowly, painfully and without a fragment of remorse. And I hate myself for being too afraid of him to run. I despise that I was too terrified to try to kill him. And I will never forgive myself for allowing him to imprison my very soul so that he could abuse me the way that he did. Sture, I swear to God . . ."

And then I just collapsed into his arms and started to cry—very softly. When it came to the story of Gordon and me, I really didn't have many tears left. Sture put his arms around me and, for the briefest of moments, I felt like I had found a sanctuary from the madness that was the planet Earth.

"How badly did he hurt you?"

"How badly did he hurt me?" I almost spat out the words. I sat up suddenly and faced Sture as the car continued its way uptown to our fateful destination. I took off my wraparound sunglasses. I could see from the look on his face that Sture immediately regretted his question, as did I. But there was no turning back now. In our three weeks together, we had never even mentioned Gordon. Now it was time for Sture to know what he had to know.

"Sture! How badly did he hurt me? I don't even know how to begin to tell you what that creature did to me.

"Do you see my eyes? Do you like my eyes? Well, the right one is glass, Sture! That's right, it's a goddamn fake eye from the time that idiot clocked me with a table lamp and I forgot to duck. I don't even remember the details, he kept me so fucked up on pills and liquor and coke, but I do remember being flown in a private plane to a very discrete clinic in Switzerland, just outside of Geneva, and that was where the procedure to replace my eye took place. You see, my real eye was damaged beyond repair." I put the sunglasses back on and could see the appalled look on Sture's face, but I couldn't stop.

"But I wish that the beatings were the worst of it. He beat me what seemed like every day. Usually punches, sometimes kicks, sometimes with whatever was close at hand. He usually didn't hit me in the face because he wanted me to be able to come out in public with him whenever he wanted to show me off.

"But the beatings were not the worst of it, Sture. Not by a long shot. He would make me take so much cocaine and so many painkillers that after a while, he didn't have to make me anymore. I wanted the coke. I needed the painkillers. And I would do anything for them. He basically turned me into his personal drug whore, abusing me and degrading me in horrible, filthy, disgusting ways that make me sick to even think about.

"He would tie me up and rape me. He would burn me. He would make me lie in my own filth—and in his filth—for days at a time. And then he would laugh at me and make me feel like I was less than shit. He made me feel like I deserved to be treated like that. He wanted to break me, Sture. He wanted to break my spirit. He thought that he owned me. He thought that he owned my soul. He was like the devil on earth and I couldn't get away.

I couldn't get away because I was afraid, and I couldn't get away because I hated who I had become.

"When Gordon almost killed himself down in New Orleans, at first I didn't know what to think. He was hurt and I was glad. But he was alive, and I knew, just knew, that he would come back to visit even worse punishment on me just for hoping that he would die. I was that afraid of him.

"And when Paul called me up and helped me find a way to get out of New York and live in California, far, far away from Gordon, it was like a gift from God. The only catch has been that since that monster is still alive, I have to get the hospital reports on him. I visit his hospital room when I come to New York just to make sure that the son of a bitch is still in a coma. But I have to tell you; I wouldn't set foot in that hospital room alone—ever.

"You would have to know Gordon like I do to know that it's not beyond him to come out of this 'irreversible coma' just so he can inflict more damage and pain on me. But this is the first time that I have ever gotten a call like this. And please forgive me for what I am going to say next, Sture, but I hope that he is going to die tonight. I have prayed for him to die every day for years, long before his little adventure in New Orleans, and I hope that the doctors have called to tell me that he is going to die tonight." And with that, I stopped.

I felt like a hundred pounds had been lifted off of me. I had flushed the hate and vitriol that I had for Gordon out into the open and now Sture knew the real me. For better or for worse.

"There's nothing to forgive, Kenitra." As he put

his arms around me again, I could see that he had tears welling up in his eyes.

I have no idea why I also remember the incredibly small details from that evening. I recall that my hair was damp from my quick shower and that I had not had time to make even the briefest attempt at makeup. I noticed that the streets were wet and slick from an early autumn shower, which gave the city more of a dreamlike quality than usual.

As we drove across First Avenue, we passed what seemed to be a minor traffic accident. The police were trying to separate a turbaned taxi driver from what appeared to be a six-foot-tall, two-hundred-and-fifty-pound transvestite. The accident didn't seem to have caused too much damage to the taxi or to the Volkswagen Beetle into which the sequined, wig-wearing transvestite managed to squeeze him/herself with, I noticed, very stylish, four-inch Jimmy Choo stiletto high heels. Nevertheless, despite the minimal damage, the two drivers were beyond irate and seemingly about to resort to violence.

While we were stopped at a red light, I adjusted my sunglasses and continued to observe a few more snippets of yet another urban vignette courtesy of the Gotham City Players. I saw both drivers gesticulating in a wild and increasingly dangerous manner. They were shouting unknowable curses and imprecations at each other, and the two harried police officers were clearly getting tired of the whole scene.

That's when the transvestite pivoted on one of his/her high heels and hauled off and slugged the cab driver with what had to be a stunning left hook. With his/her other hand, he/she grabbed his turban, which began to unravel as he sank to his knees, seemingly knocked senseless.

For what seemed like the slowest two seconds in the history of the planet, the cops stood motionless as the transvestite held the taxi driver upright by his unraveling turban while getting ready to unload another blow to his head. And then it really got interesting.

Just as the light was about to change, the taxi driver miraculously regained consciousness and grabbed the transvestite around both of his/her legs and rose up off the ground, giving a pretty good imitation of a linebacker tackling a wide receiver in the open field. The cab driver, however, was somewhat hampered by the fact that the transvestite was still holding a handful of his turban, which continued to unravel and which was still attached to his head.

Nevertheless, he found the will and the strength to continue to rise off his knees. Amazingly, he lifted the transvestite right off the pavement, and they both shot up and over the top of the Volkswagen Beetle, landing on the other side of the car in a hopelessly hilarious tangle of legs, arms, an unraveling turban, a flying wig and rocketing sequins.

I remember noticing two things as the light finally changed and our car drove off, taking me to my next appointment with destiny. I remember the two policemen leaping over the Volkswagen after the battling pair, hats flying and nightsticks at the ready. And I remember that the transvestite was not wearing any underwear.

I couldn't help but laugh out loud at the Keystonian scenario. First it was a giggle, then a chortle and then an uncontrollabe laugh. Sture looked at me like I was crazy. And then he started laughing, too.

I guess the stress and strain of the situation had us both wound so tight that we needed a release. There was no time for a drink. Or sex. So that little burlesque performance on First Avenue had to suffice.

We laughed like silly schoolchildren. And I am sure that the driver must have thought that we both had lost our minds and that he was taking one or both of us to New York Hospital for psychiatric observation.

"Are we going to the Payson Pavilion?"

When the driver actually asked us whether we were going to the psychiatric wing, we both stopped laughing—for a moment. Then what he meant by his question registered with both of us simultaneously and we started laughing again, harder and harder. We laughed until tears were pouring down our cheeks and we were gasping for breath. It was almost impossible to answer the understandably bewildered man's question.

"No, driver. We are going to the main hospital entrance." The paroxysms of laughter made me feel like my sides were going to split. And for a few brief moments, the laughter took me a million-million miles away from Gordon and New York Hospital.

It was a good feeling. And as I recall, it was the last good feeling that I would have that night.

CHAPTER 19

Gordon

Every Beat of My Heart

After our little adventure at the Purple Dragon, the Dark Lord and I started going uptown at least two or three times a week. It wasn't like I had shit else to do lying in that motherfucking hospital bed. The worst part was not being able to move or speak while being able to hear and see everything.

I could see the tubes and wires and monitors crawling all over my body, under my arms, up my nose and between my legs, and I did not feel a damn thing. I could see the doctors coming around every few hours, poking, prodding and shining those fucking lights in my eyes. From their comments, I gathered that they couldn't see any reaction or response from me even though, every time, I tried my damnedest to shout, blink, wink, flinch or wiggle or do something to let the doctors and the whole fucking world know that I was alive.

I heard the nurses and orderlies when they were checking my vital signs or changing the sheets or bathing me. I heard them laughing and joking with each other, ignoring me like I was just a piece of furniture. I had heard the doctors tell them that talking to me might help my recovery by eliciting some kind of response from me, but those useless motherfuckers never said a word to me unless the doctors were around.

When the doctors were around, they were like Heckle and Jeckle, yapping and laughing and chatting with me just like they had been instructed. When left to their own devices, however, they did just what they had to do and nothing more. That meant bathing me, changing my sheets, and making sure that my tubes and wires and monitors were functioning properly.

I remember one time when they were changing the sheets, somebody fucked up and I fell onto the floor—face first, as I recall. That caused a bit of a ruckus, and I had to laugh to myself at the commotion that my accident caused.

It seemed like every doctor and nurse in the whole goddamned hospital showed up in my room. People were running around shouting orders, reading my charts and checking my vital signs like they were really concerned.

But they weren't fooling me for a minute. The only things that concerned them were their own asses and what might happen if a lawsuit came out of this little mishap.

As it turned out, the only injury I suffered was a broken nose. And since no one came to see me with any regularity, the hospital—the doctors, the nurses, the orderlies and the administrators—conspired to keep the whole incident out of my file. Since I wasn't going anywhere, my nose healed on its own, and all was right with the world.

Of course, I shouldn't say that no one came to see me. That fucking-ass bitch wife of mine would come about every three months to see if I was dead yet. I could see in her eyes that that was what was on her mind.

She had to know that if I ever got my ass out of that hospital bed, I was going to make her suffer so fucking much that she would beg me to kill her. I still can't understand why my blood pressure and heartbeat did not elevate when she walked into the room with that slick snake motherfucker Paul Taylor. She was probably fucking him, too.

Not that I could blame Paul if she was fucking him. Kenitra was a knucklehead and a troublesome bitch—with a capital "T." But that was still some of the best pussy that I had ever had. And some of the best head, too. And after a good beatdown, she would do anything, and I mean anything, that I wanted her to do.

They obviously didn't realize that I could hear every word that they said in my presence. So it didn't take me long to figure out that Paul had somehow found the ten-million-dollar rainy day fund in the Bahamas that I had put in Kenitra's name several years earlier. And they both seemed to be pretty pleased with themselves that they had taken *my* money and transferred it to an account some fucking where so that she could live like the motherfucking Queen of Sheba somewhere in California.

I do have to hand it to that bitch; however. She never stood too close to my hospital bed. She had enough sense to know that if she did, somehow, someway, I would find a way to get my hands around that pretty throat of hers and strangle her ass right there on the spot.

Sometimes I would try to count the days for her visit, trying to time her quarterly visits by the calendar on the wall in my room. I would wait and wait, and finally she and Paul would appear at the door and take a step—just one step—inside the room.

And that's when I would concentrate. I would focus. I would try to send telepathic messages to Kenitra to come over to my bed. That's it . . . just . . . a . . . little . . . closer. That's it, just a little closer so that you can get a good look. Just a little closer so that you can see that I'm still alive. Just a little closer so that I can strangle your cheating, lying, thieving, whoring, pretty black ass. Just a little closer . . . please . . . just . . . a . . . little . . . closer. . . .

But I had to hand it to the bitch. She always did have serious survival skills. She knew how to fake that she had passed out or was unconscious when I was beating the shit out of her or tying her up or fucking her in the nastiest, and most degrading ways.

She always had good survival skills. And I figure that whether or not she could hear my telepathic messages, or just read them in my eyes, she had enough good sense to stay the fuck away from me.

CHAPTER 20

Diedre

Darn That Dream

From the moment that Paul got the call from the hospital, every terrible, horrible memory about Gordon and his betrayal came bubbling to the surface of my mind. I remember it like it was yesterday.

Paul and I were still in bed that September morning, watching *Today* to find out what had gone on in the world while we slept. We were still reeling from learning the night before of Gordon and Ray Beard combining forces to support the mayoral candidate opposing the incumbent mayor whom Gordon had proposed that Morningstar support. We were further shocked and dumbfounded by the news report that morning.

In a shocking development in the New Orleans mayoral race, local police announced the discovery

*early this morning of the body of the victorious
mayoral primary contender, Percy Broussard. The
candidate was discovered with two of his financial
supporters, Gordon Perkins and Raymond Beard
of New York, both of whom are in intensive care in
local hospitals in New Orleans. The three men
were found in the suite of a local hotel where a victory celebration had been held a few hours earlier.
All three men were found naked, and the door was
locked from the inside.*

*The cause of Mr. Broussard's death is unknown
at this time, but a reliable source has told NBC
News that a kilogram of cocaine and several bottles
of vodka were found in the suite. Mr. Broussard
appears to have died from cardiac arrest, and
Perkins and Beard are suffering from severe drug
overdoses. This report will have to be confirmed
after an autopsy is performed on Mr. Broussard
and further toxicological tests are performed on
Perkins and Beard.*

*NBC News has also learned that police respond-
ing to an anonymous call discovered documents
that clearly implicate the Broussard campaign in
a plot to forge documents and falsify testimony related to recent charges against Mayor Percy Lodrig
and his father.*

*The Lodrig campaign is almost certainly going
to demand a new primary election, and it would
seem, even at this early point, that Prince Lodrig
will be reelected mayor of New Orleans.*

Paul and I found small comfort in his ignomin-
ious demise. By the time we learned that Gordon's
lying ass was in an intensive care unit somewhere

in bayou country, we were too involved in trying to ensure the survival of Morningstar to spend too much time caring about him.

But I remember that from the very beginning, I thought that Gordon simply was too evil to die and that he was going to visit additional plagues on all of us as long as he lived. And, God forgive me, I wished that he would die. And die is exactly what he did not do.

For the past three years, Paul had been the point man for seeing that Kenitra was liberated from Gordon, the ten-million-dollar secret account in the Bahamas being an absolute godsend. And for the past two years, I watched Paul take the calls from Gordon's doctors, informing him of the minimal changes in his condition.

But I knew. Gordon was not going to die. And I knew that someday, somehow, Gordon would revive and would find a way to torment us once more.

And that is why I was more than surprised when Paul got that late-night call summoning him to New York Hospital because Gordon's condition had taken a dramatic turn for the worse. There is something maniacally awful and symmetrical about late-night calls from hospitals. The calls never bring good news, and the calls are never ever forgotten.

Paul started to move with a sense of orderly madness, moving fast to get dressed and ready to go, without any seeming rhyme or reason to his pace or order of getting ready. At times like this, Paul usually did not have a lot to say.

"I think I'm coming with you." I started to figure

out what to put on Paul Jr. and what I was going to
wear. Clearly, time was not our friend, but I was
also used to moving fast at a moment's notice.

"What about Paul?" Paul stopped as he was
putting on his scarlet knit pullover, which I had
bought for him at Paul Stuart for his birthday. The
expression on his face registered a surprise that
puzzled me for a moment.

Paul had never known me to be the homebound
wife or homebound mom. And now, with a medical
crisis involving the co-conspirator who posed the
most danger to the investment firm that I headed,
Paul expected me to stay at home and wait for his
call? Paul could be loveably insane at times, but
this was not one of those times.

"Paul, sweetheart." I spoke in slow and measured tones. We did not have time for an existen-
tial rationalization of our relationship—again. But
I know that at times, I fervently wished that I could
understand how that man's brain worked. At that
moment, I had not a clue.

"Paul, Paul Junior is not made of Steuben glass
or Cuban sugar. I will wrap him in a blanket after I
get dressed and the three of us will ride down to
the hospital. Did you really think that your 'wifey-
poo' would sit here with our baby while you faced
this crisis by yourself? Aside from the fact that you
shouldn't have to do this alone, Jerome and I are
the principals of Morningstar and we need to be
there for whatever the hell is happening at that
goddamn hospital. And we need to be there
tonight. And you, my fine feathered protective lu-
natic husband, had better call Jerome so that he is
not looking to kick your ass in the morning."

"Did I ever mention that you have a way with words?"

"Not lately, *mon cher.*"

"That's because, though you have been blessed with many skills and talents, you were obviously unavailable when tact and discretion were being passed around." Paul was kind of smiling as he resumed dressing.

Frankly, it didn't matter to me whether he wanted me to come or not. I *was* going to the hospital. But the last thing that we needed at that point was another battle in the War of the Roses. I prayed that he was going to use the sense that the Good Lord had given him.

"Diedre, when you are right, you are right. I'll call for a car and get Paul ready while you get dressed. I don't know what I was thinking."

My silent prayer had been answered. As I started getting dressed, I smiled to myself. I was pretty certain that he didn't know that Sture would be there, too.

It was going to be a very interesting impromptu late night gathering. And, it was really not much of a surprise to me that the events of the evening would be courtesy of one Gordon Stallworth Perkins.

CHAPTER 21

Jerome

Cristo Redentor

At fourteen and twelve, my boys, Jerome and Channing, were certainly old enough to be left alone at one in the morning as I got dressed to head out from my home in Hastings-on-Hudson, about forty-five minutes outside of New York City. There really was no need to try to get a sitter at that time of the night, and I am sure that my two guys would have taken it as some kind of supreme insult if I had done so. I did, however, wake Jerome to let him know that he was "officially in charge" and that I would be back in time for breakfast. I also took the precaution of engaging the security system for the house and informing the security company's monitoring desk as I left for downtown.

Paul had been particularly terse and tense in letting me know about the call that he had gotten from the hospital and the need for him to go to Gordon's bedside in the middle of the night. Given the fact that Paul would rarely use a sentence if he could use a paragraph instead, I figured that the doctors had not given him much more than a summons over the phone and, most importantly, he must have thought there had been a fairly serious and ominous turn of events.

Ninety-nine percent of the time, I trusted Paul's judgment implicitly, and this was one of those times. When I hung up the phone, I never hesitated. I checked on the boys, got dressed, secured my home, got in the car and headed down from Westchester County to Manhattan. As I made my way over to the New York State Thruway, I called from my cell phone and advised the twenty-four-hour dispatching desk at Teterboro Airport that Paul and I would not be flying to Los Angeles later that day.

My Mercedes-Benz practically drove itself, and at that time of the night, there was barely any traffic on the highway. The relative solitude on the road gave me time to reflect and to think about my conversation with Diedre at the office.

I truly had it set in my mind that I would never have any contact with Ray Beard again. When I received that chickenshit letter from him announcing his departure from the firm, I just knew that there would never be a reason for us to speak again. Still, looking at the whole thing objectively, I could understand his reasons for making the business decision that he made, even if I didn't agree with that decision.

But, after he pulled the supernaturally craven

stunt of secretly teaming up with Gordon to betray Diedre, Paul and me, I had to restrain myself from spending time and energy on thoughts of revenge and vengeance. Indeed, it was Charmaine who counseled me to just move on and leave Ray Beard alone. It was Charmaine who predicted that there was a terrible karmic consequence that he would have to face, she was proven right. And as a result of the New Orleans Fiasco, Raymond Russell Beard III was left humiliated and partially paralyzed. His long-term future was predicted to center around an excruciating regimen at a rehabilitation facility and what was once a promising career was reduced to shards.

I could not have plotted a more succinct or fitting revenge. Ray could have faced the physical and psychological rigors and challenges of rehabilitation, especially with Monique at his side. He was certainly brilliant enough to find a way to resuscitate his career and reinvent himself by means of a half dozen other professional pursuits. But the humiliation—that was something else again.

We all have our faults. And sometimes, those frailties can end up being the seeds of our destruction. In Ray Beard's case, the seven deadly sins were all wrapped up in his pride. Somewhere along the line, his self-confidence and self-esteem had morphed into an arrogance and conceit that absolutely warped and twisted his judgment and clouded his mind when it came to matters of the greatest importance.

Ray just could not comprehend the fact that the universe did not revolve around Raymond Russell Beard III. He really thought that everyone in his circle of affinity made every major decision with him in mind. As a result, he perceived insult when none was intended. He saw praise when it wasn't there. And he always thought that he was on the verge of discovering some kind of plan, plot or intrigue involving the people that he knew that somehow had him as the central focus.

"Paranoid" would probably be a good word to describe that aspect of Ray's personality, but I am not a clinical psychiatrist and I certainly would be the last one to cast the first stone when it comes to being suspicious of my surroundings and other people. But Ray always seemed to *believe* that his best interests were served by keeping an eye on the whole world because the whole world was out to get him.

As I look back, the true turning point in the relationship between Ray and me came when Paul thought up the Morningstar concept right after Winner Tomlinson's memorial service and we excluded Ray from the subsequent merger discussions. I am sure now that at that point, every twisted conspiracy theory rattling around in that twenty-four-carat brain of his was confirmed for all time.

I am sure that it was crystal clear to him that some of the most important people in his life were plotting against him. I am also sure that he figured that he was being excluded from future merger discussions because Paul, Gordon, Diedre and I were somehow intimidated by his obvious brilliance, never taking the time to realize that the merger discussions needed to be held solely between the principal owners of the three firms.

And, I am also sure that he figured that the entire Morningstar progression confirmed in his mind his long-held suspicion that his place as my right-hand man and closest personal and professional friend was illusory at best. I had neither the time nor the interest to try to assuage Ray's hurt feelings at the time, and I am sure that he felt that my unwillingness to provide him with some kind of reassurance could mean only that we were never the professional brothers and personal friends that he had thought we were.

My conversation with Diedre at the office was the first time that I had really given Ray and the whole tragic turn of events any serious thought in quite a while. Since we had gotten the news from New Orleans, most of my life had been wrapped up in Morningstar, Charmaine's illness and death, and my efforts to try to make sure that Jerome Jr. and Channing were able to live something resembling a normal life. I had closed my mind and heart to Raymond Russell Beard III, so there was simply nothing to think about.

And now, I had something to think about. Diedre would never be on anybody's list of pushovers or soft touches. In the few years that we had worked together, I had come to know her as an extraordinary judge of people. She had a seventh or eighth sense that seemed to tell her who was worthwhile and who was not worth the time— regardless of pedigree, references or documentation.

It was probably never a really good idea to try and bullshit her, and from what little I knew of Monique Jefferson, I doubted that Monique was trying to pull off a stunt like that in any event. So, when Diedre suggested that we consider giving Ray Beard a chance to work at Morningstar, I didn't have to give her proposal much consideration. If she thought that it was a good idea for our business, I was prepared to support it.

I did, however, have to take a moment to look inside myself because my visceral response was to reject Ray and to have nothing further to do with him. I had not survived the mean streets of Philadelphia and the academic back alleys of Yale and Columbia and the trench warfare of Wall Street by giving the people who would harm me second chances.

My survival instincts were finely tuned to avoid and eliminate betrayal and deception. And my success has been a testament to my policy of avoidance and elimination.

As I took the highway toward the Bronx and could see the lights of Manhattan shimmering over the horizon, as if some alien mothership was just over there, I had a chance to give some more thought to the turn of events involving Ray. After all, there had been many times in life when I had had to exercise my own judgment to look after my family, my business and myself.

But I have always known that judging people has many hidden pitfalls, starting with the fact that the faults that we see in others are sometimes simply a reflection of our own. And I also have come to realize that being the one to cast the first stone is a good way to end up under an avalanche of recrimination and regret.

There was no question in my mind that Ray had

been absolutely wrong. In my view he had been a traitor and a betrayer, a liar and a thief, who had run off with my trust and my hopes for him. I didn't feel that it was my role to forgive him—but I tried to figure out how I could forget his misdeeds, especially since they were so personally hurtful.

And that's when I realized that I was wallowing in the same slough of egoism that had caused Ray's downfall. In being brutally honest with myself, I realized that my biggest issue with Ray was not that he had betrayed Morningstar and my partners, but that he had betrayed *me* and had hurt *my* feelings. My biggest issue with Ray was personal, not business, and that realization hit me like a slap across the face.

In point of fact, Ray had made some very poor decisions. Leaving my firm so precipitously was certainly one of them. His linking up with Gordon was certainly a doomed prospect from the beginning, as Gordon was able to mask his predatory nature with a veneer of friendship that Ray probably needed because he perceived me as betraying him in the whole Morningstar process. And Ray had certainly paid a very high price for his mistakes. And one payment involved the termination of our friendship and personal relationship.

Ray Beard was still a young man with a lot to learn. Ray Beard had been brutally tutored as to the consequences of poor decision making and was smart enough to have learned from his Job-like experiences. Ray Beard was still an exceedingly brilliant businessman and corporate finance technician.

I realized what Diedre must have seen during her conversations with Monique: that if I could put my hurt feelings aside, Morningstar had the opportunity to add an asset to our management team. And, I thought, if I could stop thinking about my hurt feelings for half a second, I might have an opportunity to renew a valued professional and personal relationship.

As I steered my car onto East River Drive heading to my rendezvous with Paul, Diedre, Kenitra and Gordon, I realized that second chances were few and far between. I decided to trust Diedre's judgment, I decided to trust my judgment, and I decided to believe in Ray Beard once more.

CHAPTER 22

Gordon

Can You Read My Mind?

The Dark Lord came to the hospital once again, with my street gear in hand as usual. By now I was used to the fact that whenever he came to visit, nobody on the hospital staff noticed him and no one seemed to mind when he helped me disengage from my tubes and wires and monitors.

At one point, I thought it strange that I could just walk out of the hospital whenever I wanted to, but I guess that as long as my allegedly comatose ass was back in the Special Intensive Care Unit by dawn, it was okay. I felt like I was in the middle of some kind of fucking vampire story, and the crazy thing is that I was cool with it.

We started to get a regular routine going. As soon as I had finished getting dressed, we would go downstairs on the elevator and right out the lobby. No one would ever say a fucking word to me. As a matter of fact, no one even seemed to notice the Dark Lord and me sashaying out the front door as if we owned the whole motherfucking hospital.

The Dark Lord usually arranged for a gypsy cab from East Harlem to be waiting for us. It was always the same car and it was always the same driver—Esteban Escondido. Esteban, who liked to be called El Steve, was an Ecuadorian brother from someplace outside of Quito, as best I could figure out.

El Steve was cool. He knew exactly when to show up and he knew to always have about a quarter of an ounce of Colombia's finest ready for me. I needed those seven grams of coke after being cooped up in that hospital for days at a time. And I needed to have some coke around to make sure to get the party started with a couple of bitches that I was planning to see at the Purple Dragon that night.

The ride uptown was almost always the same. El Steve drove straight up First Avenue while I snorted some blow. The music on the car stereo was pumping sounds by Jay-Z and Missy Elliott and Ja Rule and some other miscellaneous rapper motherfuckers who I didn't know. Meanwhile, the Dark Lord and I would usually try and figure out how much fun we could have that evening.

But this night was going to be a little different. In addition to the bitches and the blow and the Rémy at the bar of the Purple Dragon, we had some business to conduct. I had always had an entrepreneurial urge, ever since my first newspaper route as a kid in New Rochelle.

Then there was my car-washing and lawn-care enterprise that, by the time I graduated from high school, employed twenty of my New Rochelle High School classmates. I started investing in the stock market during my freshman year at Howard University and, by my sophomore year, I had made enough money to buy one of the photocopying franchises in Washington, DC, near the campus. By the time I graduated, I owned four other franchises, in Maryland and Virginia.

I sold those franchises and used the proceeds to continue to build up my stock portfolio. While I attended the Tuck School of Business at Dartmouth College in New Hampshire, I continued my stock market investments and did some speculation in the real estate market near the Hanover, New Hampshire, campus, a market that was just starting to heat up in the late seventies.

So, by the time I came to New York City with my MBA and a healthy stock portfolio and more than a little cash in my bank account, I was ready to make some real money. And ever since, during my stint at Goldman and when I founded and ran my own firm, I always have had other business interests going.

There has always been my personal stock portfolio. But there have also been real estate investments in New York City, all over the United States and in Europe and South Africa. There is the tool-and-die manufacturing concern in Detroit with the close relationship with General Motors and Ford in which I have had a silent majority interest for well over a decade while a very popular former member of the Detroit Tigers major league base-

ball team has been the public face as president
and (titular) chief executive officer.

I have invested in some successful movies and a
couple of Broadway plays, and I was an early in-
vestor in Apple *and* Microsoft. And all of my successful investments have actually brought in more
cash than all of my successes as an investment
banker. Not that anyone but me knows that full
story.

I always engaged the parallel services of several
law firms and accounting firms. And I am the only
one who knows about the *other* bank accounts that
I have set up, in places like Switzerland, Dubai,
Costa Rica and the Fiji Islands.

All of the accounts are in my name. All of the accounts, that is, except a few that I set up with alternative identities in case I ever needed to be
someone else in some other place. And one account I set up using the name of that dumb bitch
wife of mine.

And it is that one Bahamian account, with ten
million fucking dollars that that goddamn motherfucking asshole Paul Taylor happened to stumble
upon after I had my little mishap in New Orleans.
And it was by listening to Paul and Kenitra chatting in my hospital room that I learned that Kenitra was now living in the high cotton, off my
money. I made myself a promise that one day, Paul
and Kenitra would pay for that little stunt.

There would be time for that, but in the meantime, rolling uptown as G-Perk with my only true
friend, the Dark Lord, I had some new business in
mind. It was okay to hang out at the Purple
Dragon and check out the babes and drink Rémy

and snort some coke in the back room, but I have never felt *complete* unless I was trying to make some money. And it didn't take too long before a real moneymaking idea came to light.

There were always a few lightweight drug dealers rolling through the Dragon selling their nickel and dime bags and loosies (marijuana joints) to the patrons. Ernie Argentina was cool with the commerce as long as no one was too obvious or too stupid about it and as long as these minor merchants paid him a small management fee.

After hanging out there for a while, however, I noticed one particularly smooth operator who never seemed to actually put his hands on any money or drugs, but who seemed to be the vortex for a continuing stream of traffic. I slipped Ernie a C-note and asked him to make an introduction. Within moments, I was seated at a table with a slim young brother named Duke.

Duke was well dressed and elegant in a Purple Dragon sort of way. He was about six feet tall and brown skinned with a shaved head. He was not a big brother—"lithe" would be the first term that came to my mind. But he carried himself in a way that suggested more than a passing familiarity with the martial arts and the art of self-defense—and offense. He favored knits and leather instead of the usual denim/baseball cap/do-rag attire (like I was wearing), and he always wore sunglasses. I decided to get down to business right away.

"The name's G-Perk." We were both trying to figure out where this conversation was going.

"I know. Duke here." We shook hands perfunctorily, and we each took a sip of our respective drinks. I noticed that he favored Corona beer with a wedge of lime in the bottle. For a moment, I felt like I was in some kind of fucking Japanese tea ceremony.

"Duke, I've got some cash and I want to turn it over. You interested?"

"Yeah, I guess I'm always interested when the subject is cash." By his bland, noncommittal response, you would have thought I was talking about the weather. As the saying goes, "He was so cool, ice wouldn't melt in his mouth."

"Yeah, that's right, Duke. I have some cash, and I hear that you might be in the kind of business where some cash might come in handy." I was trying to get a sense of the young brother, who was probably not more than twenty-five. He was playing it cool, as well he should. The question was whether he was smart enough to recognize opportunity when it was sitting right across the table from him.

"Depends on what kind of cash you're talking about, G-Perk. You seem like a down brother so I'm not going to bother with a whole lot of bullshit. I pay enough money in this part of town to know every undercover cop around. So I know you're not a cop. If you are some kind of snitch or a plant or a turncoat motherfucker, I will find out, and I will personally pop a cap in your old ass.

"Go on, Duke." I was starting to like the brother already, although I wasn't crazy about the "old ass" reference. He was handling this situation much the same way that I would have if I were on his side of the table. We continued the conversation. I made sure from my tone of voice and demeanor that he knew that he wasn't intimidating me in the least.

"Okay then. As long as we are straight on that. If you can bring me ten G's, I will give you twenty G's in two weeks. You ask me no fucking questions and I will tell you no fucking lies. Do we have a deal?"

There was a certain electric intensity to this Duke that I enjoyed. We were definitely going to do business.

"No, we do not have a fucking deal." It was, however, my style to always try to keep the other motherfucker off balance. I could see from Duke's expression that my ploy had worked.

"What? Well, fuck it then, old motherfucker, I don't . . ."

"Hold on, Duke. Slow your roll. I don't have time for any small-time bullshit, with you or any of these other Mickey Mouse motherfuckers in the Dragon. So no, we don't have a deal—yet." I knew that I had Duke's attention for about another ten seconds.

"How's this for a deal? I will bring you a hundred G's tomorrow and you will bring me two hundred G's in two weeks. And I will give you a hundred G's every two weeks for the next two months. After that, we'll see."

I could see a small muscle twitch on the side of Duke's jaw. He was now in the deep water and he knew it. He could either swim back to shore or risk fucking around with the sharks. I wanted to know if the boy had heart right away.

I could almost see his mind working. He had to know that if I had one hundred thousand dollars to put into his drug business, I probably had a whole lot more. He also had to know that if I had that kind of money, I also had the resources to track him to the ends of the earth and skin him alive if he tried to fuck with me. Plus, everyone in the Dragon knew of my encounter with the Gate-keeper of the Bar Stool, and Duke had to know that it was not a good idea to fuck with G-Perk.

Duke also had to be thinking about what kind of world he would be living in with a hundred large in his back pocket. He would be moving up the food chain in the drug world in Harlem, and someone was not going to like that. In fact, there was a good chance that some unhappy chappy would want to put a bullet right through that smooth, shaven skull of his. But that was not even almost my problem.

As for Duke, he knew the basic rule of business: no risk, no reward. It was just that in this case, the risk was certain death if he fucked up.

Duke took just another moment to consider the consequences of my offer and his response. And then, for the only time in our relationship, he took off his glasses, revealing a pair of blazing hazel eyes. He put his hand out over the table where we were sitting and looked me in the eye.

"G-Perk, it's a deal."

"Cool, my man. I will see you here at this time tomorrow night with the cash." It was that simple. And with that, I finished my Rémy, paid my tab and Duke's, said good-night to Ernie Argentina, and strolled out of the Purple Dragon along with the Dark Lord. It was time to get back to the hos-pital and figure out my next move.

I got into El Steve's car, which was waiting out

front on 125th Street, and we headed downtown. The Dark Lord and I considered my options all the way back to New York–Presbyterian Hospital and, by the time I settled back in my hospital room, I had a plan.

Despite the coke and the exhilaration of doing drug deals and carrying on with the crazy bitches that seemed to always be around the Purple Dragon, I was real tired when I got back in my hospital bed. I usually went right into some kind of deep, dreamless sleep even though my eyes would be wide open.

It would usually be a few hours before I could start seeing through my open eyes again, but on this September night/morning, all hell seemed to break loose just as soon as my head hit the pillow. I guess the saying about "no rest for the wicked or the weary" must be true. As if I could give a shit.

At first, I had no idea that all the commotion was about me. But, as I saw nurses and doctors running around my bed like they were in some kind of Chinese fire drill, I quickly figured out that something was happening with all of the wires and tubes and monitors and me. And, from the expressions on their faces, I was not having a good evening.

Since I could move neither my eyes nor my head, I had to depend on people walking past my restricted field of vision to figure out who the fuck was in my room. I could see the Dark Lord occasionally pacing across the room at the far end. And, every now and then, a nurse or doctor would almost run by on his or her way to who-knows-where.

I could pick up only bits and pieces of conversation among the doctors and nurses. I heard the words "diminishing vital signs" and "organ failure" and "elevated heart rate and respiration." I clearly heard one doctor say, "Contact the next of kin right away."

None of this sounded very good to me. But the Dark Lord didn't seem to be too worried, so I wasn't worried either. That is, until I saw that jack-leg preacher, the Right Reverend Very Reverend Quincy Holloway, come across my sightlines.

That was when I knew I might be in real trouble.

CHAPTER 23

Paul

Concierto de Aranjuez

One of the things that first attracted me to Diedre was that she defied stereotyping. Usually that has been a good thing. She has always been gorgeous—but plainspoken and accessible. She has always been brilliant and creative and also capable of cold calculation. And despite the caricatures created about women being unable to get dressed or to get moving quickly, she was almost always ready to go before me when we had to go somewhere.

Early that September morning was one of those times when she was ready before me—again. She was on the first floor of our town house calling for the car service while I was still throwing on some clothes. Of course, I had a credible excuse. I was the one who had gotten Paul Jr. out of bed and helped him into some sweatpants, a sweater, socks and sneakers.

Getting a totally unconscious two-year-old dressed was like trying to mold slightly warm Jell-O. There was no cooperation from my little man. Indeed, he remained oblivious to my efforts to get him prepared for the trip downtown to the hospital, clearly preferring to remain in the dreamy world inhabited by small children that I call Babyland.

Finally, with Paul Jr. and me being dressed for the late-night mission, I found a light blanket for him and a leather jacket and Basque beret for me, and headed downstairs. The car service that Diedre had called was waiting outside, and within minutes, we were on Harlem River Drive heading south to FDR Drive, with New York Hospital and Gordon Perkins as our destination. I could certainly have thought of better things to do in the middle of the night.

New York is certainly the City That Never Sleeps. But the nocturnal animal that is New York late at night is a very different beast indeed. The air is clearer; the lights are crisper in their incandescent efforts to pierce the eternal nighttime darkness. Every shadow, every person, every corner, seems to have its own story. This evening's journey was no exception.

Paul Jr.—or PJ, as Diedre and I sometimes called him—was amazing in his ability to sleep soundly no matter what the location, no matter what the circumstance. We were truly blessed in that from the day that he came home from the hospital, PJ slept soundly through the night, interrupting his slumber only in response to his as-yet-incomprehensible pain of hunger pangs. But those hunger pangs came on a very clear schedule, absolutely calibrated to the size of his capacity to hold breast milk or formula. Once Diedre and I got in synch with his timing, we were able to sleep pursuant to a schedule as predictable as any that you would find at Grand Central Station.

On that night, the only sounds that could be heard in the backseat of the car were the light purr of Stan Getz playing "Desafinado" on the local jazz station, CD 109, which I had asked the driver to put on the car radio. The sound of the car's tires, briefly but endlessly kissing the dry pavement as we made our way downtown, is also a sound that I remember.

Since it was late and we didn't want to go through the drill of putting a car seat in the back of the car and almost certainly awakening our heir, Diedre placed PJ against my chest and strapped us both in with the harness seat belt. So the other sound that I remember from that night was my son lightly snoring somewhere over my heart.

As we rode past East Harlem, I espied on the right side of the car, the large brick complex that used to be Benjamin Franklin High School, one of the finest public high schools in the city back in the day. It was a school that represented a portal to success for many sons and daughters of Puerto Rican immigrants—sons and daughters who went on to become lawyers, doctors, successful business owners and, in one case, personal assistant to Jerome Hardaway, co-owner of Morningstar Financial Services.

I don't know why it occurred to me that night—
probably because I didn't feel like thinking about
Gordon Perkins, a subject that never elicited pleasant thoughts in my personal universe. But, for whatever reason, I recalled Jerome telling me about his
assistant, Berta Colon, yet another promising graduate of Benjamin Franklin High School.

Berta was a brilliant student in high school, with
a ticket for success reserved in her name. In her senior year, she received a four-year scholarship to
Mount Holyoke College, and she was literally on
the verge of taking her first step toward her life-
long ambition of becoming a lawyer who would
represent the rights of poor people in East Harlem.

Unfortunately for Berta and the people of East
Harlem, in her senior year, she also met and fell in
love with Hector Colon, a member of the community revolutionary group known as the Young
Lords. Three months before graduation, Berta was
pregnant. A week before graduation, she got married. And with the birth of her son, Hector Jr., and
the descent of Hector Sr. into the omnivorous and
insatiable maw of heroin addiction, her dreams of
Mount Holyoke College and a law degree and
serving as the avenging avatar of the poor people
of East Harlem went the way of the buffalo: virtual
extinction.

Jerome had told me that after Hector Colon
died, Berta had started working in the entertainment
business. She worked for a talent-management-and-
booking agency, handling various administrative
functions and duties. That is, she did that line of
work until the stress and toll of being a single par-

ent with a road job finally made her hit the breaking point.

Hector Jr., who was a brilliant student, sometimes without even trying, started being a serious disciplinary problem in school. Finally, when Berta was on the road and got a call about Hector being suspected of starting several fires, she simply quit her job on the spot and went back to New York to look after her son. She took temporary secretarial jobs until she landed the position as Jerome's assistant.

She was now an integral part of Jerome's professional life and, therefore, a key part of the Morningstar operation. Jerome trusted her without reservation, and over the few years that I had seen her in action, I knew her to be much more than a secretary and receptionist. She really orchestrated the daily functions of Jerome's office and everything that mattered at the firm. And she was fiercely loyal and protective of Jerome.

In the meantime, Hector Jr. straightened up and learned to fly right. After a stint at a special private school for children with disciplinary challenges, he enrolled at Deerfield Academy and graduated with honors. He was now in his sophomore year at Duke University, and he had aspirations of becoming an investment banker like Jerome, whom he simply idolized.

I have no idea why seeing Franklin High School at two o'clock in the morning set off memories of Jerome and Berta and Hector Jr. I imagine that, in part, it was because I wanted to think of anything other than the reason for our journey along the banks of the East River in the middle of the night.

From the time that Gordon Perkins had been flown to New York City in an air ambulance, he had remained in a comatose condition. Since he was totally unable to communicate his condition or his wishes, I assisted Kenitra in getting the New York State Supreme Court to appoint her as Gordon's guardian. The irony of Kenitra being the guardian of her principal abuser wasn't lost on anyone familiar with the facts.

The reality, however, was that on a day-to-day basis, I was the contact person for the hospital and for anyone else who had to discuss any matters concerning Gordon's condition or his interest in Morningstar. And yet another irony was that, in addition to the Bahamian bank account in Kenitra's name into which Gordon had secreted ten million dollars, he had also put his ownership interest in Morningstar in Kenitra's name, having forged her signature on a document designating her as his proxy on all matters related to that stock interest. Now, with Gordon in a coma, Kenitra was an owner of Morningstar on paper and in reality.

Kenitra was truly the silent member of the triumvirate that owned Morningstar. She deferred to Diedre and Jerome on all matters involving the firm. I always figured that she was so glad to have been freed from the soul-leaching dungeon that was her life with Gordon that she would have deferred to Mickey Mouse and Donald Duck if they would just leave her alone and not cheat her out of her interest in the firm.

On several occasions, Jerome and Diedre had discussed the prospect of buying out Kenitra. But the reality was that it was more fair to Kenitra (and a lot less of a burden on the firm) to pay her a share of the profits for the time being and to buy out her interest in a few years, when the value of Morningstar promised to be exponentially greater than it was at present.

The human brain can be a fantastic piece of machinery. But no one has yet been able to fathom the reasons why the conscious, sentient mind will go off on tangents that cannot be explained logically. How, for example, my mind went from Franklin High School to Berta to Jerome to Hector Jr. to Kenitra and Gordon Perkins would be a challenge for a whole battery of psychiatrists. Fortunately, I was not on the therapist's couch. And, in any event, Diedre was there to abruptly summon me back to reality.

"What do you think the doctors are calling you about, especially at this time of night?" Diedre had this habit of looking directly ahead while speaking if we were in a car or airplane. It could be annoying, quite frankly. But it was dark and it was late, and I had come to learn to accept small faults and small blessings, as rare as the latter seemed to be lately.

"I really have no idea. The last I heard from the hospital, Gordon's situation was stable. At the rate he was going, and with continued intensive care, the doctors thought that he would probably live another fifty years. A hell of a thought." God forgive me, but I could not help but note the twist of fate that rendered Gordon insensate but that still kept him in our lives. PJ continued to snore almost imperceptibly. Our conversation, the commotion of driving, and the occasional honking horn—

none of that seemed to disturb his slumber in the least.

"You know that the court requires a quarterly medical report regarding his general medical condition as well as the probability of resuscitation or recovery. Ever since he was rolled off that plane from New Orleans, he hasn't moved a muscle or responded to any outside stimuli. His heart, liver and vital organs have stayed remarkably healthy, and he has physical therapy five times a week to help him keep some kind of flexibility and to keep his muscles from becoming atrophied. Interestingly enough, the most recent reports have indicated a surprising return of muscle tone." I now had Diedre's full attention, and she turned to speak to me.

"How on earth is that possible? I thought you just said that he hasn't moved a muscle in over two years. I never got further than Biology at Wellesley, but I remember that muscle tone can be maintained only with some kind of exercise involving some kind of resistance."

"You remember your biology correctly, Diedre. The only explanation that the doctors have come up with is that Gordon has been going through some kind of deep dream sequence and has been flexing his muscles during those dreams—kind of like doing a series of isometrics. At least, that's how it was explained to me." Hearing myself trying to explain Gordon's condition, I realized once more how strange this situation had been. And now, it seemed like we were entering yet another bizarre episode featuring Gordon Perkins and the rest of us.

What the hell was going on anyway? Was he dead? Was he alive and getting ready to awaken? Was he awake and ready to wreak havoc in all of our lives yet again? I unconsciously held PJ a little tighter and sent a wordless prayer skyward.

CHAPTER 24

Sture

How High the Moon

After laughing ourselves silly at the sight of the battle *royale* on First Avenue, Kenitra and I settled down into some kind of contemplative silence as the car continued north towards New York Hospital and a fateful rendezvous for the both of us.

During our few weeks together as friends and lovers, Kenitra had said very little about Gordon. That was, until that night, when she revealed the awful story involving the loss of her eye and the other unspeakable abuse that he had caused to cascade upon her like some endless torrent of evil. It was almost too much to believe that one person could be that bad for so long.

I had heard all kinds of stories about Gordon over the years. They were gruesome, ghoulish and unimaginably creative. But all the stories were told

by someone who had heard the story from someone else, and there was very little that I truly believed.

When I looked in Kenitra's eyes, I saw something more than fear. I saw a look that almost
seemed as if she were pleading to be rescued because she was trapped—horribly, horribly trapped.
Sometimes, her eyes were reminiscent of the ones
that you saw in old photographs of German concentration camp victims—the eyes of a person who
knew that she was doomed and did not have even
a fraying fragment of hope. And, as it turned out,
everything that I saw in her eyes had been a true
reflection of the horrific reality of her life with
Gordon.

I hated Gordon for all the terrible things that
he had done to Kenitra. I hated him because he
had done them without remorse and without caring about the consequences to her or to himself.
And I hated Gordon Perkins because he had
somehow escaped any punishment or retribution
for his sins.

His comatose state seemed to mock everyone
and everything that he had touched with his hate-
ful presence. He might be in a coma, but he had
not suffered. He had not felt the lash of guilt
across his back, and no pain had been inflicted to
cause him to beg for mercy, if not forgiveness.

As the car pulled off of First Avenue into the circular driveway of the hospital, I found that I had a
capacity for hate and revenge that I never knew existed inside of me. Gordon didn't just deserve to
die; he deserved suffering and vengeance, and as I
stepped out of the car and helped Kenitra out,

holding her fluttering butterfly of a hand, I silently prayed that God would find a way to finally recognize the evil that was Gordon Perkins.

And then we were in the hospital elevator, headed to the eleventh floor, where the Special Intensive Care Unit was located. We followed a labyrinthine path to get to the unit itself once we got out of the elevator. Kenitra stood erect and serene, but she held my hand with a strength that let me know that she was barely holding on to her emotions.

"I'm with you, Kenitra. Whatever it is, I'm with you all the way."

She squeezed my hand even harder as we approached the nurses' station, never saying a word.

I am not sure what either of us expected to see as we answered the summons from Gordon's doctors that night. In looking back, I probably anticipated seeing one or two very officious and very serious doctors. If I had really thought about it, I might have anticipated that there might have even been an administrator or two, just in case some kind of decision had to be made by Kenitra that night.

And, indeed, there were actually four very officious and very serious doctors who, because of their demeanor and their number, approximated a white-jacketed phalanx of bad news in my battered imagination. There were actually five hospital administrators present as well, which was a sure sign that something extraordinary was going on. And there was one other clear sign that could not be ignored.

Standing in the middle of the hallway leading to

Gordon's room was none other than Reverend Quincy Holloway. The same Quincy Holloway who had pretended to carry the stigmata of wounds received at the scene of Martin Luther King's assassination, that were proven to be false. The same Quincy Holloway who had pretended to rescue a U.S. Army Ranger in the Amazon forest, even though the true story revealed that Reverend Holloway spent his time at a luxury resort in Bahia while the Ranger managed to free himself by virtue of pure serendipity. That Quincy Holloway.

Improbably, it was Quincy Holloway who stood in the hospital hallway, holding a microphone and getting ready to be interviewed by the camera crew that he had brought with him. It was more than amazing that he was there, at New York Hospital, at three o'clock in the morning. It was absolutely unbelievable. But there he was, and Kenitra and I stopped in our tracks at the sight of the five-foot two-inch presence of Reverend Holloway in front of us.

I had no idea how he had managed to be there. Kenitra had no idea who might have told him about the latest developments in Gordon's condition. And neither of us knew what to do next. It was as though our truly bizarre world had now taken an otherwordly turn.

Thankfully, at that very moment, Paul and Diedre materialized in the hallway behind us. They must have gotten on the elevator right behind us.

I was never so glad to see Paul in my life.

CHAPTER 25

Gordon

In a Silent Way

All the commotion around my hospital room made it impossible for me to sleep when I got back from the Purple Dragon and my meeting with Duke that night. Most of the time, particularly at night, I was unable to close my eyes, but I was also unable to move my eyes, or turn my head or move any other muscles. As a result, I was condemned to watch my life go by through a rather small-sized television screen. Having seen several doctors and Reverend Quincy Holloway scurry past my line of vision, it seemed like a good idea to pay closer attention to my surroundings.

Having heard words like "organ failure" and "septic shock" was bad enough. But hearing a reference to "last rites" and seeing Reverend Holloway started to actually get me worried. After all was said and done, I figured this fool might actually stumble upon a way to get me killed in this mother-fucking hospital, particularly if my death would get him some publicity. I knew that the Dark Lord would always be by my side and on my side, but he was usually reluctant to intervene directly in my affairs, so it was a good idea for me to pay close attention to the current events at New York Hospital. I listened as carefully as I could to every conversation that was held anywhere near my bedside, as, at that point, no one really believed that I had a conscious bone in my body.

"Reverend Holloway, I am going to have to ask you again to please remove yourself from the premises and to take your camera crew with you." The lead doctor of the team of physicians that was treating me sounded like he knew his argument with Holloway was a lost cause, but he needed to go through the motions, just for the record.

"I am here as Mr. Perkins's pastor and spiritual advisor. I am also here to make sure that a cruel and heartless decision to remove him from life support doesn't take place. I am like a shepherd, and a good shepherd never abandons his flock." Holloway was clearly just getting warmed-up now. The good doctor didn't stand a chance going up against the self-proclaimed good shepherd.

"Mr., I mean Reverend, Holloway. First of all, I don't know how you were able to get into this hospital, but you are trespassing." The doctor was starting to ride the waves of righteous indignation. And I was trying to figure out how the good shepherd had found out about anything that was going on concerning my medical condition. The doctor continued in that indignant tone that doctors adopt when they feel that their sacred healing world has been trespassed upon by the heathens, by the pagans, by the nondoctors.

"Secondly, Reverend, I am sure that no one from this hospital has consulted with you in an official capacity with respect to Mr. Perkins's condition. You are not a family member or a designated legal representative of his interests, and I simply will not discuss his condition with you as a matter of New York State law." I am sure that, in his mind, that last statement concluded his discussion with Quincy Holloway and he would now simply evanesce, like some midget-wraith in a bad dream. He was about to learn how very wrong he could be.

As I lay there, a mute observer of this near-comedic scenario, I tried to focus on two items—one very important, the other a matter of idle curiosity on my part. Being totally immobilized in my hospital bed for almost two years had sharpened my ability to focus and think, since that had been all that I could do, and at that point, I was thinking about how Quincy Holloway and a camera crew had made it to my hospital room.

I have never been averse to publicity. It usually worked to my business advantage, with the notable exception of all the press coverage of my downfall in New Orleans. And, if there had been some discussion outside my room regarding taking me off life support, it is possible that this impeccably dressed gnome of a preacher might have saved my life. But that still didn't explain how he got to the hospital on that night at that time.

I tried desperately to focus on the problem. Consciousness and lucidity seemed to come and go, and I wanted to get to the solution before I drifted off to someplace else, like the Purple Dragon. I tried to think some more, and then it hit me. The answer was so obvious, I would have slapped myself for not seeing it sooner. It was a matter of simple deduction. For a moment there, I felt like goddamned Sherlock Holmes.

Anyone who knew anything about that little motherfucker knew that Quincy Holloway was a grade-A cockhound. His ministry was in third place in the order of his personal priorities, far behind priority number one, which was his deep and abiding and constant pursuit of pussy. Priority number two was his eternal quest for cash and more cash. But, in point of fact, it seemed that fucking was what he thought was his purpose on earth, and it was an aspect of every major event in his life.

The reason that his lie about being at the site of Martin Luther King's assassination was so despicable is that he was fucking some white freak of an heiress in California. The reason he was trying to rescue that U.S. Army Ranger in Brazil is that he was fucking the lost soldier's very attractive mother, and the reason he didn't find the Lost Ranger, as the young man came to be known, is that he was fucking every thong-wearing Brazilian bitch he could get his little midget hands on at the Bahia resort that he accidentally parachuted into when he was supposed to be looking for the soldier.

So, trying to figure out what the Right Reverend

Quincy Holloway was doing in my room was a simple proposition. It was either a matter of following the money or, more likely, of following the pussy.

There was no way for me to look around the room, but nothing stopped me from looking around my mind. I scoured my memory for some clue, some hint of a factoid, something that would link Quincy Holloway's presence to some pussy that was someplace in this hospital. And that's when I figured it out.

From snippets of conversations that I heard her have with Paul Taylor, I knew that Kenitra stayed at the Waldorf-Astoria when she was in New York—presumably to make sure that I was still in a coma and unable to track her down and strangle her cheating, thieving bitch ass. I also knew that Quincy Holloway had been living in a suite at the Waldorf for years courtesy of the generosity of his many supporters in his globally based congregation. That little motherfucker always depended on the kindness of strangers and, strangely enough, strangers always managed to accommodate him.

Clearly, Holloway must have seen Kenitra traipsing through the hotel. I am sure that the dumb-ass bitch figured she was incognegro walking around with a pair of sunglasses, and I am sure that Quincy saw right through that disguise and figured out why she would be in town at all. The good reverend might have been a degenerate cockhound, a minor-league thief and a major-league charlatan, but he was not stupid.

I figured that it wouldn't have taken much deductive reasoning for him to decide to follow Kenitra to find out where I was being warehoused.

Once he had that figured out, all he would have to do would be to get somebody on the hospital staff to feed him the information that he needed regarding my exact whereabouts and condition. For Quincy Holloway, getting that kind of information from one of the nurses would have been a piece of cake.

A number of the nurses were black women, and the overwhelming majority of his global ministry consisted of black females. While several of the nurses that I saw looked like clear winners of the Mike Tyson Look-alike Contest, I could recall seeing several truly attractive nurses pass through my field of vision—nice asses, great bodies, dreamy eyes. Hell, I would have fucked more than a couple of them if I could have gotten my fucking head off the pillow.

And, as I thought about it a little further, I do remember hearing a couple of the nurses chattering about getting some of that hospital cocaine to take to a private party that "the reverend" was having at some hotel in midtown. It didn't take a genius to add one and one and come up with two. And now I knew how Quincy Holloway came to be outside my hospital room, but I still couldn't figure out why he was there.

It wouldn't be long before I found out.

CHAPTER 26

Diedre

Straight, No Chaser

What I remember most about that evening is the sheer, improbable madness of the entire scene at the hospital. I was never more thankful that Paul Jr. was a heavy sleeper.

As Paul and I exited the hospital elevator on the floor where the Special Intensive Care Unit was located, we found ourselves literally two steps behind Kenitra and Sture. They were holding hands and not walking very briskly towards the nurses' station. Kenitra was emanating an extremely high level of tension. There was no doubt and no question why.

Gordon had traumatized her mind, body and soul, and no matter what she might do to recover and rebuild her life, she could never be around Gordon without being embraced by the cold and

pitiless arms of Pure Fear. I was so glad to see Sture
there with her. She absolutely did not need to be
alone in a situation like this. I knew that Paul,
Jerome and I were there for her as well, but she
had told me about the special relationship that she
had started with Sture, and I was glad for her when
she told me. I was even happier for her now, in the
hallway of the hospital.

"Kenitra, Sture, let's talk for a moment before we go down the hall." I was hoping that I
didn't make it sound too urgent, although the
stress of the situation was beginning to be contagious. When Kenitra turned, I could see the
fear and anxiety all over her face, and I had
never seen Sture look so drawn and concerned.

"Diedre, Paul, I'm so glad you are here." Kenitra
flung her arms around my neck and began sobbing and weeping. I put my arms around her trying to comfort her, and for a few minutes, Paul,
Sture and I stood there in silence. That was when
Paul eased away to try and find a cot or small bed
for PJ in one of the rooms usually used by the rela-
tives of patients.

While he was gone, and while Kenitra was trying
to compose herself and Sture and I were trying to
comfort her, events started commencing at opposite ends of the corridor. On one side, we saw
Jerome coming out of the elevator, tall, serene,
wearing a dark fedora and a suede jacket and a
somber expression. He seemed to take in the entire scene as Kenitra lifted her head from my shoulder and mouthed "hello" in his direction. Jerome
nodded, but he seemed to be looking at something behind us.

I turned in the direction in which he was looking. In another place and at another time, it would
have been an hilarious sight evoking peals of
laughter. Even under the circumstances, I cursed
myself for even beginning to smile, but I couldn't
help it.

Coming down the hospital hallway was the elfin
preacher Quincy Holloway, engaged in what
seemed to be a furious conversation with several
doctors and hospital administrators. Arms were
flailing; voices were alternating between shouts
and fierce, hissing whispers. And behind them
were the bright tungsten lights of a video camera
crew, which was seemingly taping the entire encounter.

Surrounding this bizarre tableau were several
nurses and orderlies who were dumbstruck by the
apparition before them. I also saw a couple of
rather huge beefy bouncer types lurking in the
background that I assumed to be part of the hospital security staff. I would have bet that it would not
be long before the good reverend would be igno-
miniously jettisoned from New York Hospital.

That was a bet that I would have made if the situation involved anyone but Quincy Holloway. The
tiny reverend had made a career out of extricating
himself from situations that would have struck
down mortal men. Staying in a hospital without
even a fig leaf of authority was mere child's play
for him. The staff of New York Hospital had no
idea with whom they were dealing.

After all, it was Quincy Holloway who, when it
was discovered that he had lied repeatedly about
being at the scene of Dr. King's assassination, ini-

tially accused *Time* magazine, which had first printed the story, of racism and persecution "in the manner of the slave master."

When that didn't resonate with anyone with an IQ over fifty, he called a press conference with a couple of noted black psychiatrists in tow. It was then that he introduced to the world the concept of "Black Grief." Essentially, black grief was supposed to be a special kind of mental affliction suffered by the postslavery psyche of African Americans that magnifies the impact of any psychological or emotional trauma.

So, Holloway confessed to misrepresenting his presence at the King assassination. He blamed Black Grief for the entire misunderstanding, claiming that Black Grief made him *think* that he was in Memphis on April 4, 1968, even though he was in a California hotel suite with a white heiress well known for her sexual appetite and diverse tastes in men—and women.

Amazingly, Holloway lost very little popular support after his so-called confession. And after taking the hit on the King episode, the press assumed him to be bulletproof and essentially left him alone. His various exploits and adventures since then had only added to his fame and his bank account, and he had ascended into the celestial heavens of celebrity, seemingly for all time.

When he appeared at the hospital that evening, he had just arrived back in New York after having spent the previous month engaging in a hunger strike in Mount Vernon, Virginia, in front of the plantation home of George Washington. He had been leading a campaign to have Mount Vernon de-listed from the National Register of Historic Places unless it was relabeled a "concentration camp for African Americans."

His opening line had been that "Mount Vernon is black America's Auschwitz," and one had to admire his creativity in coming up with a campaign and a slogan that were sure to get on the news every evening. And while there was no chance that Mount Vernon would be de-listed, there was every chance that Quincy Holloway would be on television every day and that the nation—indeed, the whole world—would follow the progress of his hunger strike.

When he had ended his hunger strike a few days earlier, promising to return "until justice is done," he was reported to have gained eight pounds during his ordeal. While he vehemently denied those reports, he certainly didn't look like a man who had been hungry for the past thirty days when I saw him in New York Hospital that night.

I started to feel sorry for the doctors and the hospital administrators.

CHAPTER 27

Paul

Expect a Miracle

I had found a nurse who was nice enough to let me put PJ in one of the small bedrooms reserved for the families of patients. I had just finished wrapping him in a blanket and returning to Diedre, Sture and Kenitra when I saw Jerome coming down the hallway. And that was when, as I waved hello to him, I heard all the commotion down the hall—commotion centered around Reverend Holloway and a gaggle of doctors and hospital administrators. Clearly, this was going to be a night to remember.

I had known Quincy Holloway for too long to be totally surprised by his presence at the hospital at three in the morning. In retrospect, it would have been surprising if he weren't there. I knew immediately that he must have gotten some word about

Gordon's condition, but I couldn't figure out why he was there at that moment in time.

"Let me see what the story is . . . I'll be right back." I spoke quickly to Diedre, Kenitra and Sture. Jerome walked with me over to the madding crowd that was centered on Holloway, the whole scene shimmering under the false daylight-bright camera lights and being recorded for eternity by the video camera crew that had accompanied the reverend.

Seeing the tiny reverend in such an agitated state, arguing vociferously with the doctors and hospital administrators, somehow reminded me of a bantam rooster preparing to do battle with a couple of dull hound dogs. And these were hound dogs that had no idea of what to do next. I could see it in their eyes.

And when the doctors and administrators turned their eyes toward Jerome and me approaching the *contretemps,* I could almost read their minds: *Sweet suffering Jesus on a cross! What now? First, this midget minister with a camera crew at three in the morning. And now, these two tall, serious black men coming our way. Thank God they're well dressed. But what do they want? And where is security when we need it?*

The doctors were Indian and the administrators were white. None of them were happy. But clearly something was going on that kept them from just having the approaching security guards toss everyone out onto First Avenue, sorting out the facts later. I was hoping that I could introduce some element of sanity into this particular imitation of Bedlam.

"Pardon me. I'm Paul Taylor, counsel to Mr.

Perkins's wife, Kenitra Perkins. The courts have also appointed Mrs. Perkins as Mr. Perkins's guardian. She and I were asked to come here this evening, as some medical emergency required our immediate presence." I tried to speak calmly and with firmness that I hoped would begin to settle things down. When I saw that Quincy Holloway recognized my voice and quieted down as he turned around, I knew that I had a chance of turning down the volume.

"I am here with Mr. Perkins's business partners, Ms. Diedre Douglas and Mr. Jerome Hardaway, and given the urgent nature of the message that we received, we would appreciate an immediate briefing." I was looking straight at Holloway as I said this.

Quincy Holloway was one of the few short people I knew who really thought that he was a tall person in a short person's body. He drew himself up to his full height, just slightly past five feet, and while motioning to the camera crew to turn off the video and the lights, he attempted to assert the legitimacy of his presence.

"Paul, Jerome, I am so glad to see some brothers with some *sense*. Maybe you can explain to these godless gentlemen that whatever his sins in the past, Gordon Perkins deserves to have a spiritual advisor at his bedside during these urgent moments." With his grandiose gestures and grandiloquent phrasing, he made one believe that one of the original apostles had been dispatched by the Great Redeemer to look after the New Prodigal Son, none other than Gordon Perkins.

"Reverend Holloway, as you mentioned, this appears to be a very urgent moment, so allow us to speak with the doctors and hospital representatives, and then we can figure out how you can best minister to Gordon."

Quincy Holloway and I had been through too much too many times for us to spend too much time in a choreographed debate. We both knew that he was pushing his luck, as usual. We both also knew that Quincy Holloway was capable of creatively manufacturing trouble for anyone who didn't try to help him get his way. So, without further conversation, there was an unspoken agreement that I would see what I could do to address whatever concerns he had as soon as we all found out what the hell was going on with Gordon.

"Paul, I have always known you to be a brother possessed of good judgment. My colleagues from the media and I will wait with proper courtesy and respect while you and your people sort things out."

Quincy was smiling as if he had already won a victory, and in point, he had. Our presence and brief conversation had legitimized his presence in front of the New York Hospital representatives, who realized, with some finality, that arguing any further with Reverend Quincy Holloway was a losing proposition. On the other hand, I am sure that they experienced some feeling of relief because now the good reverend was our problem.

I wasn't too crazy about Quincy now being "our" problem. On the other hand, I was reminded of an expression that I had heard in South Africa during one of my many business trips there: "When you are trying to eat an elephant, you cannot do it all with one bite." In other words, when you had a big problem to solve, you had to solve it in bits and pieces. Sending Quincy Holloway down the hall was one small bite.

"Thanks for understanding, Reverend. Gentlemen, could we go somewhere quiet so that you can explain to Mrs. Perkins and me the nature of the crisis? And actually, given the circumstances, I think it would be appropriate for Ms. Douglas and Mr. Hardaway to also be in attendance."

"Whatever will let us get down to the reason for our meeting is fine with me, Mr. Taylor. Right this way." One of the hospital administrators, who I later learned went by the name of Alfred Kennedy, seemed to take charge and led us to a quiet alcove area that had several chairs and a small couch. With the air of an Elizabethan courtesan, he motioned us in the direction of the sitting area, and our little party of five—Kenitra, Sture, Jerome, Diedre and I—walked the short distance to be seated and to finally find out what all the fuss was about.

As we walked away from Quincy Holloway and his camera crew, I subtly signaled for him to wait and not to follow. I have always had to hand it to the tiny reverend. He may never have been the smartest player in the game, but he always had good instincts. And at that point, his instincts correctly told him to play it cool for the moment. And so he acknowledged my direction and stepped back to have a few words with his crew.

It took a moment for all of us to get situated and for introductions to be made. When the formalities had been dispensed with, it was time for the physician who was in charge of Gordon's case, a

Dr. Vijay Krishnamurthy, to explain why he, and
New York Hospital's finest thought that it was so
important to meet at three o'clock in the morning
to urgently discuss Gordon's condition.

Dr. Krishnamurthy was a native of Bangelore,
India, tall, bespectacled, mustached and elegant
without seeking to impress the world. Extremely
dark, in the manner of many natives of the Indian
subcontinent, he was dressed in a pair of crisply
pressed slacks and a white medical jacket, neither
of which looked as if they had ever been worn before. He stood before us and took out a fine linen
handkerchief to clean his glasses—a process that,
under the circumstances seemed to take forever.
He finally finished clearing his vision, and then he
cleared his throat.

CHAPTER 28

Sture

In a Mellow Mood

From the time we got off the elevator at the hospital, it seemed to me that Kenitra and I had stumbled into a kaleidoscopic whirlwind of sights and sounds and people and voices. Since we were already wound as tight as guitar strings, it didn't take a lot for us to quickly approach being unhinged. I know that I felt as though I was trapped in a nightmare inside of a circus inside of a hospital.

I thought that Kenitra might permanently damage the circulation in my left hand, which she was holding tightly. I had always suspected that Gordon, and his memory, had a special hold over her. There was no way that she could have lived with such a fearsome person and not been permanently terrorized and traumatized. And after she had told me some of the gruesome details of their relationship during the ride from the hotel to the hospital, I was amazed that she could summon the will to be in the same building with him, even if he was in a coma.

Knowing what little I knew about their relationship, I was feeling queasy at the mere thought of the things that man had done to her. I can only imagine what she was feeling as we sat down in that small alcove to listen to Dr. Krishnamurthy.

The doctor spoke in the clipped, lilting tones that characterize the speech patterns of most Indians that I have known. He looked around the room at all of us as he spoke. Jerome, Paul, Diedre and I all were paying close attention. But it was clear that his message was intended for Kenitra, whose eyes were still veiled by her sunglasses and who still had not loosened her surprisingly viselike grip on my hand.

"As you are aware, at the time of his original, ah, accident, Mr. Perkins suffered a catastrophic episode involving temporary heart failure occasioned by a massive ingestion of stimulants—stimulants that we believe were cocaine-based. The consequence of the heart failure was a severely diminished flow of blood to the brain, resulting in conditions that we find in patients who have suffered a massive stroke." The doctor's cadence and tone were unchanging, but I could sense a certain tension and urgency in his voice.

As he continued, the only ambient sounds that I remember hearing were the occasional beeps coming from the various monitors and machines that were attached to Gordon Perkins, in the room just a few yards down the hall.

"When Mr. Perkins was brought to our facility, his vital signs were barely perceptible, and our original diagnosis was that he had suffered irreversible brain damage and that he would never awaken from the comatose state that he entered almost three years ago." It was not clear whether the doctor paused again for dramatic effect or to make sure that all of us were listening to what he was about to say. I glanced over at Kenitra. She was like a mahogany statue, not a muscle moving, her gaze riveted on the doctor, her hand still clenched around mine.

"Until recently, Mr. Perkins's condition was stable. His vital signs have stayed constant, and his brain activity has been barely perceived by our most sensitive monitors. Our physical therapists have done all that they can to ensure that his muscles do not completely atrophy, and his overall musculature is not bad, given the fact that he has not voluntarily moved from a hospital bed during all this time.

"We have actually observed the occasional tensing of his muscles during times when his minimal brain waves have increased almost imperceptibly. The minimal movements and even more minimal brain waves could be indicative of some kind of dream process occurring—a real indication of brain activity." It was at this point that Kenitra became even more tense, as if bracing herself for an avalanche of bad news.

"However, in my opinion, this activity, if I can call it that, can only be described as illusory and ephemeral. There is absolutely no possibility that Mr. Perkins will ever recover from the brain damage that he has suffered, and there is even less possibility that he will ever regain consciousness. To put it simply, he will never come out of this coma." I thought that I felt Kenitra's death grip on my hand relax, if ever so slightly.

"Dr. Krishnamurthy, we certainly appreciate your updated diagnosis. Our concern regarding Mr. Perkins's condition has remained constant over these three years." I could sense that Paul was about to ask the question that was on all of our minds.

"But doctor, with all due respect, what event has occurred that required you to call us in the early hours of the morning? Exactly what is the emergency?"

"I was just getting to that point, Mr.— Mr. Taylor is it? Yes, yes, yes. My colleagues and I apologize for the lateness of the hour, but in the last twenty-four hours, we have begun to observe the onset of organ failure. His vital signs, which have been relatively constant, have started to definitely move downward. I am of the opinion that if we do not take immediate extraordinary steps, Gordon Perkins will be dead within the day." Dr. Krishnamurthy paused to take a breath before answering the remaining questions that his stunning statement had sprinkled around the room. Once more, it seemed as if Kenitra relaxed ever so slightly. I almost felt as if I could read her mind: *Please, please, God, please let him die. Forgive me for what I'm thinking, but please, God, please let him die. I just can't live with him still being alive, even like this. Please let him die, God. Please.*

"Well, doctor, whatever the issues might be, perhaps you should get to the point so that Mrs. Perkins can take a moment or two to consider whatever options you are going to present to her. I assume you are going to give her some options?" Diedre always had a way of getting to the point, and it was probably a good idea for her to have stepped in before the good doctor went off on a lecture tangent as if we were a bunch of first-year medical students longing for enlightenment.

"Yes, yes, of course. Please forgive me for rambling. My wife says I do that all the time . . . my, my, I am doing it again." The doctor started to get flustered, took a deep breath and settled himself down.

"The human body is meant to function on its own. Life-support systems are meant to be temporary aids and not the basis for a patient staying alive indefinitely. What happens with some patients, and what has happened with Mr. Perkins, is that the human body can become overly reliant upon the various monitors and life-support systems that medical science can provide. The organs can become 'lazy,' in laymen's terms. Once that happens, the body will die within a relatively short period of time." At this point, he paused to let his words sink in. He certainly had our attention, and at that point, I don't know that any of us knew where the doctor was heading with all of this.

None of this sounded like good news for Gordon, of course. The question now was whether any of this would constitute good news for Kenitra and the rest of us.

CHAPTER 29

Kenitra

Desafinado

As I listened to Dr. Krishnamurthy, I felt like I was in some kind of insane movie scene—a bizarre and horrible scene that was being played out as a comedy. Only I wasn't laughing.

It wasn't just that I loathed Gordon. It wasn't just that I feared him, even with him being in a coma and seemingly sliding off towards the open arms of Death. I wanted Gordon to die, and I hated myself for that. But I still had been praying for his death for all those years.

I prayed for him to die when he was beating me. I prayed for him to die when he was raping me—raping me in the "traditional" way and then, in his more depraved moments, with sex toys, champagne bottles and anything else that he could get his hands on. I prayed for him to die when he caused me to lose my eye. And I prayed for him to die every time he fed me cocaine and pills and alcohol.

And when he almost died as a result of his escapade in New Orleans with Ray Beard, I thought that my prayers had been answered. From what little I could make out of the medical reports, there was just no way that the bastard could live after the damage that he had visited upon himself.

In fact, I remember sitting in that very same alcove at New York Hospital listening to the very same Dr. Vijay Krishnamurthy explain to Paul and me that Gordon's expectancy of survival could be measured in months, if not weeks, if not days. But even that rosy prognosis kept me in New York City only long enough for Paul to get my finances in order and to help me buy my condominium unit in Venice Beach. Now that Gordon seemed to be powerless, I wanted to be sure to be as far away from him as possible. That's because as long as he was alive, my life and my sanity were in danger. So, like Diedre, Paul, Sture and Jerome, I waited and listened to hear what the doctor had to say next.

"The best course of action that I can recommend—indeed the only course of action—is to remove Mr. Perkins from life support immediately. There is, of course, a certain risk attendant to such a course of action. Indeed, he may die as a result of being taken off of the life support and monitoring systems. But I assure you that there is no chance that he will live for more than another two days at the most if he remains on life support."

We were already paying attention, but now we

were literally hanging on his every word. And it seemed as if his every word was directed at me.

"Doctor, let me see if I understand what you are telling us. If my . . . husband stays on life support, he will die and there is no chance of his living for anything more than another two days. But if you take him off life support, he may live, but he may die."

"Exactly. You now understand the situation perfectly, Mrs. Perkins. Obviously, your witnessed consent to his being taken off life support is needed for us to move forward. However, as I have tried to explain, time is not our friend in this situation, and if we are going to move forward in this fashion, then we must do so quickly. Otherwise, any decision that you make will be moot and will have no bearing at all on your husband's condition."

I tried to let the words sink in. In what seemed to me to be another cruel twist of fate, my prayers for Gordon's death might be answered. If I left him on life support, he would certainly die. If I had him taken off life support, he might die. And, he might live. Either way, the decision regarding his life and death was in my hands. If he died, I would have to live with that guilt for the rest of my life. If he lived, that monster might walk the earth again and try to befoul my life once more. If he lived, I would most assuredly die, by his hand or my own.

Oddly enough, I was reminded of an ancient bit of cautionary advice: "Be careful what you ask for." I had prayed for Gordon's death for so long, it was like saying grace before meals. And now, I had the power of life and death over him, with all of its awful consequences.

"I see. Thank you, Doctor. Now I understand the need for urgency, and I appreciate your taking the time to explain this. Now, could you please excuse me for a few moments while I speak to my friends? I will give you my decision in a few moments."

"Yes, yes, of course. My colleagues and I will be in the hallway. I wish I could say to take your time, but I'm afraid that time is of the essence." And with that, Dr. Krishnamurthy and the other doctors and Mr. Kennedy and the hospital administrators left the alcove and gathered down the hall outside of Gordon's room.

I could hear Quincy Holloway and his camera crew milling about at the other end of the hall. Everyone in the alcove was silent for a moment. I am almost certain that we were all thinking the same thing. Could we all be witnessing the end of Gordon Perkins?

CHAPTER 30

Paul

Maiden Voyage

That evening at the hospital, I found it hard to figure out if bizarre things happen when Quincy Holloway is around or if the mighty reverend is the cause of bizarre things occurring in the first place. Whatever the case, Reverend Holloway's presence turned a very compelling and difficult situation into a semiclassic scene from the eternal theater of the absurd.

Quincy smelled the imminence of some significant event the way a shark smells blood in the water miles away. As I approached him, I could see a look in his eyes that would best be described as feverish. He knew that something was going on, and being that he was the Right Reverend Quincy Holloway, he assumed the right to be a part of that something, whatever it was, whatever it was going to be.

"Quincy, I . . ." I hesitated as I tried to figure out what I was going to say. I noticed Quincy's camera crew bustling in preparation for springing into action. It seemed that the tense conference in the alcove was turning out to be the proverbial quiet before the storm.

"They're going to do it, aren't they, Paul?" Quincy did not believe in beating around the bush.

I leaned over so that we could speak to each other without raising our voices. I needn't have bothered.

"Do what, Quincy?" Playing dumb has never been my forte, as I flatter myself that I have no natural aptitude for the role. In any event, it was a futile ploy in this situation.

"Paul, Paul, you know the old expression 'Don't bullshit the bullshitter.' It's too late at night *and* too early in the morning to be playing these kinds of games. They're going to pull the plug on Gordon, aren't they?"

Although there was more than a foot difference in height between us, he managed to look me directly in the eyes, and at that moment, I knew that my only strategy with Quincy was to play it straight.

I put on my most solemn face and continued, trying to figure out how this conversation could possibly have a positive outcome. It wasn't looking good for the home team.

"Quincy, it's a pretty rough time for Kenitra and everyone else. Yes, they are going to take Gordon off life support. Ironically, and incredibly, it's his only chance to live. That's the whole, sad story."

"In that case, I would like to go inside Gordon's room with you to lead a prayer for his recovery—with my camera crew, of course." He said this in such a matter-of-fact tone that I had to give him points for sheer nerve, even though he was lacking even a modicum of respect or decency.

"Quincy, are you out of your mind? If the doctors don't throw you out of Gordon's room, Kenitra will probably have a cataleptic seizure on the spot. This is a bad enough scene without your becoming the ringmaster of the circus. The answer is no. You cannot come into Gordon's room, and your camera crew for damn sure can't film anything."

I felt myself starting to get agitated with Mini-Meddler, and that is probably why I missed his signal to his crew to turn on the camera lights. Suddenly, the hallway was flooded with the light of day. Looking down, I could still see the reverend, now backlit. And I knew that a video camera was aimed directly at me, and I could see a microphone edging its way into my field of vision.

"Paul, we have always found a way to get along. Let's not stop now. Things have been a little slow for me lately, and I need to send the wire services and networks some tape of me in action. Now, you can be a part of that tape, standing in the doorway preventing me from giving spiritual aid and support to Gordon Perkins in what may be his last few minutes on earth, or you can let me come in the room there and be just a small part of the proceedings." Quincy was smiling, but his eyes were not.

I noticed the nurses and doctors moving urgently, and what looked like resuscitation equipment was being moved down the hall and positioned right outside Gordon's room. They moved with a purpose that indicated a serious turn of events was about to take place. Looking over my shoulder, I could see that Jerome, Kenitra, Diedre and Sture were outside Gordon's room. Dr. Krishnamurthy was conferring with his colleagues for what was probably one last time before taking the irrevocable act of removing Gordon from the tangle of wires and monitors and tubes that had consisted of his life support system for almost two years. I didn't have a lot of time to converse with Quincy.

I knew that he was dead serious in his veiled threat to make my colleagues and me look like pagans who were inhospitable to the ministrations of the sincere Reverend Holloway. And I also knew that there were an untold number of ways in which Quincy could make life difficult for all of us if we couldn't work out some kind of accommodation—and quickly.

I was amazed at the number of corporate titans who would quake in their Johnston & Murphy shoes at the mere thought of the Reverend Quincy Holloway leading a picket line or a boycott in an effort to gain some kind of recognition, a contract for a colleague or a contribution to one of his favorite causes. The Quincy Holloway Crusade being the leading one. Quincy could prove to be a formidable foe on the media battlefield, and as a result of his forays on behalf of innumerable causes, real and imagined, he had a Rolodex that gave him access to clients and investors and contacts

who would probably not hesitate to give Morningstar Financial Services and me a hard time if that
meant not getting another call from Quincy Holloway for a year or so.

All of this was unspoken, of course. Quincy
knew that I knew he was a charlatan and a *poseur.*
And I knew that Quincy knew that he could make
life unnecessarily difficult for everyone except
Gordon if he didn't get his way. Right then and
there. So I had to make a decision.

"Quincy, you can come into Gordon's room.
You can put your spiel on tape before going in, but
no cameras in the room. None of us has any interest in calling the press about any of this, so when
we leave the hospital, you can take your tape and
your commentary, and do with it as you please.
Take it or leave it."

I tried to give a note of finality to my "offer" to
Quincy. I had to look down to look into his beady,
hungry eyes. I could see that he knew that it was
the best deal he was going to get without escalat-
ing the level of threat that he had been insinuat-
ing. I held my breath waiting for his response.

"I'll take it, Paul. And thank you for being so
reasonable." His smile could have melted butter
on a stack of pancakes a mile away. "Please let Kenitra and your colleagues know that I will be right
there. I assure you that you won't even know that I
am here."

With that, Quincy turned to a waiting microphone and began what seemed to be a prepared
monologue explaining how even the rich and the
powerful were in need of his spiritual healing. As I
turned to finally head towards Gordon's room, I

heard him mention something about "answering the call of the Lord" once more. Love him or hate him, the Reverend Quincy Holloway was an original. And in some bizarre way, it was only fitting that he would be at New York Hospital with a camera crew for what might be Gordon Perkins's last few hours on earth.

Somehow, it all made sense.

CHAPTER 31

Kenitra

Body and Soul

Once I had told Dr. Krishnamurthy my decision to take Gordon off life support, I felt a strange sense of relief. Gordon was surely the seventh level of hell in my life, and he always would be the culmination of every nightmare I had had since I was a little girl. Over our years together, he had methodically stripped me of my values, my self-esteem, my confidence—everything but my will to survive.

And it was my will to survive that had kept me alive and relatively sane through the beatings and the cursings and the forced ingestion of too many drugs and too much alcohol. It was my will to survive that had allowed me to pray for relief and to hope for his downfall and my escape.

And just when it seemed as if I were at the bottom of a hole that would soon be my grave, Gordon met his downfall in New Orleans. It seemed a cruel twist of fate that he would fall into a coma but that he wouldn't die, that he would not completely disappear from my life. Instead of becoming a dead, dusty memory that I could shelve away in the attic of my brain, Gordon persisted in being a part of my life by remaining alive.

Going to California, living in Venice Beach, enjoying life with friends, having affairs in the open without fear or suspicion—none of these aspects of real life could rid my days of the reality of Gordon. As long as he lived, he would haunt my dreams and my consciousness. As long as he was alive in that Special Intensive Care Unit, there was a chance that he would awaken. And so, there was a chance that one day, while I was walking down the street or brushing my hair in the morning, I would feel his bear paw of a hand grip my shoulder from behind, and I would be dragged back into the maw of misery and shame and pain that had been my life until his fateful day in Louisiana.

It was the not knowing that was so maddening about Gordon's condition and my own situation. Not knowing, when I woke up in the morning, if this would be the day that he died and I would finally be free. Not knowing, when I woke up in the morning, if this would be the day that he would awaken from his coma and recover to haunt my life and hunt me forever. Not knowing, when I went to bed in the evening, if it would be my last peaceful night on earth, because if Gordon recovered, the nightmare that had been my life would become my life once more.

When I was at the Waldorf-Astoria earlier that night lying in bed with Sture, when the phone call from the hospital came I felt the kind of fear that I knew as a little girl, when the bogeyman in my bedroom closet was always close at hand in the deepest hours of the night. And as we dressed and got ready to go to the hospital, I somehow knew that a simple ending, culminating in Gordon's immediate death, was just not in the cards. There was never a chance that anything involving Gordon and me would be so cut-and-dried.

In another place and time, with someone else as the main character, all of this would have been some kind of bizarre and semifunny tragicomedy. But this was, of course, me, the formerly abused and now estranged wife being awakened in her lover's arms by her comatose beast of a husband's doctors, summoning her to the hospital in the middle of the night.

And there was me, the formerly abused and now estranged wife daring to believe that the dream that she had been harboring deep in her heart of hearts, the dream that her comatose beast of a husband would die, was about to finally come true. At the time, it seemed like a perfectly simple dream and a perfectly attainable dream.

And then, at the moment of absolute truth, the beast of a husband doesn't simply die. Rather, the formerly abused and now close-to-liberated wife is given the life-or-death decision over the beast—finally holding the life of her tormentor in her hands.

It seemed like some kind of bizarre comedy written by a madman with too much time on his hands. At the time, I remember looking into Sture's eyes and seeing the reflection of the dawn of laughter in my own eyes. Of course, there was absolutely nothing funny about anything that was happening. But since I didn't know whether to laugh or cry at the possibility of my finally being free from Gordon, I preferred laughing.

CHAPTER 32

Sture

In the Wee Small Hours

As we all walked away from the alcove, the doctors and nurses hustled and bustled into Gordon's room. You didn't have to be a medical expert to know that something important was about to happen.

And now that we had learned the cause of the late-night distress signal, and now that Kenitra had made the most important decision of her relationship with Gordon since she decided to marry him, there was nothing left to do but wait. So we did. Right outside Gordon's room, with Diedre and Jerome and Paul standing nearby.

We were waiting now to see if Gordon would live or die. But I knew in my heart of hearts, and I knew from looking into Kenitra's eyes, that this wasn't quite true. She was waiting for Gordon to die so that she would be free of the specter of Gordon somehow materializing in her life again. She was waiting for Gordon to die because that was the only way that she could be sure that he would truly be gone from her life, if not from her nightmares, forever.

And I was waiting for Gordon to die as well. There was no denying that I was in love with Kenitra, and I was beginning to believe that she loved me, too. And there was no room in our romance for Gordon and his monstrous aura.

Every man probably has something more than a passing interest in the men that his lover might once have loved. Since speculating about past lovers can lead a man into the land of the truly mad and distracted, with no known escape, it's usually best to leave that particular brand of history alone.

But as long as he lived, Gordon was not in the past. He was very much in Kenitra's present, and in mine. When I was with Kenitra, when she was in my arms, when we were making love or taking a shower together, it was like Gordon never existed. And the rest of the time, he was like some mythical chimera that may never really have existed and who certainly had no place in everyday life.

But then there were those times when I could see the pain bubble to the surface of her consciousness, occasioned by the most innocuous remark or occurrence. I could see the fear in her eyes every now and then when the phone rang or when there was an unexpected knock on the door.

It was as if Gordon was lurking somewhere deep in the shadows. But like any predator, he never really went away. He hunted. And he hunted patiently. And now that I was Kenitra's lover, I was also his prey.

It wasn't a pleasant feeling. And I wanted him to die. So he would be gone. Forever.

"Do you want to take a walk, get some coffee or something? Waiting right here can't be the best thing to do."

"I'm sure you're right, Sture." Kenitra looked up at me and removed her sunglasses, and I could see the fear that even being on the same floor with Gordon made her feel. "But I want to know—I *need* to know—what's next in my life. If Gordon dies, I will never have to be in this hospital again. So I want to wait for him to die, so that I can walk out of here and never look back, or come back."

I really didn't know what to do at that point. I wanted to hold her and comfort her. But there would be no real comfort until Gordon was dead. I wanted her to know that I would protect her with my life, but Gordon had taken on the stature of a force of nature in her life. My offering to protect her would have made as much sense to her as my promising to shield her from crashing meteors or cancer or earthquakes. There was no protection that I could offer.

"You know what's so crazy about all of this, Sture?" Her question took me by surprise.

"Everything?" My answer wasn't far from the truth, as far as I could see. Everything about this night seemed to be coming straight from the pages of a madcap celestial script that just kept us all guessing.

"Yes, everything. But I have to tell you, in a strange but very real way, I am glad that everything is coming to a head. If Gordon dies tonight, I'll be free . . . we'll be free. If he lives past tonight, I will make sure that he never sees me again, and that will be fine with me also." She put her glasses back on and squeezed my hand yet again. "I'm just so tired of living on the razor's edge, Sture. I want to live without worrying about Gordon, without thinking about Gordon, without being afraid of Gordon."

"Frankly, my dear, I don't give a damn . . . about Gordon. I only care about you. So, let's make it up as we go. That's all we can do anyway." I held Kenitra in my arms and gave her a light kiss on her forehead. It was all I could say. It was all I could do.

"Let's go down the hall and get some coffee. Let's hope sentry duty doesn't take too long."

CHAPTER 33

Gordon

For All We Know

The Dark Lord was just getting ready to leave when all the fuss started. At first, I didn't know what the fuck was going on, and I never liked that feeling. We had just gotten back from my very successful meeting with Duke.

I was very sure that I had picked the right guy to get my new business operations going. Duke was going to make a lot of money, and I was going to make a lot more. No question about it. All it was going to take was some time, and G-Perk was going to rule the drug trade in Harlem—at least, the cocaine trade. When we got that far, I would see whether that would be enough for me. It probably wouldn't be, but that would be something to deal with at another point in time.

I was about to relax and savor the memory of

the rest of the evening after I finished my business with Duke. I had asked Ernie Argentina to get a couple of the miscellaneous bitches who always hung out at the Purple Dragon to ride with me and the Dark Lord on our way back downtown to the hospital.

But first we went in the private backroom, which Ernie had opened for us, and we had some fun with several grams of coke that the Dark Lord put on a small dish along with a straw and a bottle of Rémy Martin that Ernie considerately provided.

Ernie Argentina was an interesting guy. Late one rainy evening when there were only a couple of customers, I asked him what a seemingly intelligent and seemingly educated guy like him was doing working as a bartender in a total dive like the Purple Dragon.

It turned out that Ernie was indeed an educated guy—a very well- educated guy. He was from Ohio, just outside of Akron, and he had gotten a basketball scholarship to attend Duke University. Although he hurt his knee in his freshman year and never was a real contributor to the Duke basketball team legacy he worked real hard at his studies and wound up going to Harvard Law School.

And then his story got real interesting. Ernie decided that enlisting in the United States Marine Corps would be a good career move. He didn't take into account the exigencies of the Vietnam War, however, and, even though the war was coming to a close, he found himself stationed at the U.S. embassy in Saigon.

And so he was there for the madcap, insane and truly apocalyptic abandonment of Vietnam, with

American helicopters evacuating the final contingent of U.S. personnel from the roof of the embassy. Incredibly, Ernie had a framed news photo of the last helicopter leaving the rooftop, and upon careful examination with a magnifying glass, he pointed himself out, frantically pushing a Vietnamese woman and child out of the door of the helicopter.

When he returned to civilian life, he tried to make a living selling phony penny stocks to his Duke and Harvard classmates. But to hear him tell it, after his experience on the rooftop of the U.S. embassy in Saigon, he wasn't really into scamming.

And so, he made acquaintance with "the boy who makes slaves out of men," as Marvin Gaye once put it. Ernie became a godforsaken heroin addict for about ten years. And then, he said, he simply got tired of being a down-and-out junkie, and he kicked his habit and tried to find some way to work and support himself. And that was how he wound up as the bartender at the Purple Dragon. It was a great story for that rainy night, and I filed it away. Someday, Ernie might be useful for something besides lining up tackhead bitches that wanted to snort coke and give head.

As usual, the Dark Lord took my clothes and put them away, and helped me get situated back in my hospital bed. Getting all the tubes and wires hooked back up had gotten to be a pretty routine thing for us, and within minutes, I was back in my comatose condition. As far as anyone knew, I hadn't moved an inch. I had all these motherfuckers fooled. As usual, I would have the last laugh on all of them.

That's why I never liked not knowing exactly what was going on around me. And that's why I didn't like all of that unanticipated hustle and bustle around my bed without anybody saying a damn thing, not a fucking word. It was like they were carrying out some well-thought-out plan that had already been decided at some other point in time. And that's when they started removing the wires and cords and tubes that the Dark Lord and I had just put back in place. Since I still couldn't say a damn thing, all I could do was watch.

It was with amazing speed and skill that the doctors and nurses freed me from all of the medical tethers that had been a part of my life for almost two years. I watched them, admiring their handiwork and wondering what was going to happen next. And then it occurred to me. Perhaps they knew about my trips to the Purple Dragon with the Dark Lord.

Maybe there was a camera somewhere that revealed that I really had not been in a coma, that I had just been biding my time, plotting my comeback, plotting my revenge against Paul and Diedre and Jerome and, most of all, absolutely most of all, that beautiful, one-eyed bitch whore of a motherfucking wife of mine—Kenitra.

They would pay. They would all pay. But first, I had to officially get my ass out of the hospital bed. And I had to be sure that the move to take me off life support was not some kind of trick.

And that's when things got crazy. I could have sworn that I could see Kenitra through the window that looked out from my room onto the hospital hallway. And she was being held in the arms of fucking Sture Jorgensen, and he had just kissed her on her forehead.

And there was that stuck-up, holier-than-thou Jerome Hardaway. And there was that smart-ass Paul Taylor. And there was that know-everything bitch Diedre Douglas. It was like a convention of my enemies, right outside the door of my hospital room. Why were they there?

And then things suddenly got very dark. It was like I was cast into some kind of tunnel with a light at the end. And I could have sworn I heard something that I had not heard for over thirty years. It couldn't have been, but it was.

It was the voice of my father.

CHAPTER 34

Paul

I Only Have Eyes for You

From the time that I got the call from the hospital until the moment that Kenitra gave her consent to Gordon being taken off life support, I thought that everything was proceeding routinely, given the circumstances. After all, in my view, it was only a matter of time before the day came that Gordon would have to live or die on his own.

And I thought that Kenitra made the best decision for herself. By giving Gordon a chance to live, however slim that chance might be, his almost-certain death would not be her choice or the result of her decision.

Yet, as soon as Kenitra made the decision, I started having the feeling that things were going to go wrong—horribly wrong. I started feeling that the smartest thing that Kenitra could have done

was to keep Gordon on the life support systems if
that meant that he would die. Suddenly, the
thought of Gordon surviving, being alive, walking
among us again, was just too awful a chance to
take, especially for Kenitra.

I was about to walk over to where she and Sture
were standing to tell her what I was thinking when
I heard it. Actually, we all heard it. One of the
nurses gasped loudly and covered her mouth in
shock at what she saw. Instantly, all eyes turned to
Gordon through the window. And it seemed as if
Gordon had turned his head toward us, and his
cold, reptilian eyes were looking right back at us.

Dr. Krishnamurthy had assured me on several
occasions that, although Gordon's eyes were almost always open, he was unable to see, and that
he was not conscious in the least. I tried to remember that advisory from the doctor as I looked into
Gordon's eyes and saw what I could have sworn
was a flicker of recognition and a flash of hate.

Kenitra and Sture took a step backwards as Gordon turned to look at them. It was almost as if they
thought he might come right through the window.
Jerome and Diedre both froze in their tracks. And
we were all transfixed by what we saw next. And I
know that I will never forget it.

After Gordon slowly scanned the scene outside
his hospital room, his eyes rolled up so that only
the whites could be seen. As the last tubes were removed, he turned his head back onto his pillow so
that he was facing the ceiling. He started to
breathe heavily, as if he were running a race or
were engaged in some kind of struggle. He also
started to foam at the mouth, which was just be-

fore the convulsions started. It was a horrible sight to see. And then it got even worse.

The convulsions caused Gordon to flail and thrash in his bed, and two orderlies had to stand by to make sure that he did not throw himself onto the floor. The blanket and sheet that were covering him were thrown across the room as if hurled by some unseen hand. And, as the convulsions progressed, the foam continued to pour from his nose and mouth, and his eyes remained rolled up in his head so that only the whites were showing. Dr. Krishnamurthy and his colleagues stood by the bedside watching Gordon with shocked eyes.

As a nonmedical person, it was clear to me that Gordon was about to die before our very eyes. Kenitra looked like a rabbit trapped in the presence of a wolf or other all-powerful predator. She couldn't have run if she wanted to, and she certainly didn't want to stay to see anything more than she had already seen. She was trapped.

Jerome, Diedre, Sture and I watched without knowing exactly what we were seeing. But we all knew that Gordon would not be alive on this planet for more than another few moments. Quincy Holloway and his camera crew, who had been mercifully silent and unobtrusive up to this point, sprang into action. The video camera lights came on, and Quincy started praying very loudly.

And then Gordon started to shake and vibrate as if a couple of giants had taken hold of his hospital bed and were trying to dump him onto the floor. He shook and vibrated as if he were being administered thousands of volts of electricity, but that had not been the case. And at this point, I gave up trying to figure out what the hell was going on.

Quincy Holloway kept praying, however. And as he rambled on and on, I was reminded of *The Exorcist*. That's how crazy the entire scene was. Thankfully, the furniture did not start moving and Gordon's head did not start spinning around.

And then, as suddenly as it began, all the commotion halted. All that could be heard was the beeping of the monitors, which seemed to indicate that Gordon remained alive, although barely. Kenitra was now sobbing loudly, and Sture put his arms around her in a vain attempt to provide some kind of comfort to her. Diedre and Jerome did not move an inch.

Gordon's breathing was very faint at this point. There were no more convulsions. There was no thrashing. His heartbeat and blood pressure went from impossibly high levels to normal and then to below normal. Gordon was dying.

The video camera continued to focus its single eye on Gordon. Quincy Holloway continued to mutter prayer after prayer into the microphone that he held. The doctors and nurses said nothing. The rest of us remained transfixed. The lights from the camera made this bizarre scene seem even more surreal.

And then, Gordon sat straight up in the bed as if propelled by some kind of infernal spring-action contraption in the bed itself. This caused even Quincy Holloway to be quiet. Finally, even the doctors looked a bit surprised. I remember taking an involuntary step back. Quincy Holloway's little beady eyes looked like they were going to pop out of his head.

Gordon, still sitting up, grew very still. His eyes rolled back down, and he seemed to focus on his surroundings for the first time. He turned his head slowly to face the window where we all stood, and he looked from Quincy Holloway to me to Diedre to Jerome to Sture, slowly recognizing each one of us and beginning to comprehend his environment. And then he saw Kenitra.

He stared at her for what seemed like a full minute. And then he smiled a horrible, twisted smile. It was a smile that I hope to never see again.

"Hello, Kenitra," Gordon croaked. "Did you miss me?" Those were his first words in almost three years.

Kenitra screamed and bolted, running down the hallway as if she expected Gordon to get out of the bed on his withered legs and pursue her to the ends of the earth. Sture followed her, and Quincy Holloway and his camera crew brought up the rear chasing her and Sture.

The doctors and nurses finally moved toward Gordon and began to examine and assist him as he returned to the world of the living and the conscious. There was no question about it. Gordon was back, and all of our lives had just changed forever—again.

CHAPTER 35

Jerome

Sombrero Sam

The madness of the night that Gordon returned to the land of the living is something that I don't think any of us will ever forget. The sheer spectacle of his resurrection was like something out of a B horror movie. The primordial, visceral fear that absolutely consumed Kenitra was almost visible as she fled from the building, and I was glad that Sture was there to try to comfort her as best he could.

Once the shock of Gordon's revival was absorbed, everything suddenly took on a life of its own, and the routine of the hospital took over. Gordon was now simply another patient in need of care and attention.

The doctors, the nurses and the rest of the medical personnel sprang into action and began to minister to him, trying to make sure that his unexpected resuscitation did not put too much stress on his system. Amazingly, within minutes, Gordon had quieted down, and he was now reclining comfortably, sipping some ice water from a cup that a nurse held for him.

As I tried to take in the entire scenario, I could hear the voice of Quincy Holloway as he spoke breathlessly into the camera. He and his team had been unable to catch up with Kenitra and Sture and they had returned to position themselves outside of Gordon's room. It came as no surprise to me that Holloway, who had managed to turn the assassination of Martin Luther King, Jr. and the near-tragic disappearance of a U.S. soldier into career-building events, would turn the bedlam surrounding Gordon's recovery into another résumé item.

"Through the power of prayer and the mercy of God, we have witnessed a miracle." The breathlessness and rapture that could be heard in the tiny reverend's voice would make a casual observer believe that he had encountered some kind of religious experience. "As Gordon Perkins found himself about to cross over the threshold of death and take that eternal walk into the Great Beyond, he reached out to God, he reached out to Jesus, he reached out to me as his spiritual advisor and guide, and, working through me, God brought him back. Brought him back to his friends, and brought him back to his loving, faithful wife."

I looked at Quincy and could see that he had worked himself up into such a frenzy that he might actually believe that he was personally responsible for some kind of miracle. There were tears in his eyes (which the video cameraman was sure to focus on), and beads of perspiration crowned his forehead. He desperately clutched the microphone with both hands and looked as if his own life depended on his getting the story of Gordon's recovery out to the rest of the world.

"His loving, faithful wife, Kenitra Perkins, who kept a vigil at Gordon's bedside for these three years, was so overcome with the ecstasy of joy that she ran out of the hospital to go to the closest church to offer her thanks to God. We will be joining Kenitra in a few minutes, as I know that she will want to share this miracle with the rest of the world."

As he was speaking, Quincy looked up for a moment, and I caught his eye. An expression passed over his face that seemed to say, "What can I tell you? This is what I do." Taking advantage of any and every situation was ingrained in Quincy Holloway's DNA. His behavior was neither shocking nor surprising. It was simply what Quincy did.

All I could do was nod and acknowledge his gaze and walk away. It wasn't with disgust; rather, it was with the realization that there is a little bit of Quincy Holloway in all of us and a lot of Quincy Holloway in some of us. There clearly was very little that Quincy would not do to advance his own interests, and in the years when I was first building my career and then my own business, and now, as I was trying to manage Morningstar Financial Services, I rarely let anything or anybody get in my way.

I can honestly say that I have never cheated anyone and I have never tried to take unfair advantage in my business dealings. But I have always focused on coming out ahead, and that has meant that my competition—in school and in business— had to come in behind me. And I have never squandered my time worrying about whose feelings I might hurt as I left them behind.

And as I walked down the hospital hallway toward Paul and Diedre, I realized that, on some level, there wasn't a lot of difference between Quincy and me, except . . . there was *nothing* Quincy wouldn't do to advance his interests. On the other hand, I felt that I had my limits. At least, I hoped that was the case.

I remembered that a few years ago, soon after we had started Morningstar and had survived the New Orleans Fiasco, a senior executive from a rival firm asked to meet with me privately. Rather than go to Dorothy's By the Sea, where we were guaranteed to be seen by countless members of The Pride, the surreptitious banker suggested that we meet at Fresco by Scotto, a very stylish and discrete Northern Italian restaurant located on Manhattan's East Side.

Fresco, which is still run by the Scotto family, presents its Northern Italian cuisine in an array of dishes that helped me to change the perception of Italian food so that it encompasses a whole lot more than pasta and pizza. The Scotto family and its chefs and cooks have been featured in all of the cooking publications and shows, and the celebrity of the restaurant has attracted celebrities from around the world.

Over the years that I have eaten there, I have sat

at tables next to Katie Couric and Donald Trump
and Bill Clinton and George Steinbrenner and
Rudy Guiliani and Johnnie Cochran. And the
amazing thing about Fresco is that whoever might
be in the restaurant, it was never a big deal. People
come for the food and the wine. Unlike with other
places, people did not come to be seen.

And I guess that's why Domino Oakley thought
that Fresco would be the perfect place for us to
meet on this important and clearly secretive matter.

Domino was one of the most successful black
women in the world of investment banking. She
had parlayed her brilliance and fabulous good
looks into superstar status in the world of finance.

I remember first meeting her after I spoke as a
returning alumnus at a career forum held at Columbia Business School about ten years after I
graduated. Even then, Domino had the kind of
look that was irresistible to any man with a pulse.
As happily married as I was to Charmaine, and as
in love as I was with Charmaine, I could barely take
my eyes off Domino during my entire presentation—making my presentation a bit more chal-
lenging than I had anticipated.

It was one of those experiences that you just
don't forget. Soon after I began speaking, I saw a
woman dressed in a very red and very tight and
very short dress walk down the aisle of the audito-
rium as if she owned the entire building. Without
hesitation or recognition of the fact that she had
missed the opening remarks (as well as the beginning of my speech), she sat down in the very first
row and crossed a pair of the longest and loveliest

legs that I had ever seen, legs encased in silk mesh stockings that seemed to shimmer with promise and temptation. She looked up at the stage and fixed me with a pair of coal black eyes that could make any man feel as if he were the only man on earth at that moment. She casually tossed her very long, very black hair to the side as she settled into her seat, and I considered myself very fortunate to have been able to continue my presentation without faltering.

At the end of the conference, she casually walked up to me and asked if she could apply for a job with my firm. She had a smile that danced to a slow samba and a complexion that reminded me of coffee with just the slightest acquaintance with rich, sweet cream. And as I breathed in a fragrance that somehow reminded me of mango and chocolate at the same time, I knew instantly that the smartest and safest thing I could do would be to introduce her to one of my former colleagues at Merrill Lynch.

It most certainly was the smartest and safest decision that I ever made, and it was not one that I regretted. But I must confess that I had reconsidered that decision from time to time over the years.

In the meantime, Domino Oakley did indeed end up working at Merrill Lynch, and then at Goldman Sachs. She became a noted hedge fund specialist who was as brilliant at structuring deals and transactions as she was effective at securing and maintaining high-profile clients. Simply put, Wall Street had never seen anyone like Domino before.

And it wasn't long before her name was appearing in the pages of the *Wall Street Journal*, the *Economist*, *Essence* and "Page Six" of the *New York Post*. Her brilliant achievements on Wall Street were almost overshadowed by the glamorous side of her life, as she was linked romantically to several high-profile entertainers and sports figures, as well as at least two senior Wall Street types who were supposed to be as happily married as I was.

From the moment she came to New York from her hometown of St. Louis, she took the local chapter of The Pride by storm. Eligible and not-so-eligible men thought nothing of almost groveling in her presence. Many of the single women sought to be her friend in the hope that her glamour and brilliance were contagious. The married women in The Pride simply despised Domino, for all that she represented to them was Danger with a capital "D." A real and present danger to the marital comfort zone into which they had settled.

At some point, however, Domino started to tone down her act. Or maybe it was simply a matter of true love shining down on her. Whatever the case, she met and married Roger Hansley, the founder and chairman of the Hansley Group, arguably the most successful black investment-banking firm in Chicago.

And just like that, Domino was gone from New York, returning only occasionally for a business meeting or dinner or a shopping excursion. She and Roger bought a fabulous six-bedroom triplex condominium in the same building in which the fabulously wealthy Oprah Winfrey lived. They had a small mansion on the north shore of Jamaica, just east of Port Antonio, and they traveled around the world on various exotic holidays.

And along the way, Domino applied her special brand of genius in hedge fund transactions and other arcane areas of financial services to the Hansley Group. In short order, the very successful firm was even more successful, and to tell the truth, the Hansley Group and Morningstar were soon running neck and neck as the two small investment firms with the brightest futures—regardless of the color of the owners.

Roger and Domino were one of the true power-sharing couples in The Pride, and then something happened. I truly don't have the time or inclination to keep track of the latest bedroom and backroom adventures, but even I heard the rumors about Domino becoming involved with the twenty-something caretaker of their estate in Jamaica.

Things got really crazy when Roger made an unexpected visit to Negril and encountered Domino and the caretaker naked and embracing in the hot tub, which overlooked the ocean. This led to Roger and Domino separating and living in separate condominiums in Chicago, while tongues nearly wagged out of the heads of the nosy and the curious. And then crazy became just downright bizarre, like something straight out of the supermarket tabloids.

According to some published (and unpublished) reports, Domino brought her Jamaican boy toy back to Chicago. About two weeks after he arrived in the United States and started to get settled, Domino arrived home unexpectedly (here we go again—it's always good to call ahead, I guess) to find her Jamaican friend entangled in an undeniably romantic position with her (male) hairdresser. Aside from throwing her new friend (and her hairdresser) out of her home, she had her friend deported to Jamaica and braced herself for the inevitable onslaught of embarrassment and gossip.

So, it was in the aftermath of all this madness that Domino suggested that we meet for lunch at Fresco. I arrived at the restaurant early and was sipping a Tio Pepe sherry, chilled with a twist of lemon, having been warmly greeted by a few of the members of the Scotto family who were always there. A few minutes after I settled into my seat with my aperitif, Domino arrived.

One always sensed Domino before actually seeing her. The stirring in the front of the restaurant made me aware that someone special had arrived, and that someone special turned out to be Domino. As she headed toward my table, it seemed that all the eyes in the restaurant were on her.

"Jerome, it's so good to see you again." She was as beautiful as ever. She wore a tasteful Donna Karan suit. It was a subtle shade of purple with white piping. Her only accessories were a string of pearls and matching earrings. It was all the accessorizing that she needed. I inhaled that almost-forgotten fragrance of mango and chocolate, and for a moment, I was lost in thoughts that had no business at a business luncheon.

"Domino, the pleasure is mine. I am glad that you were able to squeeze me into your busy calendar." My attempt at humor was well received, and her smile in response lit up the already-bright room. I helped her into her seat, and she ordered a matching Tio Pepe.

We exchanged pleasantries as we studied our menus. We talked about people who we knew in the world of finance. I told Domino about my sons and about Charmaine's death, and she offered her sincere sympathy. There was not much point in saying too much about her misadventures with Roger in Jamaica, so we both left that subject alone.

I remember a lot about that luncheon. I ordered a bottle of pinot grigio to go with the *oso bucco* that Domino ordered and the broiled chicken breast dish I selected. We enjoyed our first glass of wine while continuing the banter and miscellaneous conversation. Then she put down her glass.

"Jerome, it's so good to see you. But you know that I didn't want to see you just to look into your eyes."

"Domino, you're breaking my heart. But I guess I will have to bear the pain." We both smiled, although I remember thinking something about the truth sometimes being spoken in jest.

Domino leaned forward in an almost conspiratorial manner. At that moment, I had no idea what she wanted to talk about.

"Jerome, I have a proposal for you. Let's call it an offer that you can't refuse."

CHAPTER 36

Jerome

Dolphin Dance

One thing about Domino Oakley, she didn't waste a lot of time. What had been a pleasant, meandering conversation suddenly got deadly serious. Her aura transitioned from alluring to sober and serious, totally focused on business.

"Jerome, you are one of the few people to hear this, but I am leaving Roger and resigning from the Hansley Group. Actually, Roger and I have already separated, as I guess most people who care about such things already know." It was hard not to know about these kinds of things. I have been neither a consumer nor a purveyor of gossip, but the Roger Hansley–Domino Oakley story was a featured item of conversation at most dinners, receptions and cocktail parties attended by members of The Pride. Domino confirmed the broad outline of her separation from Roger, but I had to wonder why she was bothering to tell me all of this. I didn't have long to wait.

"Since my days at Merrill, thanks to you, by the way"—she flashed those black diamond eyes in my direction, and once again, I felt myself standing in the presence of a force of nature, not sure what was coming next—"since my days at Merrill, I have always done pretty well, and I am not looking to work so hard anymore. But when I leave the Hansley Group at the end of the month, I do intend to still be, shall we say, active. I have thought about starting my own firm, but I really, really like what you and Diedre have been doing with Morningstar. To be frank, Jerome, I would like to join your team."

The ironic thing is that if she had just stopped right there, she would have been making an offer that would have been very hard to refuse. At the very least, it would have been an offer that I would have had to discuss with Diedre. But then she continued.

"You know what I have done running hedge funds and the kind of results that I have produced with repos and derivatives. What I have done for Merrill and Goldman and the Hansley Group, I can do for Morningstar. But I want to, shall we say, sweeten the pot."

When Domino had come in, I did not notice that she was carrying a small and stylish Louis Vuitton valise. It was next to her on the banquette on which she was sitting, and from it, she produced a bound report that appeared to be about fifty pages in length. She placed it on the table between us. After a suitably dramatic pause, she continued. I really had no idea what was coming, but when I found out, I could have been knocked over with a feather.

CHAPTER 37

Diedre

Baby, It's Cold Outside

Even if I am lucky enough to see PJ become an old man, I will never forget that night at New York Hospital. The dramatic scenario laid out by Dr. Krishnamurthy and Kenitra's fateful decision were enough drama for me, that's for certain.

But when Gordon was taken off life support, his thrashing and crashing around in the hospital bed was one of the most horrific and terrifying things that I ever hope to see. I didn't know if he was going to die or live. And I don't think that the doctors or nurses or anyone else expected anything like what we saw that night.

But the worst part was when Gordon actually regained consciousness. As his eyes started to focus on those of us standing by the window of his room, it was as if a demon was returning to the planet, having just left his home in Hell. He looked at each of us, his gaze moving slowly from one to another, until he fixed a baleful glare on Kenitra, who would have collapsed onto the floor if Sture had not been holding her in his arms.

When he called out to Kenitra, his raspy voice scratched out a sound that chilled all of us and fixed her on the spot for several seconds. And that was when Kenitra's survival instincts kicked in. The instincts that had kept her alive despite Gordon's worst depredations and abuse told her to get the hell out of the hospital, and when I saw her run screaming in terror toward the elevators down the hallway, I can honestly say that I could not blame her in the least.

I knew that Kenitra expected Gordon to die. We all did. None of us believed that he was going to die as soon as he was disconnected from all the tubes and wires and monitors, but we were all certain that in a matter of minutes or hours, he would pass on. I guess we thought that, in some way, we were paying our last respects to Gordon. Even though he didn't really deserve respect, he probably didn't deserve to die alone in a hospital with no one to note his passing.

And even if Gordon didn't die, we were all certain that, having been in a coma for almost two years, he would have no functioning brain capacity and would most certainly depart from his mortal existence very soon. One way or another, I was sure that we were witnessing the last days and times of Gordon Perkins.

So, when the bastard didn't die and then regained consciousness, shock and awe was my first reaction. And when he fixed his eyes on Kenitra and called out her name, my blood ran cold.

I saw Sture running after her, and it would be months before I saw her again, although we did speak from time to time. As she told me later, she had made herself a promise when she gave Dr. Krishnamurthy permission to take Gordon off life support.

She was not going to entertain even a hint of regret over what she thought was the right decision. But she had no idea that Gordon was going to regain consciousness and call her name in that very special way of his.

She later told me that as soon as he called her name, all the memories of the beatings and torture and abuse came flooding back. She felt the sewage of her past life threatening to submerge the sanity and happiness that she had been creating for herself.

She wasn't afraid that Gordon was going to jump out of that hospital bed and start beating her on the spot (although I must confess that nothing would have surprised me after Gordon revived). She was afraid that being in the presence of a revived and conscious Gordon Perkins would allow him to assert control over her once again. That was a prospect actually worse than death for her, so she ran and she ran.

She ran down the hallway. She ran out of the hospital when the elevator doors opened onto the lobby. And, with Sture in tow, she ran to the Waldorf-Astoria and packed her clothes, checked out and caught the first flight to Los Angeles, running back to her Venice Beach sanctuary.

It was downright noble of Sture to fly out to California with Kenitra as she tried to maintain a slippery grip on her mental equilibrium. Of course, as the manager of Dorothy's By the Sea, he had to take a red-eye flight back to New York later that day. So Sture joined the rest of us in being absolutely stunned and disoriented during the first days after Gordon's recovery.

Kenitra later told me that she felt as if she had not taken a single breath from the time that Gordon called her name until she was in her living room in Venice Beach looking out over the Pacific. But although she was breathing, she did not feel safe anymore. She would spend the next few months waiting, wondering and watching out for Gordon.

It was something that she would have in common with the rest of us.

CHAPTER 38

Jerome

Impressions

I don't know what it was about the fantastic scenario outside Gordon's hospital room made me recall my luncheon with Domino Oakley. Perhaps it had something to do with the upcoming meeting with Ray Beard that Diedre was arranging. Perhaps it was just my mind wandering away from a distinctly unpleasant circumstance.

Like most people, I had never been too crazy about spending time in hospitals. When I joined my colleagues in attending to the events surrounding Gordon's situation, it had been my first time in a hospital since Charmaine died. Whatever the case might be, I found myself thinking about the resolution and conclusion of my luncheon with Domino.

"Jerome," she continued, "I want to add serious

value to Morningstar if I am going to come aboard. You know what I can do managing hedge funds and derivatives, but this"—she motioned to the bound document that she had placed on the restaurant table—"is the three-year strategic plan for the Hansley Group. In it are all of the contacts, work plans and timelines that the firm will be using to surpass Morningstar and get it ready to take on the really big firms on Wall Street."

I am guessing that a look of total shock and surprise must have marched across my face. I also guess that must have been the case because a quizzical, puzzled look appeared on Domino's lovely face.

"Don't look so shocked, *Saint Jerome.*" That comment stung more than a little bit. "I helped to write just about everything in that plan, and I never signed a noncompete agreement with the Hansley Group. Therefore, what I am suggesting is perfectly legal. I have already consulted with my attorney on this. So, what do you say? Do you want me on your team or not?" And with that, she picked up her glass of pinot grigio with an elegantly manicured hand and took a sip while gazing over her glass with a pair of eyes that could make the pope give up celibacy.

To tell the truth, I was absolutely tempted to take Domino up on her offer. It was an offer that I could barely refuse. But I did. Not because of some "Saint Jerome" bullshit self-image. It's just that I have never played the game that way.

I have always been prepared to outwork and outthink my competition. I have also always believed that if I do my best, nobody will surpass me.

I would have jumped at Domino's offer to come to work with Morningstar in a minute.

She truly had a genius quality that would make her an asset for any firm with which she might associate. And, she had that star quality that you rarely find on Wall Street, and because that quality is so rare, that quality becomes absolutely brilliant when someone who has it shows up.

But being handed the Hansley Group business plan was just too much baggage for me, more baggage than I was prepared to carry into the offices of Morningstar. It was not that I succumbed to an attack of morals. I just never have wanted to win so badly that I would take what I thought to be an unfair advantage. And I thought that taking the Hansley business plan was tantamount to taking an unfair advantage.

Domino continued to look directly into my face, awaiting an answer. I knew what my answer would be. I took a moment to think of what to say.

"Domino, you are so right in saying that this is an offer that I can't refuse." She started to smile expectantly. I almost accepted her offer just so I could be assured of seeing that smile every day. "But it's an offer that I simply cannot accept—at least, not here, not now. You know that with Gordon . . . sidelined, shall we say, Diedre and I share all the important management decisions regarding Morningstar. And, Domino Oakley, your joining the firm would certainly qualify as an important decision."

Her smile was not so dazzling now. However, it remained in place, although her eyes were now focused upon me in a manner that was suggestive of an archer focusing on the bull's-eye of a target. It was more than a little unsettling, but I pressed on. I knew that there was no way that I wanted any part of Domino and the Hansley business plan in Morningstar, but I also was not interested in telling her no in such a blunt fashion.

"So, why don't you hold that thought, and that business plan, and I will take this matter up with Diedre." For a moment, those archer's eyes went blank, like a computer monitor that suddenly lost its power source. Then she regained her focus.

"Jerome, if I didn't know better, I would swear that I was hearing 'Don't call us, we'll call you,' which would really be a shame. It would be a shame, Mr. Hardaway, because I know we would get along very, very well." The way she said "very, very" made me know that her interest involved more than the Hansley business plan or Morningstar.

I did not perceive her interest with mixed feelings. Charmaine was the love of my life then, and she will always be the love of my life. I know in my heart that I was totally dedicated to her memory for every minute of my life. Nevertheless, there was something about Domino and her attention that made me feel more than special.

Even in the midst of my inner turmoil due to Charmaine's death and my dislike of Domino's business tactics, I still found something about Domino Oakley that made me hope that there would be another time and another place, and at that other time and other place, perhaps I would be the one making the offer that couldn't be refused.

"I think I understand, Jerome." Domino's voice was like a warm glove on a brisk autumn day: just pure pleasure. "But tell me, Jerome, are you familiar with the principles of bifurcation?"

"I certainly know what 'bifurcation' means, Domino, but I'm afraid that I'm not familiar with any 'principles' associated with the word."

"Well, Jerome, what I am saying is that perhaps we should bifurcate our relationship." The way she drew out the word, she suddenly made "bifurcate" one of my favorite words. "You know, we should take our relationship and separate it into two parallel aspects, business and . . . well, whatever else may come up in the future. I am sure that you have your reasons for your lack of enthusiasm for my offer, but let me give you some free advice. Don't ever, ever play poker, because your face will give you away every time." And then she smiled that magical smile of hers again, and I just knew that I would enjoy bifurcating with Domino someday.

"Domino, thanks for the offer, and I know I must sound like I am out of my mind to even hesitate. But I think your bifurcation idea is certainly one of the best offers that I have ever had, and one that you can be sure I won't refuse." We both laughed at that last comment, and what could have been an awkward moment morphed into a pleasant ending to a pleasant luncheon at Fresco by Scotto.

We both had the raspberry–passion fruit gelato. Domino had a cappuccino. I had an espresso. We finished up our encounter with some small talk and the promise to stay in touch so that we could discuss the various aspects of "bifurcation." And

she gave me her card with all of her contact details.

Domino went on to establish a suitably epony-
mous company, Domino Advisors, a financial advisory firm that had done quite well since our fateful
luncheon at Fresco. As for me, I held on to
Domino's card.

As I prepared myself to accompany Diedre and
Paul on their way into Gordon's room, I made a
mental note to retrieve Domino's numbers from
my Palm Pilot.

It was time to further explore the principles of
bifurcation.

CHAPTER 39

Paul

Nature Boy

I remember thinking that when he spoke his first words in almost three years, Gordon sounded very much like Kermit the Frog in the aftermath of a very bad drug experience. But, however ridiculous he sounded, the menace and malice were unmistakable and undeniable, and there was no room for misplaced humor. I didn't blame Kenitra in the least for running away in a panic. In fact, it seemed like the smartest thing for her to do.

After the initial madness had given way to hospital routine, the nurses ministered to Gordon as he made what seemed to be a miraculous reacquaintance with consciousness. And once he regained his bearings and his equilibrium, it was only his body's betrayal that gave away the fact that he had been inert for so long.

Dr. Krishnamurthy strode out of Gordon's room toward Diedre, Jerome and me with that same sober, self-assured and self-absorbed look about him. Now that he had shepherded his patient through the Valley of Death, it was clear that there was more to come.

After the whirlwind of events that we had all just experienced, I was through guessing as to what could be next. The good doctor addressed my concerns immediately.

"Needless to say, Mr. Perkins's recovery has exceeded my most optimistic expectations. While it is too early to be sure, I believe that he will make a rapid and full recovery. But there is something more that I feel I should share with you."

My train of thought froze on the tracks as I couldn't imagine that there could be any more "news" this evening.

"Mr. Perkins is under the impression that he has not been in a coma for almost three years. At one point, he was most insistent that he and a friend of his have been going to Harlem several times a week for the past year."

I was getting ready to file this night under the heading of "Strange But True" in my personal cabinet of memories.

"The only explanation that I can offer is that, contrary to what our various monitors and indicators have shown, Mr. Perkins has had a very active dream existence for a good part of the last year. Many comatose patients have extremely vivid dream experiences while they are unconscious, and sometimes, when they return to the world of the living, they truly believe that their dream experiences were real.

And frankly, I have never found it to be a good idea to argue with these patients. Certainly, from what little I now know of the conscious Mr. Perkins, I would suggest that the less said about his dream persona the better. But you can be assured that you will be hearing about it from him from time to time."

This was the insane cherry on the madness cake. It seems that not only were we about to be reintroduced to the Gordon Perkins that we all knew and loved, but now we also had to deal with the pesky matter of . . . what? His evil twin? Gordon times two—what a divine comedy indeed. Although I really think that Dante would have had to go a ways to come up with this particular scenario.

"Mr. Perkins has practically insisted on speaking with the three of you, and to prevent any further exertion or excitement on his part, I would suggest that the three of you go in to speak with him. But for no more than a few minutes, on that I must insist."

I tried to quickly absorb Dr. Krishnamurthy's comments, and realized that there was not much point in spending too much time trying to make sense out of the turn of events that had occurred during the past few hours. It was what it was, and there was no denying or escaping the reality of the bizarre. And so, he went on.

"I will wait outside the room to respect and observe your privacy. When I give the signal, please wrap up your conversation and leave the room. I think it is fair to say that Mr. Perkins has been through quite a bit this evening, and we do not want to add to his stress."

Later, I thought that the good doctor's comments were particularly ironic given the fact that Gordon's revival was going to add a whole lot of stress to all of our lives. It was not something that I had expected when I had awakened at home almost twenty-four hours ago. Now, I was trying to adjust to a new set of life-changing circumstances, and I knew from the beginning, it was not going to be easy for any of us standing there at the threshold of Gordon's hospital room.

Ever since his simultaneous betrayal and downfall, Gordon had, in many ways, existed in the past tense for Jerome, Diedre and me. My idea of merging the firms owned by Diedre, Jerome and Gordon was a good idea. Not realizing the depths to which Gordon was prepared to go to advance his own interests was the mistake that we all made. But that was then, and we had tried to live in the now.

And so, the three of us worked like beasts to make sure that Morningstar would be a successful firm, and it was. And I made it a personal project to work with Kenitra to make sure that she was in a position to recover from the unspeakable ordeal of her marriage to Gordon.

Except for the occasional hospital report or offhand reference to the New Orleans Fiasco, it really was as if Gordon was dead to us all. And given the nature of our memories of him, he was not recalled often, and never in a positive context. As long as he was comatose, seemingly permanently, all of us could compartmentalize the entire Gordon Perkins experience. That is, until that fateful and bizarre night.

Now Gordon wanted to speak to us, together. He had been conscious for only a few minutes, so it was hard to imagine that he would be very coherent. I didn't think that he had much to say, but I was particularly interested in his "dream existence" and Dr. Krishnamurthy's comment regarding the frequency with which comatose patients have such experiences.

It reminded me of *La Vida Es Sueño*, the comedy written by Pedro Calderón de la Barca, the famous Spanish playwright. In the play, one of the central characters commits a terrible crime, killing a man and attempting rape. For these acts, he is drugged and returned to prison.

Upon waking, he is told that the events of the prior day were merely a dream, and that his life in a dungeon is reality. During the rest of the story, this character struggles to determine the difference between life in "reality" and life in his "dreams," somehow trying to reconcile the two.

It was a quirky, interesting and entertaining play that I remember reading for Spanish Literature when I was at Dartmouth College. Trying to determine when one was dreaming and when one was awake, attempting to figure out what was reality and what was a dream, posed all kinds of metaphysical conundra that could be debated for entire afternoons, taking up entire seminar sessions.

But now, the "reality" was that Gordon Perkins was awake in his hospital room, recovering from a three-year coma and ready to re-enter the world, our world. And the "reality" was that Gordon had been living in some dream world for a good part of those three years, a dream world about which we knew nothing. But I had the feeling we were going to learn a lot, and real soon.

CHAPTER 40

Sture

Save the Last Dance for Me

The flight to LA with Kenitra was painful due to the sheer terror that seemed to consume her entire being. From the moment that she began running down the hospital hallway, it seemed as if she were certain that Gordon was right at her shoulder about to grab her by the hair or the neck and sling her to the floor so that he could renew the assaults to her body and spirit that had ended almost two years ago.

While we were in the elevator, I tried to comfort her, to soothe her blasted serenity. But there were no words for her that night, no words for her that day.

Back at the Waldorf, she packed wordlessly and with amazing, almost blinding speed. She spoke twice. Once was to ask me if I was coming with her to the airport. I told her that I was coming with her to Venice Beach. The second time was when she called the concierge to request that he arrange for two first-class tickets on the 9 AM American Airlines flight to Los Angeles and a car to take us to Kennedy Airport. And then she continued packing like a dervish who had discovered methamphetamines. It was like watching a movie on fast-forward as clothes, cosmetics, books and shoes disappeared into bags and valises.

I would have offered to help if I had thought I could be of any possible help. But that was an absurd notion. Kenitra was a woman on a mission, and the best that I could do was to keep out of her way and make sure that my few belongings were stowed so that I would be ready to go when it was time to go.

Within a few brief hours of Gordon's awakening, Kenitra and I were ensconced in seats 3A and 3B on American Airlines Flight #1, nonstop to Los Angeles. After a smooth and uneventful takeoff, I felt like I could finally speak to her.

"Kenitra, I want you to know that I meant what I said about being there for you. Now I mean it more than ever." The powerful jet engines of the Boeing 767 hummed outside the window, giving a slight vibrato to every word that was spoken. For a few moments, I wondered whether she had heard me. Then she turned from looking out the window to face me. I remember seeing the lazy cumulus clouds over her shoulder floating by. And for some godforsaken reason, I thought for a moment about angels, and wondered whether there might be at least one angel in heaven that would help me to look out for this woman.

It wasn't that my promise to protect her wasn't sincere. It was just that I had more than a passing familiarity with Gordon's reputation for cruelty, brutality and vengeance. If half the stories that I had heard were true, Kenitra had every reason in the world to run screaming down the hospital hallway earlier that morning.

And I had empirical evidence, more than just rumor or mere hearsay. I had had a passing acquaintance with one of Gordon's former drivers, Alexander Lapidoulos. Alex had told me about an affair that he was having with Kenitra that included trysts in the backseat of the car and at Gordon's vacation home in Sag Harbor, even in their Park Avenue apartment when Gordon was out of town.

I remember telling Alex that he was playing a very dangerous game. Having sex with your employer's wife could get you deported if you were in the United States on a work visa, as Alex was. Having sex with the wife of Gordon Perkins could also get you killed.

I also remember Alex telling me that he and Kenitra were in love, and that she would soon be leaving Gordon so that the two of them could go away together. Without ever speaking with Kenitra, I knew that she would have to be lying because of the improbable nature of such a move.

If Kenitra left Gordon, she would be leaving not only his money. I was sure that Gordon would find a way to get *her* money as well. And if Kenitra left

Gordon, any fool would know that he would kill her and whomever was unfortunate enough to be her partner in cuckholding him.

And Alex turned out to be that kind of fool. At least, I think that was the case, because after a few months of repeatedly warning him that he was in grave danger and that he needed to rethink his romantic ambitions, I heard that Alex was found dead in his Queens apartment. The police ruled his death a murder accompanying an apparent break-in, and his killer was never found. And I immediately believed that there was nothing random about Alex's death, and that the cold, quiet hand of Gordon Perkins was hard at work in that instance.

All these thoughts were rushing through my brain like some kind of madcap stampede of panicked imaginings, heading lemminglike toward pure hysteria. I took a deep breath and tried to pull myself together.

"Sture, you don't have to say that. And you don't have to stay with me any longer. Gordon is my problem, and he doesn't have to be yours as well. It's not too late for you to just step away. I'm a big girl, and I will find a way to take care of myself, even if I have to run around this world for the rest of my life."

There were tears in her eyes as she spoke, and I knew right then that if I didn't love her before, I loved her now, more than ever. And I knew that there was no way that I was going to leave this woman.

"Kenitra, you have to know me better than that. Do you think these past few weeks have been just a fun fling for me? I told you that I have given you my heart. I have told you that I love you. Haven't you been listening?"

"Haven't *you* been keeping up with the latest news, Sture? That bastard son-of-a-bitch motherfucker is back. Gordon is alive, Sture! He's alive, and I'm so afraid. And I don't want to live in fear for the rest of my life. I thought that those days were over, and now he's back!" With that, she buried her face in her hands and turned her head toward the window, sobbing softly but relentlessly.

There are times when the right word or phrase can make all the difference in the world for a person. And there are times when there are no words, whether it's at a funeral, a wedding or the birth of a child. And this was one of those latter times.

There were no words for me to say, so I just stayed with Kenitra. We sat in silence for the rest of the flight. We held hands, and I stroked her cheek from time to time, and then we were in the City of Angels and a taxi took us to her condominium in Venice Beach.

As we stood in her living room looking at the infinite expanse of the Pacific Ocean, clouds drifting and floating toward that eternally elusive horizon, Gordon Perkins and New York–Presbyterian Hospital seemed a million miles away. And then I held her in my arms. And I kissed her.

And when we kissed again, we were already in her bed. Within moments, the episode at the hospital seemed like a really bad dream, like something that may not even have really happened. We were together now, using our arms and our bodies to protect each other from everything in the world.

And I know that for a few moments at least, I made Kenitra feel safe. And I was happy.

And then it was time for me to go back to LAX and take the American Airlines red-eye flight back to New York. I had to get back to Dorothy's just to set up a manager rotation that would allow me to come back to Venice Beach to spend as much time with Kenitra as possible. Her coming back to New York anytime soon was clearly out of the question.

As the plane lifted off the runway and headed east over the desert toward the Rocky Mountains and beyond, all I could think about was my last glimpse of Kenitra as I left her apartment. Sadness and terror lurked just behind the vestige of a brave smile that she offered, and I wondered to myself how all of this was going to end.

CHAPTER 41

Gordon

Love's in Need of Love Today

When I heard my father's voice, I figured that I was truly on my way out. I wasn't ready to die, but, of course, who the fuck is ready to die?

I have heard about ninety-nine-year-old mother-fuckers who are still not ready to die, and I certainly wasn't looking forward to the prospect.

But there I was. I was in some kind of dark tunnel. And then I heard my father's voice, although I wasn't sure what he was saying, as he wasn't speaking to me. And then, damned if I didn't see that light at the end of the tunnel that you hear about on *Oprah* and other talk shows. Every asshole on those shows with a near-death experience always seems to see some kind of bright white light at the end of a tunnel, the implication being that death is right where that light is. And there I was, seeing that light, and hearing my father's voice.

And then suddenly, I was thrown into a whirlwind, and I was seeing all kinds of images from my life. There was that whore-bitch Kenitra. There was my first father-in-law. There was the motherfucker who told me I would never be a partner at Goldman Sachs. There were my mother and my father. And there were Duke and Ernie Argentina and, finally, the Dark Lord. The images spun and blended and intersected and merged into some kind of psychedelic collage that had to be seen to be believed. There was no use resisting. I gave myself up to the madness that swirled around me.

And that was when I felt myself being spun around and buffeted, as if I was a cork caught in a tidal wave. I had no control over space or direction, and time was clearly endless. I could see some distant images, like small objects on a shore seen from the deck of a faraway ship. I could barely make out the figures, but there were moments when, looking through the haze of confusion and something very close to delirium, I thought I saw Diedre, and then the dead body of my former driver, Alex, and then Paul and Jerome, and finally Kenitra and . . . Sture. I remember thinking that I was having the wildest fucking hallucination in history.

Finally, the storm seemed to pass, and I felt that something resembling equilibrium started to return. I finally thought I knew up from down, and that fucking bright white light started to fade. I also couldn't hear the sound of my father's voice anymore.

And then I had the feeling that, although I had been seeing, my eyes were closed. So I made a Herculean effort to open them, and after enduring the sharp, stabbing pain of rays of light battering the rods and cones in my pupils, I started to focus on my surroundings.

There were the ubiquitous doctors and nurses, as well as those infernal machines to which I had been attached for God-knows-how-long. And there was a window to the left of my bed. And damned if I didn't see the Dark Lord and then the fucking Moon Pie faces of Paul and Jerome and Diedre. And damned if I didn't see that fucking one-eyed whore wife of mine in the arms of that half-assed mother-fucking Viking waiter who worked over at Dorothy's.

I imagine that my fine-feathered friends would have seen a crooked smile work its way across my face. And I was smiling because, as I croaked out a greeting to Kenitra, the Dark Lord came over and whispered the suggestion of a plan in my ear. It was a great plan. And all at once I knew that it was a plan that I was going to enjoy.

CHAPTER 42

Diedre

The Nearness of You

Jerome, Paul and I went into Gordon's room not
knowing what to expect. When it came to Gordon Perkins, expectations simply flew out the window. I am sure that we all figured that, even in his
presumably weakened state, even after his spectacular and bizarre return to the land of the living, he
still had some more surprises in store. We were not
to be disappointed.

We stood in a modified semicircle at the foot of
his bed. By now, Gordon was propped up on pillows and sipping through a flexible straw that was
placed in a Styrofoam cup full of water and ice
chips. Since his resurrection, all of the tubes had
been removed and his remaining medical tethers
were just a few monitors keeping track of his pulse
and heart rate. And for someone who had been in

a coma for the better part of three years, he looked remarkably fit.

He had certainly lost weight, and his powerful arms and shoulders seemed diminished somehow. His dark brown complexion was somewhat sallow, and there were deep, dark circles under his eyes. But his eyes glistened with alertness and energy. There was no mistaking it. Gordon Perkins was back. And I remember thinking, "Now what?" We didn't have long to wait.

"Dr. Krishnamurthy told me that I have been in a coma for the past three years, and that I am lucky to be alive. But the good doctor doesn't know the half of it." Gordon's voice had already lost that raspy, scratchy sound, and amazingly, he was starting to sound very much like his old self. Gordon's eyes moved from me to Jerome to Paul, the cause for the urgency in his voice and his gaze hard to understand.

"I know that what I did in New Orleans had to cause all of you pain and disappointment. And I couldn't blame any of you if you never forgave me. What Dr. Krishnamurthy doesn't know is that, even though I have been in a coma, not a day has gone by that I haven't thought about each of you and Morningstar, and how wrong I was to betray your friendship and your trust."

At that point, you could have colored me stunned. But Gordon wasn't through yet. He had plenty left in his bag of tricks, and it was then that I could have sworn that I heard his voice crack and quaver.

"Ever since my father died, I have always felt that it was up to me, and only me, to look out for myself. As I guess all of you know, I have had some trouble trusting other people and a lot of trouble in believing in anyone other than myself. I guess that's something of an understatement."

That's when I heard a self-deprecating chuckle as his eyes again reached to each of us in turn.

"That's why, when Paul came up with the idea of the merger of our firms into what became Morningstar, I believed in the idea more than any of you could know. I really felt that I could be part of a team, a family, and you all know that I put my whole self into making Morningstar a success. At least, that's what I wanted to do." With these words, a downcast look came across his face, and I remember thinking that if this was an act, it was worthy of an Oscar, a Tony and an Emmy.

"I can't explain my behavior in New Orleans. I really don't know what possessed me to get Ray Beard tangled up in my half-ass plot. And whatever you do, don't blame Ray. The whole deal in New Orleans was my idea and my fault, my fault alone." Gordon now stared off into space, as he seemed to be trying to get something off his chest with this full confession.

I have to admit that, along with Paul and Jerome, I was floored, completely taken by surprise. I had no idea where all of this was coming from, and I certainly didn't know where Gordon was going.

"I don't know how to explain this, but believe me, I have had a lot of time to think about this. Something just slipped in my brain so that I thought that pulling that stunt in New Orleans made sense. I just couldn't trust the fact that I had friends, real friends, and that I was truly part of a team. And so, I fucked up. Fucked up big-time."

At this point in his peroration, I could have sworn that I saw tears welling up in Gordon's eyes. I just knew that the end of the world had to be around the corner.

"I wouldn't blame any of you if you turned your back on me now. But I am asking—no, begging—you to give me another chance. If you can find a way to let me be a part of the Morningstar team again, I will spend the rest of my life trying to make up for the wrong that I've done."

It was at this point that I could have been knocked over with a feather. "Gordon Perkins" and "begging" just never belonged in the same sentence in my personal experience.

"It's a lot to ask and a lot for each of you to think about. But I figure that if a miracle could bring me back to life, then maybe there are a couple of more miracles coming down the road. I want to spend the rest of my life trying to make it up to you guys. And please, please, tell Kenitra that she doesn't have to be afraid of me anymore. I want to make my peace with her, too." Gordon paused to take a sip of ice water through his flexible straw.

It was at this point that I noted that Quincy Holloway and his camera crew were still rolling the videotape and catching Gordon's revival through the window, without the sound. I remember wondering what on earth Quincy was going to do with all the footage from this night.

"It's really too much for me to ask much of anything of any of you at this point. But I am asking that you consider my offer. I am prepared to come back to Morningstar under any conditions, financial or otherwise, that the three of you think make sense. I just want to be back on the team, and I will do anything to make that happen. You just name it."

Paul and Jerome and I exchanged glances. None of us knew what to say at that moment.

Gordon continued. "Again, all I can ask is that you think about it. If the answer is no, I will understand, believe me. But if you can find it in your hearts to let me back on the team, you can be sure that I will bust my ass for you, for all of you, and for Morningstar."

Being so newly recovered from being in a coma, Gordon quickly became exhausted. His little speech took a lot out of him and he leaned back on the pillows that were propping him up. For a few moments, there was silence in the room, except for the slow and steady beep of the pulse monitor. Paul was the first to speak.

"Gordon, if we are to take you at your word right now, then we have an obligation to each other to be as honest as possible. So, I have got to tell you that it's going to take more than a bedside conversion to get me to believe that you won't try to screw us again as soon as you can get back on your feet." Paul certainly spoke for all of us on that point. And then he continued.

"But there is no denying that you are brilliant, talented and something of a genius when it comes to the world of finance, Gordon. And if—and I say *if*—you are being straight with us, I certainly would be in favor of at least considering your offer."

From a business standpoint, Paul was right. But

I couldn't help feeling that we were all missing something. I just couldn't put my finger on it yet. And then Jerome pitched in.

"Gordon, you have been so wrong in so many ways, it's hard to know where to begin. Diedre and I have put our careers on the line trying to make Morningstar a success. Everything we own and all of our hopes and aspirations and personal resources are tied up in this firm. I am not about to say yes or no standing here in this hospital room at six o'clock in the morning. But, if you are man enough to admit that you were wrong, I am man enough to discuss your offer with Diedre and Paul. That's the best I can say right now. If you need an answer right now, then the answer is no. If you can wait a few days, which I guess you can, since your ass is going to be in this hospital for a while, then my answer might change."

"While I can't be 'man' enough, let me say that I agree with Paul and Jerome. The best that any of us can do is think about everything that you have just said. I'm not inclined to do a damn thing else. I just hope to God you are being sincere for once in your life, Gordon. The way I see it, if almost dying and being in a coma for three years can't change you, then nothing ever will."

The evening and now the morning had produced an unbelievable series of events, culminating in Gordon's revival and renewal. I found myself thinking that if it were true, wonders really never ceased.

We told Gordon that we would be back to see him in two days, and Paul went to get PJ from his borrowed bed. As we left the hospital to go home,

Paul and Jerome and I agreed that we would meet later that day to consider Gordon's offer.

Looking back, I think that we were all intrigued by Gordon's transformation, and that we all wanted to believe him, on some level.

As we left his room, Gordon thanked us and seemed to drift off to sleep with an indecipherable smile on his face, and Quincy Holloway's camera crew shut off the lights. I am guessing that they had enough footage for whatever bright idea that little hustler had in mind.

CHAPTER 43

Jerome

Our Love Is Here to Stay

That night at the hospital with Gordon had to be one of the strangest of my life. To this day, I can't decide what was the most bizarre aspect— Gordon returning from the dead or his humble act of contrition. His proposal to return to Morningstar was simply off the charts.

As I drove home to get the boys ready for school and to change so that I could get into the office, I tried to review the events of the past few hours to try to get a handle on what I was going to do. I began with that phone call and the drive down to the hospital.

I realized that I had fully expected Gordon to die that night so I had never really considered other options. Since Gordon had almost killed himself during the New Orleans Fiasco, there had

never been a need to consider any kind of revenge, vengeance or punishment. That is, except
for the occasional fleeting thought about going to
New York Hospital and standing on his oxygen
hose.

Now, Gordon was back. He was alive and wanted
to be part of the Morningstar team. From a purely
business standpoint, there was a way in which Gordon's proposal made sense. There was no denying
his brilliance—indeed, his genius—when it came
to matters of finance. And even though many of
his contacts may have moved on during his three
years of imposed hibernation, there was no doubt
in my mind that he would be a major asset to the
firm. If—and it was a huge "if"—he could be
trusted.

Diedre had pointed out that damn-near dying
and being in a coma would change just about anybody. But Gordon was not just anybody. It was almost counterintuitive to think about having
Gordon rejoin Morningstar. But there was another
point of view.

Paul mentioned the old adage about keeping
your friends close and your enemies even closer.
No matter what Gordon's real motives for rejoining Morningstar might be, it was hard to argue
against the idea of keeping him under watch all
the time. And clearly, it would be easier to do that
if he was working with us instead of plotting and
scheming against us from someplace else.

It was a hell of a logical process. But it made
sense in a weird sort of way. I gave Diedre and Paul
and their son a ride back to their home in Harlem.
It had been a long evening, turning into what was

going to be a long day. There was going to be lots to talk about and lots to do, but during the ride uptown, we sat in silence, each of us, in our own way, trying to absorb the import of the events of the past few hours.

Since it was not yet seven in the morning, traffic was still pretty sparse, and we arrived at Paul and Diedre's Harlem town house in short order. I got out of the car to open the door for Diedre and to help Paul maneuver out of the backseat.

"I guess we have a lot to talk about later today." Diedre, with her typical understatement, sounded as drained and exhausted as I felt. But I knew that she was right.

"I have some meetings outside of the office later this morning, and then I have to speak at a New York City Partnership luncheon. Let's plan to meet at four."

"Sounds about right to me. I couldn't make it any earlier in any event," Paul called over his shoulder (PJ's head was occupying the other shoulder) as he went up the stairs to the front door of his town house.

"We certainly do have a lot to talk about, so I guess we all have to give this some thought between now and then. Try to have a good rest of the day, and I will see you later."

"Drive safely, Jerome."

"Thanks, Diedre."

I headed toward Riverside Drive and then on to the West Side Highway heading north to the Henry Hudson Parkway. I listened to 1010 WINS, the twenty-four-hour news radio station, and tried to clear my head by not thinking about anything else for a few moments.

As I wound my car through the thoroughfares of Westchester, I silently voted in favor of Gordon coming back to Morningstar, even though it was certainly a reluctant vote.

I also reminded myself that I had another reconciliation to put into motion, and I speed-dialed Berta's office voice mail to ask her to set up an appointment with Ray Beard.

And then there was one other item. I was glad of one thing about the night's events. My mind had wandered to Domino Oakley, and I decided that it was about time that I made her an offer she couldn't refuse. I was glad that I kept her contact details, and I promised myself that I would call her before the end of the day.

CHAPTER 44

Paul

It's Only a Paper Moon

When we walked out of Gordon's hospital room, it seemed like a whole series of events started to go into motion in a kind of fast-forward. It's only now that I can look back on the events that took place during the rest of 2000 and 2001, and sort out the sequence and the importance of what transpired.

But even at the time, from the moment that I started to breathe the fresh morning air of the Upper East Side, I knew there were some major and minor resolutions that were going to evolve over the next few months. And some of those resolutions would have a huge impact on all of our lives.

As a crisp dawn breeze meandered through the canyons of the huge New York Hospital complex, I

carried Paul Jr. in my arms with his head resting
on my shoulder. He was an amazing little boy. I was
convinced that if he was sleeping, the entire Rus-
sian Army could march by and he wouldn't wake
up. As a result, during all of the *Sturm und Drang* in
the hospital, PJ never even *almost* woke up. It was
probably just as well that he missed all that drama.
Gordon's revival alone was probably just the kind
of experience that could require years of intense
therapy in his adult life.

When we got out of Jerome's car and into the
house, Diedre took PJ and carried him up to his
bed. He would be out of synch and out of sorts for
most of the day, and she called the neighborhood
day care center that he attended to let them know
that he would be staying home. I also called our
housekeeper, who was due to arrive shortly, to let
her know that our son would be home.

We both needed to be downtown sooner than
later, so there wasn't a lot of time to review everything that had happened. There wasn't even time
for small talk. Diedre needed to be at the offices of
Morningstar, which had recently moved to 9 West
57th Street, one of the more spectacular office
buildings in midtown Manhattan, with upper
floors that had views of the entire planet. The legendary Reginald Lewis, the leverage buyout firm
KKR Financial, and countless other nodes of financial power resided on every floor. Morningstar was
on one of the upper floors, and the duplex layout
was as spectacular as it was impressive.

My offices were further west on 57th Street, in a
decidedly more modest building. Indeed, the only
tenant of note in the building that housed my of-

fices was a Japanese massage parlor, Salon de Tokyo, located on the thirteenth floor.

The Salon de Tokyo, which was originally established to cater to expatriate Japanese businessmen, was a discrete and classy establishment that provided a shower, sauna and massage administered by a Japanese or Korean masseuse. I had been patronizing it for almost twenty years, and in that time, I had come to rely upon the soothing and energizing benefits of a well-administered shiatsu massage.

Indeed, a massage would have been just the ticket after the adventures at New York Hospital. But that was just going to have to be a dream deferred. I settled for a quick but intense workout in my basement gym, and showered and dressed as quickly as I could.

By the time I came downstairs to the kitchen, Diedre was also dressed and had just finished brewing a fresh pot of the Kenyan blend of coffee that we both enjoyed. We both sat at the marble counter in the kitchen and sipped the fragrant coffee elixir in silence as we awaited the arrival of Mrs. Bonnemere, our sitter/housekeeper, who hailed from Barbados. Many mornings, Diedre and I would take the A train downtown. This would be one of those mornings.

"How do we even begin to untangle everything that played out last night—I mean, this morning?" Diedre spoke quietly and firmly and without frustration. I knew that she was already beginning to analyze and strategize, and the thought process that she was about to apply bordered on a type of genius.

Diedre always favored stylish business suits. Today, she was wearing a light cream Givenchy suit with a sky-blue silk blouse. Her only accessory was a tasteful pair of diamond earrings that I had given her for our first anniversary some three years ago. It was hard to believe that our fourth anniversary was coming up soon.

"Well, Diedre, let's take last night apart and talk about what we know and what we know we must do." I took a sip of my coffee and debated the wisdom of warming up a couple of calorie- and fat-engorged croissants.

"You're right, Paul. Let's mark this day down." I knew I could always count on Diedre's rapierlike wit to lighten the moment. And for the moment, I was glad of it. Although many were the times that she spoke her truth in jest.

"Thank you for the compliment, my dear. Now, let's get down to basics."

"Well, first there is the eight-hundred-pound gorilla, Gordon Perkins, and his offer to come back to Morningstar."

"Check. It's still more than unbelievable to me that we are even having this discussion. But please, continue." The Croissant Team won the debate, and I put two in the convection oven while Diedre continued her inventory.

"Second, and there is no way you would know this, Ray Beard wants to work for us at Morningstar as well. Monique came to me with the proposition about a week ago, and I passed the idea on to Jerome. He wasn't too crazy about it at first, to say the least, but he reconsidered, and I think that he will want to bring Ray into the firm on some kind of conditional basis."

I felt like a character in one of those old Tex Avery cartoons, the ones that predated Warner Brothers's best work in the forties and fifties, one of those cartoons where the surprised character loses body parts—first the eyes fall out, then the ears fall off, until finally, all that is left is a pile of collapsed limbs and appendages. While Diedre had always had an advanced sense of humor, I was pretty sure that she wasn't kidding this time.

"You will have to pardon me if I ask you to repeat what you just said. Because I could have sworn that you said that Jerome was considering having Raymond Russell Beard the Third come back to work with him at Morningstar." If the first eight hours were any indication, this day was going to be one for the record books.

"You heard correctly, *mon cher.* Things have been so crazy, I just haven't had time to mention it. Besides, I can't be sure what Jerome is going to do. All I do know is that, if it were up to me alone, I would give Ray another chance." She spoke with a calmness and serenity that belied the gravity of the bombshell that she had just dropped.

"Let me see if I can get this straight. You and Jerome are seriously considering having Ray Beard join you at Morningstar. This would be the same Ray Beard who was Jerome's protégé and who stabbed him in the back by leaving him to start his own firm." I struggled to retain control over my voice and my emotions. After all, I had invested my time and hopes and dreams in Morningstar right along with Jerome and Diedre. "The same Ray Beard

who joined up with the illustrious Gordon Perkins
and tried to totally collapse Morningstar Financial
Services. Is this the Ray Beard to whom you are re-
ferring?" I felt as if I had entered some bizarre
Dada parallel universe where no sense made sense.
Could Jerome and Diedre be serious?

"Well, Paul, it appears that I may have brewed
that Kenyan coffee a little too strong this morning.
After all this time, I didn't know you could be so
high-strung." She smiled a smile that was just this
side of condescending, which in my view, was not
her most appealing trait.

"Well, my dear, obviously my horizons need
broadening. So, please proceed." I sat back on my
stool at the kitchen counter, took another sip of
my coffee and started in on my first croissant.

"First of all, Paul Hiawatha Taylor, Senior, I am
not so sure that I would describe Ray's departure
from Jerome's firm as a betrayal in the generally
accepted meaning of the word. After all, Jerome
was committed to merging his firm with Gordon's
firm and mine, and right or wrong, Ray didn't see
any room for him in the new configuration that
was about to come about. Ray got an offer from
Merrill Lynch to help him start his own firm, and,
as I have reflected on it, Ray would have been
crazy to turn it down.

"Ray didn't betray Jerome any more than
Jerome betrayed his mentors at Merrill Lynch, the
firm that gave him his first job out of business
school, to take a better offer at Goldman Sachs."
Diedre was just getting warmed up. I knew when it
was best to be quiet around her, and this was turning out to be one of those times. Also, I was start-

ing to see her point. I tried to make sense out of what she was saying as she continued.

"Ray didn't betray Jerome any more than Jerome betrayed Goldman Sachs when he left that firm to start his own. You can't crucify Ray for doing what Jerome and you and I would do—hell, have done—and would do again if the circumstances arose. So, why does Raymond Russell Beard become the poster boy for betrayal and bad behavior? Just because the precious, almighty Jerome Hardaway had his feelings hurt because his protégé grew up and flew the coop doesn't make Ray a demented imp from hell."

I was following Diedre's train of thought and logic now, but there was still an unresolved point in my view.

"Well, *mon cher*, I understand your point about Ray. And I might even be inclined to agree with you. But I am waiting for your explanation regarding Ray hooking up with Gordon. This ought to be good." I settled back to nibble on my second croissant and see what her riposte would be. I didn't have long to wait.

"I gave a lot of thought to the whole Ray-Gordon thing. But I am more than sure that the entire New Orleans stratagem was Gordon's idea, and that he presented it to Ray as a business opportunity. And, as a businessman, Ray almost had to pursue the opportunity that Gordon presented. Once he was in business and had his own firm, in competition with Morningstar, there really was no reason for him to say no to Gordon. From a strictly business perspective, it was the smart thing to do. And, from the strictly business perspective, it would have been silly and sentimental for him to let his past relationship with Jerome get in the way. I don't know why we have to hold him to a different, higher standard."

Diedre's logic was unassailable. Ray Beard was neither a sinner nor a saint. He was just another one of us, out in the great big jungleworld, trying to avoid being prey by being a predator—or, at least, by being friends with a predator.

"Diedre, I am sure that if I thought about it long enough and hard enough, I could come up with an answer to your neat and concise presentation. But, in the final analysis, I think that you are right. It's going to take a while to get used to seeing Ray Beard around again. But, as you have said so many times before, 'business is business,' and it just doesn't make sense to abandon logic and clear thinking."

And at that point, Diedre and I didn't have to agree to disagree. We were on the same page, a phenomenon for which I was overwhelmingly thankful. Mrs. Bonnemere showed up a few minutes later, and Diedre and I headed downtown on the A train as another day of adventure in the life of The Pride continued apace. As we read our newspapers—she read the *New York Times,* I read the sports section of the *New York Daily News* since we both had read the *Wall Street Journal* before leaving the house, thanks to early morning home delivery—I had the sense that this day would be only the beginning of a turn of events that would change not only Morningstar but everyone associated with the firm.

It was then that I knew that not only was Ray

going to join the firm, but Gordon was also going to return. What would happen next at Morningstar was anybody's guess.

What would happen to Kenitra was a question for which I also needed an answer. I was not prepared to sacrifice her on the altar of logic and compulsory business decisions. As far as I was concerned, she simply did not deserve to suffer anymore.

I had done all that I could to make sure that she would never be under Gordon's thumb again. But everything that I did was done while he was flat on his back in a hospital bed. Now that Gordon was on his way to rejoining the world of the living, I knew that Kenitra was going to need some more help in order to stay safe and sane and secure.

I was just about out of bright ideas at that point. But I was determined to make sure that the new and improved Gordon Perkins would not victimize Kenitra again. She was just starting to live her life and just starting to become her own person again. I knew that I would have to find a way to make sure that she could continue on her way to a better life—or, at least, to a life different from the one that she had had with Gordon.

CHAPTER 45

Jerome

Every Little Breeze Seems to Whisper Louise

When I got home, I did not have a lot of time for rest or reflection. I got the boys ready for school and out the door in time for the eight o'clock school bus. I shaved and showered, and drove myself over to the commuter rail station. As I leafed through the morning papers, I tried to form a mental image of my schedule for the day.

I planned to go through correspondence, documents and various financial reports, and then attend a morning meeting with the senior executives of an up-and-coming telecommunications company that wanted to explore the feasibility of an initial public offering. It promised to be a fascinating discussion, as the company had come up with an innovative combination of a cellular telephone, television and data-storage device.

That meeting was going to be followed by a speech at a luncheon organized by the New York City Partnership. The Partnership, New York City's version of a chamber of commerce, was composed of the leaders of the most elite companies in the city and, therefore, in the world. Morningstar had been a member for two years, and my appearing as part of a panel discussing international business strategies for the twenty-first century could only help the firm.

But my mind was not focused on international business or telecommunications. I had asked Berta to set up a meeting for me with Ray Beard at the end of the day, and I knew that Diedre, Paul and I would be meeting to discuss the matter of one Gordon Stallworth Perkins at four. I had already made up my mind on both accounts.

I had decided that Diedre was right when it came to Ray. After all was said and done, Ray was only being ambitious and aggressive, and I could not be the one to cast the first stone when it came to those traits. Gordon was another story, however.

I had also decided that having Gordon in the tent was probably better than having Gordon outside the tent, plotting and planning who-knows-what. But Gordon was the quintessential loose cannon. He couldn't be controlled, even in his recovered and presumably penitent condition. But our advantage was that Gordon was the devil we knew.

The question was how to control Gordon. The other question was, Could Morningstar survive a second go-around with him?

These thoughts were swirling around my brain as I got off the Metro North train at Grand Central Station and continued what was turning out to be a pivotal day in my life and in the life of Morningstar Financial Services.

CHAPTER 46

Kenitra

Someone to Watch Over Me

After Sture left to go back to New York, I didn't leave my apartment in Venice Beach for about a week. He had promised to come back in a week, and I decided to take that time to recover from the events at New York Hospital and all that they meant.

It took me a very long time to believe not only that Gordon was alive, but that he was back from his coma and would soon be living among real people again. And that look in his eyes when he called my name from the hospital bed told me that I would never be truly safe if I was ever alone with him.

I never truly understood the reason for Gordon's great hatred toward me. I came to understand that I was neither the first nor, Lord knows, the only woman that he had ever beaten, degraded or abused. But when it came to me, there was something more that motivated Gordon and that brought out the worst and the most depraved aspects of his personality. It wasn't enough for him to beat me with his fists and feet and anything he could get his hands on. Even beating me enough to make me lose an eye and a baby wasn't enough.

It wasn't enough for him to force me to consume incredibly excessive amounts of drugs and alcohol so that he could make me do every sick and disgusting and degrading act that he could conjure up. It wasn't even enough for him to get me to a point where I would beg him for more drugs and alcohol, and degrade and defile myself, so that he would let me have them.

And the verbal and spiritual and mental abuse was constant. And not only was it never-ending, it never had any rhyme or reason.

But it was the hatred that flowed from some deep dark pool of vitriol that resided deep in his soul that I never understood. In the early days of our relationship and then our marriage, I had never given him any reason to resent or dislike me, much less to hate me. Gordon was never an easy person to be around for an extended period of time, but I tried to be loving and affectionate and caring. And those efforts just seemed to infuriate him all the more.

When the beatings and the rest of the hell began, it came from out of the blue and then just never stopped. But over time, the source of the hatred didn't matter. I just knew that, to stay alive, I had to be aware of that hatred and on the defensive at all times.

When Gordon went into his coma, it was as if he had magically, miraculously and mercifully disappeared from my life. And after Paul helped me make my way to Venice Beach and made sure that I was financially independent, it was as if I was leading an enchanted life. I felt safe, and so I felt free, and because I felt free, I began to live my life again.

Laughing was no longer a daring act. Having fun and enjoying myself was no longer a rare pleasure. Dancing, dining, swimming, even cooking and smiling, all became new, delicious pleasures, which I savored and devoured hungrily and greedily. And then, along came Sture.

I had seen Sture around for several years, of course, but I still don't know what prompted my bold, brazen hussy routine at Dorothy's By the Sea that night. Maybe it was the champagne. Maybe I was horny. Maybe I was just lucky for the first time in a long time. But whatever the reason, that first night at the Waldorf with Sture renewed my membership in the world of pleasure and happiness.

I found myself smiling for no reason and enjoying the feeling. I had almost forgotten what it was like to look forward to tomorrow. I certainly had forgotten what it was like to remember yesterday with warmth and pleasure. And because of Sture, I started to believe that there actually might be something called love in this world.

And then came the phone call at the Waldorf in the middle of the night, and I sometimes wonder what might have changed if I hadn't untangled myself from Sture and the bedsheets to answer the phone.

That call and the ensuing insane circus at New York Hospital changed my life, and once again, I found myself mistrusting tomorrow. Once again, I started cursing myself for believing that I had a right to happiness and pleasure and random enjoyment.

I fled the hospital that night and New York City that morning not because I thought that Gordon was going to get out of that bed and try to throttle me. I ran because I did not want to be on the same planet with that beast when he was awake and conscious and mobile again. Knowing Gordon, I was sure that he had any number of targets for revenge, vengeance and sheer cruelty, and I was sure that Jerome, Diedre, Paul, Sture and I would figure into whatever demonic scenarios he might devise. The fact that we were the first faces that he saw when he came out of his coma was probably just coincidental to our being the objects of his plotting and scheming, with the possible exception of Sture.

As soon as Gordon rolled his pitiless, soulless eyes in our direction and saw that we were together, I knew that Sture would be someone that he would hate. It wasn't that he was jealous in some faux romantic kind of way. It was more a matter of territorial imperatives and possessions. In Gordon's world, I belonged to him, just like his cars and homes and furniture. He had marked me, just like a wolf or a dog or a bear marks his territory. And the fact that Sture had presumed to enter his territory and try to steal his possessions was enough to ensure eternal hatred and the continuous stoking of the fires of revenge.

I felt a moment of remorse and fear for Sture at that point because it wasn't fair that he was about to get caught up in the maelstrom that was Gordon's wrath and vengeance. He should at least have had a chance to make a choice, and when we left the hospital and I was packing at the Waldorf, I told him point-blank that he could leave, and leave me, and I would understand, because Gordon was not somebody to be trifled with.

"Sture, you haven't signed any contracts, and we haven't exchanged any vows. You don't need me to tell you that you are free to go. You *are* free to go. And if you have the sense that God gave you, you will go, because I promise you, you don't want to be around me when Gordon gets out of that hospital bed. I don't care if we are in Venice Beach or Fiji." My hands were shaking as I tried to pack and collect my belongings. I couldn't look at Sture as I was speaking.

"I know you think you are doing the right thing by telling me . . ."

"Think? Think, Sture? It's not what I think. It's what I *know*. Look at me! I am scared to death, and I am running like a scared jackrabbit just because that bastard woke up. You have no idea what he might do if he decides to come after us. I know he's coming after me. You don't have to be a part of what's going to happen next."

I cursed myself for the tears that were now flowing down my face. Weakness wasn't going to help matters, but I felt so weak. And then Sture walked over to me and held my hands. It was the sweetest and most tender touch that I had felt from him during the past few wonderful, magical, sensual weeks that we had spent together.

"Kenitra, to borrow one of your expressions, the only thing I have to do is be white and die. I *know* I don't *have* to stay with you. I *want* to be with you. And I don't know what kind of man I would be if I ran away from the most wonderful woman I have ever known because I was afraid that another man might not like it."

I couldn't suppress the smile that started to dawn when I heard Sture's "be white and die" line, but I also couldn't suppress the feeling of warmth and emotion that his words elicited from the very depths of my soul.

"Look, Kenitra, we have talked about our mutual friend Alex Lapidoulos. I have told you that I don't think that his death was the result of a random crime. You also know that I think Gordon arranged the whole thing when he found out that you and Alex were having an affair." Sture reminding me of the stupid and sordid fling that I had had with Gordon's driver reminded me once more of how low-grade and sleazy I had become because of Gordon.

"I know that you will never be safe alone, and I will never be happy without you. So, let's cut the drama and get to the airport so that you can get back to Venice Beach and we can start to make a plan. Gordon's not the only one capable of coming up with a few plots and plans, you know."

And then, Sture smiled that very special smile of his and held me in his arms, and I truly wanted to believe that everything was going to be all right, even with Gordon alive and well.

All of these things were going through my mind, including the fact that, in the final analysis, Paul and Diedre had each other and Jerome was eminently capable of taking care of himself. I had to consider myself very lucky to have Sture in my life, and as I awaited his phone call to let me know that he was driving from LAX to my apartment, I felt the flicker of a glimmer of a sliver of a speck of hope that everything might work out for us after all.

It turned out that I was right in that everything did work out for us. Things worked out for Sture and me, but certainly not in the way that I expected. The several months after Gordon's revival produced surprise after shock after surprise.

CHAPTER 47

Paul

Here Comes That Rainy Day

Looking back on the events of the several months following that late night/early morning at New York Hospital, I wouldn't blame someone for thinking that they were a work of fiction, if they weren't so true. The major thing that happened was that Diedre, Jerome and I decided to let Gordon rejoin Morningstar, although it became my job to structure the terms and conditions and penalties that Gordon would have to accept if he was going to get back on the team. I couldn't believe my amazing good fortune.

After that pivotal meeting, which didn't take long, Ray Beard and Jerome met in what I later understood to be a very direct and to-the-point encounter. It didn't take long for either of them to say what needed to be said, and the upshot was that Ray Beard was slated to join Morningstar, effective immediately.

Gordon effected something like a reconciliation with Kenitra. Not that they got back together or resumed a relationship. Not at all. Instead, Kenitra later told me that Gordon called her several times, apologizing and asking for her forgiveness, and that he promised her that he was going to dedicate his life to being a good person in an effort to make up for all the terrible things he had done to her and to so many other people. She told me that she was so stunned that all she could do was accept his apology and his promise to leave her in peace and to never try to see her or contact her unless it was a matter of urgent importance.

Quincy Holloway took the videotape of "The Resurrection of Gordon Perkins," as he liked to call it, and sold it to CNN. Somehow, he also managed to sell the same tape to BBC, Fox News and CBS, keeping the several payments and not getting sued. He truly was a miracle worker.

The Mighty Reverend also took advantage of his latest chapter of fame by marketing himself as a combination faith healer and spiritual guide. Within no time, he was appearing in packed arenas and stadiums and convention halls, healing the sick and preaching a very special message about the power of prayer and its direct connection with success in the material world. Borrowing heavily from the theories expounded by John Calvin a few centuries earlier, Quincy featured a series of sermons that basically told his listeners that if they prayed the way that he taught them to, with an accompanying fee to maintain the good works of his ministry (including his suite at the Waldorf-Astoria Hotel), they would get rich.

I would never have believed that there would be hundreds of thousands of reasonably intelligent people who would feel that praying with Reverend Quincy Holloway would make them rich. But that turned out to be the case. Combined with his faith-healing routine, which worked best on those with psychosomatic illnesses, Quincy Holloway became an even greater force on the faith circuit.

Jerome, as a romantic, turned out to be hilarious and entertaining at the same time. After Morningstar started to operate on its new basis, with Gordon and Ray Beard both contributing their special brands of talent and genius to help the firm achieve even greater success, he let me know over drinks one evening that he had started dating Domino Oakley. For someone who usually tried to come across as phlegmatic and impassive, Jerome was positively beaming when he started to talk about Domino and how happy he was to be seeing her. It would turn out to be a very interesting relationship.

Diedre and I continued trying to be good parents and decent spouses. Fortunately for PJ, we were good at the former. The stresses and strains of work and unrealized ambitions and just life in general made our relationship increasingly tense, although there were still those times when the magic between us was more than reminiscence. But those times were getting fewer and fewer, and by September 2001, we had even discussed the

possibility of seeking some kind of couples coun-
seling to find out if there was some kind of way
that we could get along better instead of separating or divorcing.

As things turned out, our need for marital coun-
seling would turn out to be the least of our problems.

CHAPTER 48

Jerome

Everytime We Say Goodbye

The day after the night and morning of Gordon's return to the land of the living turned out to be pivotal in so many ways. First, of course, there was the slight matter of all of us having to deal with a living, breathing and soon to be walking Gordon Perkins again after a three-year absence. Then there was the matter of Paul, Diedre and me deciding what to do about his request to rejoin Morningstar.

Not only that, but while I had decided in my mind to accede to Ray Beard's request to join Morningstar as well, I had not seen or spoken to Ray in the three years since his departure, and our meeting later that day was another hurdle in a steeplechase of a day. And finally, last but certainly not least, I decided to try to reconnect with Miss Domino Oakley so that we could further discuss the principles of bifurcation—hopefully over drinks and dinner.

When I returned from speaking at the New York City Partnership luncheon, there was not a lot of time to prepare for the meeting with Diedre and Paul regarding Gordon. As it turned out, the meeting was, under the circumstances, surprisingly brief. Paul, Diedre and I sat on the sofa and armchair in Diedre's office.

"In my view, there really isn't a whole lot to discuss if you want to stick to the business aspects of this whole matter concerning Gordon." Paul was the first to speak, and, as usual, he quickly and efficiently framed the issues at hand. "We all know that Gordon is a liar, a schemer and, in so many ways, a low-life son of a bitch. Of course, he was all that when the three of you decided to merge firms in the first place."

Diedre and I sat calmly, acknowledging the obvious and waiting for Paul to continue.

"The thing is that Gordon is also an exceptionally brilliant low-life son of a bitch. Furthermore, for all of his plotting and scheming, it may be in your best interests to have him and his conspiratorial ways close by, so that you can keep an eye on him. Furthermore, if you join his interests with yours sufficiently, he will be cheating himself if he tries to cheat you."

"Paul, you will have to outdo yourself as an attorney and advisor to come up with a foolproof arrangement that will give us the kind of oversight and control over Gordon that we need." I knew that I was stating the obvious, and I hated to put that kind of pressure on Paul, but it had to be said.

Paul nodded in acknowledgement, and then Diedre let out a deep, long sigh and spoke in that very direct, almost stern manner that she adopts when she wants to be very clear on a point.

"Look, I know that I am always the one who insists on staying focused on the business aspect of whatever matter comes over the transom. And I will be the first to say that the idea of having Gordon rejoin Morningstar almost makes me sick to my stomach." Even though she never raised her voice, the tension that she was experiencing in her effort to control her emotions was obvious to Paul and me as she pressed on. "I should have my head examined for saying this, but I still think we just have to bite the bullet and find a way to work with Gordon." As she said "find a way," she looked directly at Paul as a way of reiterating what I had already said.

"Okay, okay, you don't have to hit this mule over the head too many times. If you want Gordon in Morningstar, there are a number of conditions and controls I can put in to make sure that he will be tied down, as much as the law will allow." Paul paused and looked at both of us for a moment before continuing. "Just remember that this is Gordon Perkins we are talking about. We all know that he will continue to plot, he will continue to lie and he will continue to be someone that you will have to monitor twenty-five hours a day, and that probably won't be enough. But if you can use Gordon and his skills and his contacts for a couple of years, you can employ an exit strategy at your option—

which I will put into the partnership documents—
and get him the hell out of the firm."

I usually don't spend a lot of time engaging in
plotting. I have always been a direct-action sort of
person. But I had to admire, appreciate and finally
accept Paul's proposal. Clearly, it was the only way
that we could have a chance of avoiding another
near-disaster like the New Orleans one.

"Well, then, I guess it's a done deal, as the saying
goes." Diedre let out another deep sigh and
leaned back on the couch. We all felt some kind of
relief at the fact that we at least knew what we were
going to try to do.

The devil was going to be in the details. And the
details were going to be Paul's personal project for
the next few weeks. I didn't envy him his job in all
of this. Actually, at that moment, I was feeling only
relief and not much in the way of exhilaration.
And that was the beginning of Gordon coming
back to Morningstar. It was that simple.

Paul excused himself and went back to his offices. After a few minutes of going over some
Morningstar administrative matters, I also left
Diedre's office and headed down the hallway to
my office, knowing full well that the next item on
my agenda was not paperwork. It was Ray Beard.

CHAPTER 49

Gordon

Criss-Cross

As soon as I floated my "proposal" to Paul, Diedre and Jerome, I knew that they would accept. I just knew it, because the fact that they would even listen to me after all that had transpired told me that there was a way to work out a deal, and if there was a deal to be made, I have always found a way. As soon as they left the room, I started to think about three things that I knew I would have to do.

First, I knew I had to listen very carefully to the doctors to find out how I could get my black ass out of the hospital as soon as possible and get back on my feet again. Dr. Krishnamurthy had already explained to me that I was lucky to be alive, and that I was going to have to commit myself to intensive rehabilitation if I wanted to get back to anything like normal.

Second, I needed to come up with a plan to settle my accounts with Kenitra and Sture—as well as to sort out my plan of action for when I returned to Morningstar Financial Services. I knew that motherfucker Paul Taylor was going to come up with all the belts and suspenders and bells and whistles that he could think of to try to tie me down when I did get back to Morningstar. I had no intention of playing second fiddle to Jerome or that bitch Diedre, or to anybody else. But I was willing to sign off on any arrangement they proposed just so I could get my feet on the ground. But there would come a day when they would learn once more that it made no sense to fuck with Gordon Perkins.

Third, I had to figure out a way for G-Perk to monitor and manage his new business arrangement with Duke and Ernie Argentina and the rest of the crew. I knew that the distribution and sale of cocaine would not necessarily be compatible with my reprise as an investment banker and partner in Morningstar Financial Services. It was going to be a delicate balancing act, to say the least. I needed to strategize with the Dark Lord, and the sooner we talked and came up with a plan, the better.

But first things had to come first. And getting out of that hospital and back on my feet again was going to require a lot of willpower and dedication. I had no doubt that I was going to fully recover in record time, and over the next few weeks, I continually amazed the doctors and the nurses and the rehabilitation specialists and the therapists as I regained my strength and the full use of my faculties.

The doctors in particular were absolutely certain at first that there was no way that someone who had been in a coma for three years could fully recover from its effects in less than six months. They had too much data, too much research and too much knowledge to even consider the possibility that they could be wrong.

But they didn't know me, and I managed to tell them to take all that fucking data and research and knowledge and stick it up their asses by eating full meals within a couple of days of waking up. I was walking to the rehabilitation center in the hospital within a week.

The rehabilitation therapists and specialists were accustomed to so-called miraculous recoveries. But even miracles didn't begin to explain why I didn't have to relearn walking and talking, and why, within just a few more days, I was able to go online and access bank accounts of mine that neither Paul Taylor nor any of Jerome Hardaway's security geeks had been able to locate, recalling all the passwords and complicated protocols as if I had just awakened from a thirty-minute nap instead of a lengthy coma.

Instead of the guarded estimate of three months for my departure from the hospital, I was back in my Park Avenue home within three weeks. I made arrangements for home-care attendants and a private physical therapist to greet me upon my arrival. Having given my personal attorney the authority to negotiate my return to Morningstar with Paul, I was back at a desk, working the phones and get-

ting back into the world of investment banking
and corporate finance, within two months of my
awakening. It was like I had never been away.

It turned out that, if the truth be told, Jerome
and Diedre had done a masterful job at running
Morningstar since my departure. They were incredibly professional at bringing me back into the
fold, and I did everything that I could to make
sure that they had no reason to doubt their decision. I did everything that I could to avoid making
waves in those early months, and I kept myself focused on renewing contact with my network of
bankers, corporate officers, politicians and ap-
pointed officials all over the country.

Soon, I was able to start bringing deal opportunities to Morningstar, and after my first few clos-
ings started bringing in fees—some municipal and
some corporate—I could sense that my new former partners were starting to get comfortable with
my presence. It was exactly what I wanted.

All the time that I was working on rebuilding my
banking career and getting into a comfort zone at
Morningstar, I was also plotting out my own course.
Years earlier, I had set up two separate identities
for myself, complete with social security numbers,
passports, credit cards and fully funded bank accounts. Absolutely no one knew all the details
about these identities and their appurtenances.

That was why, after my misstep in New Orleans,
Paul figured that he had found all the money that
I had stashed away when he found the offshore accounts that I had set up in Kenitra's name. Even
though it cost me ten million dollars, it couldn't
have worked out better for me because, once Paul

found those accounts and could locate no others that could be traced to me, he stopped looking.

At the time I set up these rather elaborate backup personas, I didn't have a particular plan in mind. But I knew that it was a poor rat that had but one hole, and I was never going to be that kind of rat.

Using passwords and some other elaborate protocols that I had established with some banks in Switzerland, Grenada and Costa Rica, I soon had access to all of the cash that I needed to put the next aspect of my plan together. It was a plan that started coming together as soon as Paul, Jerome and Diedre walked out of my hospital room, and every day that I worked on it, I was sure that it was a plan that was going to rock their little world.

CHAPTER 50

Jerome

Boplicity

I learned very early in my professional career that the small things can count for a lot. That is why I have always dialed my own phone calls rather than having an assistant or secretary make the call, with the recipient of my call waiting until I can be brought to the phone. The direct touch, and the absence of presumption in such a simple act can elicit a positive response, and it's really so simple.

It has also been the reason why, when guests come to visit me at my office, I have never, ever had a secretary or assistant come out to escort them to my office. I have always taken the time to demonstrate a little bit of personal courtesy by coming out to the reception area and greeting my visitors and bringing them into my office or the conference room myself. It can be the little things that can sometimes mean a lot.

And that is how I happened to walk right past Ray Béard the afternoon that he came to my office. When my assistant, Berta, let me know that he was waiting in the Morningstar reception area, I quickly concluded the phone call that I was making, put on my suit jacket and headed down the hall to greet Ray. I had already made up my mind to follow Diedre's advice and stay focused on the business aspect of his coming to work at Morningstar.

I was so focused that, when I walked into the reception area, I was surprised when I didn't see Ray. I thought that he might have gone to the men's room, and I started to pick up the phone to ask Berta if she knew where Ray might be.

But I suddenly froze as I was about to dial Berta's number. In the corner of the reception room was a gaunt, almost frail man struggling to raise himself on a cane so he could greet me. I was more than stunned. The last three years had taken a toll on Ray Beard, and at that moment, it was clear to me that, if he had committed any sins in leaving my firm or hooking up with Gordon, he had paid for them many, many times over.

He must have lost at least fifty pounds since the last time that I saw him, and I guessed that he had probably gained some weight in his recovery. Ray was tall, well over six feet, and he had always had an athletic build and an erect, confident carriage that had helped make him the object of attention whenever he walked into a room. He had always been clean-shaven, but now he had a beard and a mustache, and he wore his hair long and pulled back in a kind of Japanese samurai ponytail. He also wore thick, horn-rimmed glasses. The broken man who was struggling manfully to get up from the chair in which he had been sitting. It was Raymond Russell Beard III, returning from a six-month coma, brought on by a massive stroke occasioned by a cocaine overdose and followed by almost two years of physical therapy.

As he walked toward me, I could only hope that the shock that I felt didn't show on my face. I realized that the reason I was standing there holding a phone in my hand asking Berta to help me locate the man standing in front of me was that I absolutely wouldn't have recognized Ray Beard on the street if he had walked up to me and slapped me in the face. He appearance had changed that much.

It was more than the loss of weight. It was more than the cane and the beard and the glasses and the ponytail. It was as if he had undergone a complete metamorphosis and become a different person. The self-confidence, the obvious pride, the hubris—all of them were gone. And in their place was a clearly humbled man making his way toward me, leaning heavily on a cane and extending his hand toward me.

"Long time no see, Jerome." His smile was a little forced, and I took his extended hand and held it and shook it for what seemed like a full minute before I could speak.

"Ray, it's been much too long. Let's go to my office so that we can talk. I guess it goes without saying that we have a lot to talk about."

"That might be the understatement of the year. Thanks for seeing me. You're right, though. It's been much too long. Please lead the way. I'm moving a little more slowly these days, but I get to where I need to go."

We both smiled, and at that point, it was as if the past three years and the disappointment and dismay and anger and frustration simply flew out the window. We were both three years older and, hopefully, a little wiser, and maybe that's really what made the difference in the final analysis.

We walked back to my office, and I headed over to the chairs at the small conference table in the corner, as I thought those chairs might be easier than the sofa for Ray to negotiate. After we both sat down, I poured a glass of ice water for each of us. For a moment, neither of us spoke. While Ray had requested the meeting via his wife, Monique, speaking to Diedre, who had spoken to me, I figured it would be easiest and simplest for me to start what could prove to be an awkward conversation.

"Ray, we could spend a lot of time getting to the end of this conversation, but I'm going to cut to the chase. You know that Monique spoke to Diedre, and I have to tell you, I was more than surprised to hear that you had even an interest in coming to work at Morningstar. And, to be honest, my first reaction was that I couldn't see how it could possibly work for you, or for Morningstar or for me." I could see Ray visibly tense up, and I knew immediately that he thought I was heading in a different direction than I had in mind. There was no need for suspense in this particular scenario, so I got right to the point.

"Diedre and I had a very long conversation about all of this, and I have given this a lot of thought. We would like to invite you to join Morningstar as a managing director, effective immediately. I think that it's best that you and Diedre work out the precise financial terms and details, but we will be more than fair because we really want you on the team. You are smart and bright and talented, and we know that your special skills in financial markets will make Morningstar an even stronger firm than it is right now."

"Jerome, I . . . I don't know how to thank you enough." Ray's voice caught, and I could see that he was visibly overcome with emotion. It was emotion that I could feel as well.

"Ray, Ray, please don't thank me. You can believe we are not doing you any favors. Like I said, you are a real talent, and Diedre and I would be the losers if we let an opportunity to bring you on board go by." I could see Ray start to relax, and a smile began to work its way across his face. "And another thing, and let me just say this. There is no reason for us to go into why you thought it best to leave the firm, and no reason to go into why you linked up with Gordon. I have come to understand that you were pursuing the best opportunity for yourself in starting your own firm. And, as far as Gordon is concerned, well, he just came out of a coma early this morning, and if everything works out, it's my guess that he is going to be joining

Morningstar as soon as his health permits. So, we all need to focus on how we can get this new team working together so that we can all make some money."

I could see that the news about Gordon coming out of a coma *and* joining Morningstar was a shock for Ray. And his surprised reaction approximated the way the rest of The Pride and Wall Street re-acted when word started to get around. I could also see that Ray greeted the news that Gordon would also be joining the firm as something of a mixed blessing. But, to his credit, he stayed fo-cused on the outcome that was most important to his interests at that particular point in time.

"Whew! There's a lot going on at Morningstar these days, that's for sure. Jerome, all I can say right now is that I thank you, Monique thanks you and Jerome Russell Beard thanks you." He spoke the last name with a wink and the first genuine smile I had seen since we shook hands in the re-ception area.

"I'm not sure I caught that last part, Ray."

"Jerome Russell Beard. That will be the name of our son. Monique will be giving birth to our first child in about four months. We found out about a month ago that it was going to be a boy, and Jerome Russell is the name that we chose. Monique wanted to surprise you after the birth, but I couldn't help jumping the gun."

It was one of those occasions where speechless-ness was the only possible reaction. What Ray was telling me, of course, was that he had decided to name his son after me long before he knew that he would be rejoining me at Morningstar. It was a humbling moment, and one that I simply will never forget.

"Ray, you and Monique honor me in a way that I could never have expected. I hope you know that I have always wished you the very best, and let's just say that I am sure that our chapter two is going to make chapter one look like buttons and pennies in comparison."

We both laughed genuinely, and we finished our conversation with some further talk about how the firm was doing and some of the projects that I thought would be of interest to him. After another thirty minutes of conversation, we wrapped things up, and I escorted Ray through the reception area to the elevator.

We shook hands and embraced warmly. It was like welcoming back a long lost brother. I was genuinely glad that Ray and I would be working together again, and as we bade farewell and the elevator door closed, I knew that a very good thing had happened. And, it turned out, I was right.

Ray Beard had lost none of his genius for structuring corporate mergers and acquisitions and various types of creative financings. He quickly enhanced the ability of Morningstar to serve as financial advisor to major companies on all sorts of matters, domestic and international. And as his work became more successful, his strength seemed to return.

It wasn't long before he started gaining weight and that prideful carriage began to return as well. After a few months, right about the time his son was born, the beard and the mustache and the ponytail disappeared. But the real transformation came about a year later, when he got some contact lenses and the thick horn-rimmed glasses vanished. And then one day, I noticed something about Ray as he walked into my office. The cane was gone, too.

Raymond Russell Beard III was back. But that all came later. As the elevator door closed, I had to head back to my office to finish one more item on my list for the day.

I had promised myself that I would call Domino Oakley before the day ended.

CHAPTER 51

Gordon

Can It Get Any Better?

My plan for Jerome and Diedre, and therefore for Paul, was really quite simple. I was going to settle for nothing less than the complete downfall and destruction of Morningstar. I wasn't sure how to make that happen right away, of course. That's why it was important for me to start working with Morningstar again, to learn everything about the firm and its clients and accounts and strategies.

It was also important for me to start accessing my secret personal bank accounts because I soon realized that one element of my plan's success would require me to have my own firm again. But not right away. Even though I had gotten out of the hospital in record time, it was going to take a while for me to regain my full strength. It was also going to take some time for Diedre and Jerome to become truly comfortable with my return to Morningstar.

I wanted them to be really comfortable. I knew that neither of them would ever truly let down his or her guard when it came to me, but for what I had in mind for them, it really didn't matter. The day would come when they would realize who the true genius was. The day would come when all of their hopes and dreams would be just ashes at their feet.

And when that happened, I wanted them to know that it was me who was responsible. Not bad luck. Not a wrong turn of events. I wanted them to know that it was Gordon Perkins who had beaten them, that it was Gordon Perkins who had broken them.

And while I couldn't wait for that happy day, I was also prepared to wait and be patient, like a true predator stalking his prey. A true predator is patient and focused. And while I worked at Morningstar every day and also continued my extensive rehabilitation regimen, I stayed patient and focused on Diedre, Jerome, Paul and Morningstar, my true prey.

When I found out that Ray Beard was joining the firm, it made the scenario all the more delicious. I had been able to turn Ray against his former mentor and the rest of them once before, and I was sure that I could do it again. Once again, I had to bide my time and make sure that I brought him into my plan at the right moment.

If I brought him in too early, some fucked-up sense of loyalty or guilt might cause him to spill his guts to Jerome and spoil the whole plan. If I told him too late, he might not be able to serve any purpose at all. So I stayed in my patient-predator mode.

While I was busy with the details of my plan and trying to get back to work at Morningstar, I didn't have a lot of time to give Kenitra and Sture much thought. It wasn't as if she didn't deserve a serious beat-down for leaving me in that fucking hospital for three fucking years. And it wasn't as if she didn't deserve another beat-down for fucking Sture and who knows who else.

But they were going to have to wait. I would have time enough for them after I brought down the House of Morningstar. In the meantime, I asked Paul to send word to Kenitra that there were no hard feelings on my part, that I would leave her alone and that she had nothing to fear from me anymore. And then I hired a private investigator, who was able to find her in Venice Beach after a one-week search.

I knew that my peace offering to Kenitra would only make her more afraid, and that was good enough for me at that point in time. I knew that any communication from me would have her looking over her shoulder every time she went out and staying up late at night at home thinking that every sound she heard might be me at the door or coming through the window. It was enough for me that she stayed afraid of me. I would take care of her later.

One puzzling item, however, was my business dealings with Duke. It wasn't long after I got back to my place on Park Avenue that I established a re-

liable connection for coke, which was delivered to
my apartment by livery cab. It was like ordering
pizza. And the Dark Lord started dropping by reg-
ularly, helping me to work out my plans for Morningstar, and for Kenitra, and for everybody else who
needed to be taught a lesson.

Soon after I started being able to get around on
my own, I suggested early one evening that the
Dark Lord and I go up to see Duke at the Purple
Dragon. I had heard nothing from him for several
weeks, even though I had arranged for my initial
investment to be delivered to him as we had
agreed.

So we took a taxi up 125th Street, where the bar
was located. I was more than surprised. I was
shocked to see that there was no sign of the Purple
Dragon. There was only a boarded-up hole in the
wall. When we got out of the taxi and asked
around, nobody had ever heard of the Purple
Dragon. We were told that the bar that used to be
where the hole-in-the-wall was located had been
called the Purple Manor, but that had been ages
ago.

The Dark Lord and I headed back downtown in
silence. He did suggest that we come back later in
the evening. I didn't see what good could come
from that plan, so I said good-night to the Dark
Lord and went to sleep.

But damned if he didn't come back at about two
in the morning with my G-Perk gear, right down to
the Timberland shoes and gold chains and baseball cap. After I got dressed, we did up about a
gram of coke and then went downstairs, where El
Steve was waiting in his livery cab. And when we

headed up Park Avenue and turned west on 125th Street, we found the Purple Dragon, sitting there as bold as fuck.

We got out of the car and went inside, and there was Ernie Argentina behind the bar, already starting to pour my favorite Rémy. And there was Duke in the back, seated at a table, almost seeming to have been waiting for my arrival.

I said my hellos to Ernie and went to the back to sit down with Duke. We shook hands, and he smiled warmly. It was good to be back.

"Haven't seen you in a while, G-Perk. Thought you might have gone fishing or something."

"No, motherfucker, nothing like that. I just had some other business, that's all. How is everything?" Duke knew exactly what I meant. I wanted my fucking money. He didn't disappoint me. There was a shopping bag—Macy's, as I recall—directly under the table. He slid it toward me, and I saw that there were some old clothes visible on the top.

"Under those old clothes is your money plus one hundred K. We have been doing great business since you were last here. Are you going to let me buy you a drink?"

"Nah, that's cool, Duke. You just keep up the good work."

"I heard that, G-Perk!" We high-fived and finished our drinks, and then the Dark Lord and I said good-night to Ernie Argentina and got into El Steve's Lincoln with three miscellaneous bitches that we picked up at the Purple Dragon. We went back to my apartment on Park Avenue and had a ball for the rest of the night, feeding the bitches cocaine and coming up with the wildest and freakiest shit for them to do. The Dark Lord and I were very creative that night, as I recall. The only thing was, when the Dark Lord and the bitches left and I woke up later in the morning to go down to Morningstar, it seemed as if no one had been there and that I had never gotten out of the bed.

It was something that I could never quite figure out, even though the same thing would happen over and over. I would go by the Purple Dragon during the day, and there would be nothing there, only the ruins of the Purple Manor. Then I would get up from sleeping in the middle of the night and go to the Purple Dragon as G-Perk accompanied by the Dark Lord and driven by El Steve, and get drinks from Ernie Argentina and do my business with Duke. But when I would awake at home the next morning, it would be as if I had never gone anywhere.

I didn't have a lot of time to reflect on these mysteries, however. I had my plans for Jerome, Diedre, Paul and Morningstar to execute. Having Ray Beard would actually make things a little easier. But I was sure of one thing: The days of the House of Morningstar were numbered. I was going to make damn sure of that.

CHAPTER 52

Jerome

No Room for Squares

By the time that Domino Oakley and I actually went on a date, it was already the summer of 2000. The delay in our first social rendezvous was caused by all the usual reasons. She was busy, and then I was busy. Getting Ray Beard reacquainted with the world of finance was child's play compared to trying to structure an effective modus operandi when Gordon came to work at Morningstar about six weeks later.

But we did manage to meet for lunch, both of us deciding that Fresco by Scotto would be a great place to resume our discussion of the principles of bifurcation. And what a discussion it turned out to be.

Domino came to lunch wearing her almost-blue-black hair up, somehow making her carriage even more erect and regal. She wore a tastefully short skirt, peach in color, as I recall, with a matching pair of heels with straps that snaked up her impossibly long and beautiful legs. A canary yellow blazer, a string of pearls and a nearly sheer beige blouse completed her ensemble, and I was enchanted all over again.

While waiting for her to arrive at the restaurant, I felt like a schoolboy on his first date. I didn't realize how lonely I had been since Charmaine's death until I had lunch with Domino that warm, sultry afternoon.

We talked about her new firm, Domino Advisors, and how it was doing quite well. She had just taken up office space in the World Trade Center, and she raved about the wonderful views and its proximity to Wall Street and the World Financial Center. It also sounded as if she had recovered from the bitterness that surrounded her divorce and the misadventure of her Jamaican love affair with the down-low youngster.

And success suited her just fine. She didn't just exude beauty. She exhaled the possibility of sensuousness with every breath. We didn't get very far into our lunch before I found myself wanting to see her for dinner that evening and for breakfast the next morning.

We talked about the drama and adventures that seemed to stay a part of the Morningstar story. There was, of course, the dramatic resurrection of Gordon. And there was the almost as dramatic return of the prodigal Ray Beard. As we talked about it, I realized that some aspects of the past several months were so fantastic as to be unbelievable. And sometimes, we just had to laugh.

And then she let her hair down and started to laugh. And the gorgeous jet black hair flowed down to her shoulders. And listening to Domino laugh was, for me, like listening to a gentle brook in a Zen garden. And, to tell the truth, at that moment I wanted to listen to her laugh forever.

Our luncheon once more concluded with a combination mango–passion fruit gelato, with a slight difference from our previous luncheon. This time, we were sitting side by side, and we shared the gelato from a single cup with two spoons.

What made her special was that she made me feel special in a way that I had just about forgotten. There were certainly the dawning rays of passion spilling over the horizon of my consciousness. There was no denying that. But there was so much more.

Domino made me feel like she was interested in me, not just in Morningstar or the latest deal or the latest word on The Pride. She had a way of looking at me that made me cancel out the rest of the planet so that I could hang on her every word. She had a way of looking at me that made me hope that the moment would never end.

As was the case the last time we were at Fresco, Domino had a cappuccino and I had an espresso. And then it was time to leave. She had a late afternoon flight to Chicago, and I had a Little League game to catch in Hastings-on-Hudson. We walked east to Park Avenue to find her a taxi, as I was going to walk back to the Morningstar offices on 57th Street. And that's when it happened.

She slipped her hand into mine as we walked. It felt like the most natural thing in the world. And then, without saying a word, she turned and raised her face to mine and kissed me. At that moment, the world stopped spinning on its axis. My heart, however, spun like an ever spinning top, whirling around and around.

"Jerome, if you are as smart as I think you are, you won't say a word right now. Just listen." I guess I must have nodded my head like an obedient beast of burden.

"I think we could enjoy being together. I'm sure of it. I'm willing to give it a try if you are. I have always been attracted to you, Jerome. But now that we are bifurcating, I am just going to be bold enough to say that I want to be with you. Is that okay with you, *Saint Jerome*?"

Domino made "bifurcation" sound like something that was done in bed or on a bearskin rug in front of a blazing fireplace. As we continued east toward Park, once again walking hand in hand, I knew I had to say *something*. I wasn't used to being tongue-tied. But then again, I wasn't used to being with Domino.

"Domino, I don't know where you got that 'Saint' business, but I would like to spend some more time with you, too. So, if you can tear yourself away from Chicago and get back to New York City by Friday night, we can bifurcate all weekend."

We had stopped walking again so that we could

look directly at each other. It seemed that, even with the parry and thrust of double entendre and all the jocularity, something serious was going on, and we both knew it. Domino fixed me with those black-black eyes of hers, and I felt as if I were looking into the depths of some kind of bottomless black diamond mine.

"Jerome, I will be back from Chicago Friday afternoon. I recently purchased a town house in Battery Park City. If you can arrange for your boys to be otherwise engaged, why don't we bifurcate at my place? I'll cook if you bring the wine."

"Domino, if you cook, I'll bring a case of wine, although I'm not such a bad chef myself."

"Just bring a healthy appetite."

"I'm starving already."

"So am I, Jerome, and if you don't flag a taxi for me soon, I am going to be late getting back to Chicago and we'll both be hungry for the weekend."

Her smile seemed to come from another galaxy of pleasure, and I was already counting the moments until Friday as I flagged down the taxi. I opened the door and we kissed briefly once more, then I closed the door and she was gone.

And then she was back. And on that weekend in the summer of 2000, both of our lives changed. We made an easy and quick transition from lust to love to comfortable companionship. After a few months, she started spending time with my sons, who were as quickly enchanted as their father. Being with Domino was not always pure reverie, but the good times so far outweighed the tense times that soon we were spending every possible moment together.

By the summer of 2001, I felt comfortable enough for the boys to accompany Domino and me to the Cap Jaluca resort in Anguilla during the week before Labor Day and over the Labor Day weekend. It was one of the most wonderful weeks of my life, and as I lay on the confectioner's sugar-like sand with no phones, faxes or computers in sight, I felt it was almost possible to leave behind everything that being a partner in Morningstar entailed.

CHAPTER 53

Jerome

Eronel

Even as Domino and I started what turned out to be an all-consuming romance, I still had to take multiple business trips, both locally and to London. The trips to London were occurring with greater frequency, as Morningstar was becoming involved in more and more transactions that had a foreign nexus. In fact, going to London was starting to become a regular part of my routine and something I really didn't mind.

I recall starting to make those trips to London soon after Morningstar started getting high marks for some of the successful international deals in which we were involved. The routine that I soon established involved my taking a late-night British Airways flight out of Kennedy Airport, arriving early the next morning at Heathrow Airport. By flying first class, I was able to sleep in a reclining seat that became a bed, with drawn curtains that almost made me feel as if I was in my own private bedroom forty thousand feet over the Atlantic.

As soon as I exited Customs at the airport, I would go straight to the Mandeville Hotel, which was located in Marylebone Village right next to Regents Park and Hyde Park and within a few minutes' walk of Mayfair. The Mandeville is known as a fairly hip hotel, and its accommodations remain simply flawless.

As soon as I checked in to the hotel, I would unpack my bag, return phone calls, check e-mail and then head straight for the hotel's gym. After a good forty-five-minute workout, followed by a shave and a shower, I would be ready for the day and not too worse for the wear and tear and assaults of jet lag.

I do remember that, on one of my early trips, the lawyers from the local U.K. firm that we were using took me for a proper English lunch at the centuries-old Simpson's-in-the-Strand. It was an Olde English establishment, replete with dark oak and rich leather and what seemed to be an infinite number of tables piled high with slabs of beef and lamb—shoulders, joints, loins, legs and more shoulders. Not being a heavy meat eater, it took me more than a moment to find suitable fare on the menu.

I settled for some thinly sliced roast beef and boiled potatoes, and the few mugs of the accompanying beer that we had made for a pleasant meal. When my hosts suggested dessert, I decided to be the cooperative guest, and once again I searched the menu for something that would be pleasing but not too heavy. And that was when one menu item caught my eye, and I had one of my more memorable London conversations.

"Gentlemen, being a humble visitor to London, I know I am not totally familiar with all of the customs and traditions that you have here." I was lunching with two of the most talented business attorneys—solicitors, actually—Vincent Wesley and Charles Patterson of the Rippington & Wells law firm. Both were in their fifties, and with their stocky builds, ruddy complexions and thinning brown hair, they looked like they could have come straight out of central casting.

"Jerome, from what I know of you, you have been to our little island far, far too many times to be convincing in the role of confused tourist. What seems to be the problem?" Vincent's eyes were twinkling, and a good-natured smile was on his face.

"Well, let's put it this way. I am definitely *not* about to order this item on the menu." I said this while pointing inside the leather-bound book that contained pages and pages of selections for lunch, dinner and dessert. "But curiosity compels me to ask, what the hell is 'spotted dick'? I have no idea what it is, but I am sure that neither of you two good gentlemen will ever be able to say that they saw Jerome Hardaway with a mouthful of 'spotted dick.' Still, what the hell is it?"

Vincent and Charles collapsed into paroxysms of laughter that continued for at least two full minutes. I had asked my query in the nature of a jest, but I had no idea that my question would be the source of such unbridled hilarity. After sipping some water and wiping the tears from his eyes with a table napkin, Charles was finally able to speak.

"Jerome, you should get the Queen's Cup for Comedy, truly you should! You just have to get some culture over on the other side of the pond. You really do. I don't know what's on your dirty Yankee mind, but spotted dick, my good man, is simply a steamed suet pudding containing currants. It's usually served with custard. And just for the record, my good man, 'spotted' refers to the currants, which look like spots when they are served. And 'dick,' I am sorry to disappoint you, my good man, is simply a corruption of the word 'dough.'"

At this point, impending gales of laughter would not let Charles continue, and Vincent had to pick up where Charles had left off. "So you see, you can have all the spotted dick that you want here in London, and we'll never tell." And with that, Charles and Vincent both collapsed into another fit of laughter at my expense.

"Gentlemen, let's just say that I remain firm on my original point. You will never be able to say that you saw me eating spotted dick in London or any place else." And with this, we all laughed at the silly joke and play on words that provided us with some respite from the tedium of business that day.

Over the next few years, Morningstar wound up doing a lot of business with Rippington & Wells, and I got to see a lot of Charles and Vincent. Indeed, by 2000, Rippington & Wells had opened an office in New York City, as several top London firms had done by that time. Rippington & Wells chose a suite of offices in the World Trade Center, and I had occasion to meet with Charles and Vincent in their new offices on several occasions when they came from London to New York.

There were several occasions when, after meeting with Vincent and Charles at their World Trade Center offices, I would invite Domino to join me for lunch at Windows on the World, the restaurant at the very top of World Trade Center Tower Two.

Domino and I never tired of eating at Windows on the World. It seemed like we could never go there enough.

CHAPTER 54

Gordon

These Foolish Things

It didn't take me long to get back into the swing of things. Once I got back to work at Morningstar, it was like I had never left. And as I returned to full health and full strength, I could focus on the plans I had concocted while lying in my hospital bed.

Part of the plan depended on my being enormously successful with Morningstar. As long as I was bringing in big money for the firm, there was every reason for Diedre and Jerome and even Paul to grow more and more comfortable and less and less vigilant.

And so, I dusted off my old contacts and made new contacts. Within a few months, the corporate and municipal deals were rolling in to Morningstar. Before long, we were hiring additional personnel, and while the firm already had offices in Atlanta, Los Angeles and Chicago, offices were soon slated to open in Miami and Washington in 2001. I supported Jerome's idea that we add Johannesburg as our foreign office along with London, and it was clear that all of these things would be happening, and happening soon.

I didn't spend a lot of time around Ray Beard at first. He was understandably a little gun-shy about being seen with me. Also, he was truly driven to prove to Jerome and everyone else that he had not only recovered from his physical challenges, but that he was still the golden boy who was destined for huge success.

But, as time progressed, and as success begat success, both time and circumstance brought Ray and me into closer contact. And, before too long, we were working on deals together, pitching new clients together and working on long-term strategies for Morningstar.

By the latter part of 2000, it wasn't unusual to see Ray and me working late on various projects. And no one thought anything of just the two of us going to meetings to secure new business for Morningstar. Diedre and Jerome were just too busy to go to every meeting with me. Add to the mix the fact that the new financial success that I had brought to the firm, and soon there was no reason for anyone to worry about what I was doing or where I was going. Whatever it was and wherever it was, it was clearly going to be good for the firm.

That was why, when Ray Beard and I were flying the Delta Shuttle back to New York from a day of meetings in Washington at the end of the summer of 2001, no one even began to suspect that the fall of the House of Morningstar was at hand. I had already put together a complicated and foolproof scheme, but I needed someone like Ray Beard to help me complete the plan.

Ray might have been everybody's golden boy, but it didn't take me long to bring him onto my side. By the time the flight landed at LaGuardia Airport, he was a full partner in my plan.

If everything went the way that I had planned it, the second Tuesday after Labor Day 2001 would be the last day that Morningstar Financial Services would be in business.

CHAPTER 55

Paul

Blues for Pablo

From the moment that Diedre, Jerome and I concluded our meeting at Morningstar and it was decided that Gordon could return to the firm, to say that I had my work cut out for me would have been a monstrous understatement. I had to revise literally every document related to the existence of Morningstar. And just about every change I made in an effort to protect Jerome, Diedre and Morningstar was subject to negotiation with Gordon's personal attorney.

Solomon DeSouza was a legend among practicing lawyers in New York City. Born in Spain during the civil war in that country, he had the misfortune of making a wrong turn while escaping that country with his parents. He wound up on a train to

Poland instead of France, ultimately becoming a survivor of the Warsaw Ghetto and Auschwitz.

He emigrated to the United States after the war and went to City College and Harvard Law School, and became a lawyer specializing in handling the very private matters of the rich and famous, as well as of the rich and infamous. High-ranking members of the mafia and drug overlords from Colombia sought out his services on the most discrete matters. He left it to other lawyers to appear in court and on television.

Solomon DeSouza was rarely seen in public and was never quoted in the newspapers or photographed. When waves of indictments swept through Wall Street in the eighties and nineties, there were more than a few very senior executives who found themselves on the same freight elevator ascending to the top-floor SoHo loft where DeSouza lived and kept his offices.

His specialty was negotiating and completing complicated transfers of assets, as well as structuring very private ownership and partnership arrangements. My understanding was that he had handled all of Gordon's personal business for years, and that he might be the one person in the world other than Gordon who knew exactly what Gordon was really doing at any point in time.

Working with Solomon DeSouza was like spending an eternity with Yoda, the wise and all-knowing character from *Star Wars*. He had an adage or oblique quote for just about every occasion. And he didn't just know every trick in the book. He knew about tricks and books of which I had never even heard.

Negotiating with Solomon was exhausting and educational, and I was so very glad when we finally concluded the arrangements that resulted in Gordon returning to Morningstar. But I could never shake the feeling that Solomon and Gordon had somehow gotten the better of me, even though I was sure that I had covered all the bases, dotted all the i's and crossed all the t's. It was a nagging feeling that I didn't enjoy and that wouldn't go away.

CHAPTER 56

Kenitra

'S Wonderful

Time is an amazing element. It cannot be seen or held, but it can certainly be felt. And the effects of time were nothing but positive for me after witnessing Gordon's revival at New York Hospital and then fleeing back to California. I was so very thankful that Sture came with me to Los Angeles that very first day, and I was even more thankful that he was able to start coming to California for about a week every two to three weeks.

There is very little that is good about a long-distance relationship. But I found that missing him made me want him, and that seeing him made me miss him and want him even more. We were never together long enough to find the time to argue about much. There was only enough time to savor and enjoy and love each other for every waking hour and even in our dreams.

Sture was a wonderful lover. And Sture was a wonderful friend. And although not a day went by without a shiver of fear coursing through my body at the mere thought of Gordon being alive and awake, Sture made me feel safe and Sture made me know that he would protect me. Knowing that he cared was enough to make me know that tomorrow always had a chance of being a better day. And I loved him for that as well.

By the summer of 2001, Sture had spent so much time in California that he had started to explore the idea of opening a Dorothy's By the Sea there. Actually, it was an idea that I had suggested to him as we were having coffee one morning while watching the dawn sun reflect off the western shores of the Pacific Ocean. Of course, I did have my ulterior and rather transparent motives for making such a suggestion.

"Kenitra, you do realize that the restaurant business in LA is fundamentally different from the restaurant business in New York." I always enjoyed it when Sture adopted that faux professorial tone. And I loved being this teacher's pet.

"Sture, how different could it be? After all, a restaurant is a restaurant is a restaurant, right?" I had an idea of what he was talking about, but I enjoyed our banter, and awaited his response. It didn't take but a moment.

"Well, in New York, restaurants have to succeed based on the cuisine, the quality of the food, the ambience and the presentation. In LA, there is the additional factor of celebrity. Unless and until there is sufficient celebrity support and presence, even the finest restaurant will only be a best-kept secret in this town." I knew that what Sture was saying was true, and waited for him to continue. "It would take a lot of research and a tremendous networking effort for something like Dorothy's to work out here. And, Kenitra, don't think for a moment that I don't realize that your 'suggestion' is part of a devious plot to get me to move to California. And don't think for a moment that I wouldn't do it. But under only one condition." He was now smiling that smile that made me melt like butter on a plate on a picnic table on a hot summer day. Slowly, but surely.

"And what might that condition be, Snow Cone?"

"You will have to say 'please,' and very nicely."

I had an idea of where this conversation was headed, and I put my coffee cup down and got up from the table. As I did, my robe just seemed to have a mind of its own, and it fell to the floor. I wasn't wearing anything else.

"Well, if that's the way you feel about it, come with me to the bedroom, and you will hear 'please' as many times as you like."

We both smiled, and we both headed to the bedroom. And, we both said "please" and "thank you" many times that morning.

CHAPTER 57

Paul

Coming Home Baby

During the year or so after Gordon rejoined Morningstar, so many things were happening simultaneously and quickly that I felt like I was caught in some kind of madcap hurricane where time and circumstances incessantly flew by. Morningstar remained my biggest and most important client, and with the addition of Gordon and Ray, business seemed to increase exponentially. So many new transactions required me to add lawyers to my office, and the activity was time-consuming and all-consuming.

I continued to work for other clients as well. The new and existing business kept me busy. I was extremely busy, but not extremely happy.

For one thing, it became a daily battle to find a

way to spend time with PJ. Now that his third birthday had passed, it seemed like every day and every
moment were precious. I was increasingly conscious of the passage of time when it came to my
son, time that could never be recovered no matter
how many clients I had, no matter how much
money I amassed.

He continued to be a treasure and a pleasure. It
was a wonder watching him transform into his own
person. But that person needed guidance and love
and teaching and nurturing, and it was hard to
give him all of those things when I was on a plane
to California or hunched over a conference table
on West 57th Street late at night.

He was a young black boy who would one day
become a black man in America. He was going to
be in a combat mode for most of his life, combat-
ing prejudice and bias and racism, battling self-
doubt and the doubts of others. Not only have I
always had every confidence that my son would
survive, but I have always had every confidence
that he would prevail and succeed. But it would be
a lot easier for him to succeed if I could somehow
make sure that he was prepared for all of these bat-
tles in the near future.

I tried to compensate by going home early
enough to spend time with him before he went to
sleep, and by working from my home office until
all hours of the night. I forced myself to get up before dawn on a regular basis so that I could get a start
on the business day and still wake PJ and fix his
breakfast and read to him and start to introduce
him to the learning wonders of the world—read-

ing, counting, using the computer and absorbing the world around him. Time with my son was always the best time of the day.

The brutal reality of the day having only twenty-four hours meant that I had less and less time to simply sit back and relax. Leisure time was an unknowable luxury that I vaguely remembered. I chalked that phenomenon up to the price of fatherhood and tried to move on.

Diedre was so engrossed in running the new and improved Morningstar Financial that sometimes it seemed as if we had agreed to a trial separation. Outside of the occasional meeting at Morningstar, we would see each other briefly in the morning and in the evening. I know that she was frustrated at not being able to spend even the small shreds of time with our son that I was able to carve out of a more flexible schedule. I also know that she was challenged and excited by the opportunity to take Morningstar to even greater heights.

The result of these competing challenges and demands was that we rarely saw each other. Romance and passion seemed faint and distant memories, and soon the reality was that the only things that we had in common were Paul Jr. and Morningstar.

Meanwhile, I had never seen Jerome happier or more energized. His romance with Domino Oakley blossomed, and after the enervating years of Charmaine's illness and death, he seemed like a new man. They spent as much time together as two committed professionals could manage, and as their relationship became more serious, and more public, he introduced her to his sons, who bonded with her almost immediately. She didn't become their surrogate mother or stepmother. She became the woman who made their father happy and the "other" presence to balance out all of that testosterone when Jerome and the two boys got together.

For her part, Domino seemed to enjoy her new role. She continued to be as gorgeous and glamorous as ever. But I had to confess to experiencing a feeling of shock and surprise when Jerome would tell me about weekends that she would spend bike riding and horseback riding and going to baseball games with him and the boys. Just like every aspect of life, I don't think either of them knew exactly where their relationship was heading, but they both seemed to like the direction in which it was going.

Jerome plunged into the challenges of the "new" Morningstar with gusto, and seemed to manage the presence of Ray Beard and Gordon Perkins as a new challenge that he embraced. Jerome's energy and confidence were contagious, and everyone at Morningstar seemed to be affected by them. And the results of this particular brand of contagion were obvious in the increased growth and productivity and profits of the firm.

Kenitra had found it best for her sanity to stay in Los Angeles. Gordon kept to his promise and refrained from contacting her in any way. Gordon was never to be trusted, of course, but it seemed that, for the moment, he was truly being a man of his word.

Kenitra's romance with Sture continued to blossom. Sture racked up an incredible frequent-flyer total going to Los Angeles at least twice a month, and he always returned with a smile on his face that he couldn't hide. By the end of the summer of 2001, he was seriously exploring the idea of opening a Dorothy's in Los Angeles, and on behalf of the other partners in Dorothy's By the Sea, I gave him the go-ahead to try to come up with a plan that could work.

I knew that business and pleasure were equal parts of his motivation. And we both knew that Dorothy's West would work only if it made business sense.

As everyone returned from the 2001 Labor Day holiday, it was time for PJ to start going to his first pre-K class, and it was getting close to the time for Diedre and me to figure out how we were going to live our lives and whether it was going to be together or apart.

As everyone returned from the 2001 Labor Day holiday, Jerome and Domino continued to give love and romance a good name. It seemed that their future would become as entwined as their present, and that would be a good thing for both of them.

As everyone returned from the 2001 Labor Day holiday, Ray Beard and Monique Jefferson were getting ready to celebrate the first birthday of their son, Jerome Russell, and it seemed as if they couldn't be happier. Ray became a full-fledged member of the now wildly successful Morningstar team, and Monique's television career was reaching even greater heights since she had returned from maternity leave.

As everyone returned from the 2001 Labor Day

holiday, Quincy Holloway was on his way to becoming one of the truly high income leaders of the faith industry in America. After he sold the tape of Gordon's revival to three networks, Quincy also tried to market a videotape of the event on television and through mail order. However, Solomon DeSouza had one of his particularly lethal clients place a call to Quincy on Gordon's behalf, and that particular venture was put permanently on the back shelf.

Nevertheless, Quincy Holloway enjoyed his transformation from social leader and political gadfly and conscience of America to faith healer and spiritual icon. He was planning a September 2001 premiere of a cable television program in which he would offer to heal the ill (and the gullible) on a kind of pay-per-heal basis. I had heard that early estimates of the net revenues to Quincy were in the neighborhood of one million dollars a month. Clearly, the Lord works in mysterious ways.

As everyone returned from the 2001 Labor Day holiday, Gordon continued to be Gordon. I had my monthly meeting with Solomon DeSouza to confirm that Gordon was adhering to all the terms of the revised partnership agreement, and I had just reported to Jerome and Diedre that everything seemed to be in order.

The first week after Labor Day was uneventful. The first Monday after Labor Day 2001 was also pretty ordinary, at least in the morning.

On the afternoon of September 10, 2001, everything changed. Forever.

CHAPTER 58

Diedre

Odds Against Tomorrow

There are some events that I will never forget. I will never forget my first kiss. I will never forget wearing my first pair of high heeled shoes. I will never forget the birth of my son.

And I will never forget the feeling in the pit of my stomach when I saw Jerome, Ray and Paul walk unexpectedly into my office late in the afternoon of that September Monday. The look on their faces told me at once that they were not coming to share good news. The absence of Gordon gave me a pretty good idea of what the source of the bad news might be. I braced myself.

"I'm guessing this is not an early start to happy hour."

Jerome nodded grimly as the three of them sat in chairs arranged in front of my desk.

"What on earth is the problem this time?"

"Diedre, we have some real problems—a crisis, really. But it's best to let Ray begin." Jerome took the lead in opening the discussion. I could tell that the three of them had already had some conversation on the subject at hand, and I wanted to be brought up to speed as quickly as possible. I could feel my heart beating like a trip-hammer.

"Go ahead, Ray. Tell Diedre what you told Paul and me a few minutes ago." Jerome was as angry as I had ever seen him. He almost spit the words out, and Ray hesitated for a few moments before starting. He sat in his chair staring at the floor as he spoke, never looking at any of us.

"You know I started working on projects with Gordon soon after he began working here. Jerome knows that I reported the details of everything I knew about Gordon's activities with the firm. Gordon knew it as well, and for several months, everything seemed to be going well." Ray paused and seemed to be trying to decide whether to continue.

"Then, a few months ago, while we were working on a presentation in D.C., Gordon suggested that I join him in what he called a Grand Plan. His plan entailed setting up a new firm—New Gibraltar Associates is the name—and draining all the accounts of Morningstar through some kind of sophisticated cyber-hacking arrangement that he had been setting up. He also wanted to poach as many of the Morningstar clients as possible, and that's where I was supposed to come in."

I sat in stunned silence, listening to Ray's every word. This was our worst nightmare come true.

Ray pressed on, and I continued to listen, trying to keep a grip on my nerves and my emotions and my temper.

"All of you have been so great in giving me a second chance, I thought that the best thing that I could do was play along with Gordon until we got to some critical time where you would need to know what was going on so that you could protect the firm and stop Gordon. Well, that critical time is now."

I could see that Paul was waiting with diminishing patience to get into the conversation.

"It turns out that Gordon has already set up offices for Gibraltar Associates in the World Trade Center. Ray is supposed to get key client information on disks this evening and deliver them to Gordon in the morning. I gather Gordon's hacking job is supposed to go into effect at ten o'clock tomorrow morning, at which time all of the Morningstar accounts will be drained, as well as every personal account of yours—Jerome and Diedre—that he can identify."

The plan was so unreal and so brutal that it was pure Gordon. To say I was stunned would only begin to describe how I felt. At this point, Jerome chimed in.

"Diedre, we have to move, and move quickly. I asked Paul to come by as soon as Ray told me about this, and clearly, we need to come up with a plan."

I snapped out of my dreamlike state and tried to think clearly.

"Paul, you need to call Gordon's counsel and tell him that we know about Gordon's plan and that we will exercise all of the penalties in our part-nership agreement—effective as of now."

"I already called DeSouza, Diedre. All of his lines are disconnected. I have an associate going to SoHo to check on his office, but I am betting there is nothing there but dust balls and packing boxes."

"Great. Just great. In that case, Jerome, you need to call your forensic security firm and make sure that all of our accounts—and I mean *all* of our accounts—are encrypted, protected, whatever the hell that needs to be done, and that it is done now, right now!"

"I will get on it right now, Diedre, but we need something more. Tell me what you think of this idea."

And Jerome laid out a plan that would have Ray go to the World Trade Center the next day as ap-pointed. He would go with dummy disks that, in-stead of having Morningstar details, would contain a series of viruses that would effectively cripple all of the computer operations of the new firm. That would be when we would have the federal agents come through the door of Gibraltar Associates.

And that would be the time that we would call Gordon one last time. Ten o'clock seemed like a good time for a phone call.

We all agreed, and got to work. There was a lot to do before the morning of September 11 was upon us.

CHAPTER 59

Paul

Goin' Out of My Head

Jerome, Diedre and I were in the Morningstar offices by seven o'clock the next morning. It was like we were in the middle of some military operation, and in some ways, that was the case.

I had already alerted the U.S. Attorney for the Southern District of New York, and FBI agents would be coming to the Gibraltar offices in the World Trade Center at ten. Jerome and Diedre had already completed affidavits in support of their complaint against Gordon and Gibraltar.

Jerome had been up much of the night with his security technicians. All the Morningstar (as well as his and Diedre's) accounts had been moved and protected and encrypted. Mine were similarly protected for good measure. Attempts to tamper with the old accounts would be traced immediately.

Ray had been given the dummy virus disks and was to get to the World Trade Center at nine. Then our plan would go into effect. And then hell came to earth.

As the three of us sat in silence and nine o'clock approached, we were surprised when we were told that Ray was on the line. It was much too early. I punched the speakerphone button.

"I don't know what's going on!" There was pure panic in Ray's voice, and all kinds of noise and sirens in the background. "Maybe it's a bomb! An earthquake! I have no idea what!"

"Ray, get the hell out of there now! Right now!" Paul told him the only thing that made sense. I turned on the television in my office, and Jerome bolted from the room in search of some privacy as I realized he was dialing Domino's number on his cell phone.

Within minutes, the news reports started to make some sense out of the madness. A plane had crashed into one of the World Trade Center towers, seemingly on purpose. Soon both towers were on fire, and people were jumping out of windows. Later, a jet crashed into the Pentagon. Clearly, all hell was breaking loose.

Paul ran out of the office to go the few blocks north to get PJ, who was at a YMCA pre-K class. I was never so happy to see the two of them as I was at that moment. At about the same time, Jerome came back into the office with tears in his eyes and a smile on his face.

It turned out that Domino did indeed have an early morning meeting at her offices in the World Trade Center. But she had forgotten her favorite

Bobbi Brown lip gloss and had gone back downstairs to the World Trade Center mall to get a replacement when what turned out to be the plane hit the first of the Twin Towers. Bobbi Brown had saved her life!

The FBI agents had not made it to the World Trade Center. None of them was ever at risk as a result. And no one involved in our plan had gotten to the Gibraltar offices. Jerome did check, however, and no efforts had been made to tamper with any of the Morningstar accounts that morning. Even Gordon couldn't have planned for the events of September 11, 2001.

Ray never made it into the towers either and, therefore, was able to get one of the last subways going north before the system was shut down. He made it into the office at around noon, and we all sat around the television for the rest of that terrible day. And we all wondered about two things.

We all wanted to know what was actually happening. And we all wanted to know what had happened to Gordon.

CHAPTER 60

Kenitra

Impressions

Sture happened to be in Los Angeles on September 11, 2001. It was six in the morning when the first jet crashed into the World Trade Center. We had gotten up early, planning to take a run along the beach. We just happened to catch the news on television as we were putting on our running gear. By the time the second plane hit, we were both transfixed.

The horror and the destruction were almost impossible to comprehend. The reports were apocalyptic. The sights were horrific.

And then we saw both of the towers collapse. As we continued to stare at the television in disbelief, the phone rang. There was no mistaking the voice

through the static and the sirens and the screaming in the background.

"Not yet, Kenitra. Not just yet. I'll see you again."
And then the line disconnected. And then I
screamed.

Stay tuned for a helping of
Lutishia Lovely's new series following the
hot tempers and tantalizing temptations of a
family whose restaurant is *the* place for a
tasty meal. . . .

Taking Care of Business

Coming in April 2012 from Dafina Books

Here's an excerpt from *Taking Care of Business* . . .

All was quiet on the West Coast front. And all was cozy in Bianca Livingston's world as she lay cuddled up next to Xavier Marquis, her husband and the love of her life. Had it only been seventy-two hours ago when she thought she'd go crazy?

Just three short days before this moment, Bianca had stood in the center of TOSTS—her pride and joy—ready to pull out the hair she'd decided to grow long again. The chic, quaint eatery on Los Angeles's west side, formally named Taste of Soul Tapas Style, was two days away from its one-year anniversary celebration. The place had been in chaos. The truffle, caviar, and special champagne shipments had all been back-ordered, the cleaners had destroyed the new wait staff uniforms, and the chef had been called away due to a death in his immediate family. The stress had brought on the unexpected arrival of Miss Flo, Bianca's monthly, complete with bloating, cramps, and a pounding headache. What was a sistah to do?

Put on her big-girl panties and make it happen, that's what. What other choice was there?
Forty-eight hours ago, Bianca had huddled with
her assistant and the sous chef, who'd then called
all over America until they found last-minute sup-
plies of truffles, caviar, and bubbly. After ripping
the cleaners a new a-hole, Xavier had called in a
favor from a designer friend and had ten new uniforms whipped up posthaste. Finding a selfless
bone in her weary body, Bianca had flowers delivered to the funeral home that housed her chef's
brother and Miss Flo, who'd shown up two weeks
early due to stress, had vanished just as quickly as
she'd arrived.

Twenty-four hours ago, Bianca had finished
her day at the second LA Livingston Corporation
establishment, the increasingly popular soul food
restaurant, Taste of Soul. She'd spent two hours
on a conference call with her brother, Jefferson,
and the finance department at corporate head-
quarters; overseen a fiftieth birthday luncheon for
a party of twenty-five; and soothed the soul of a
hapless vegetarian, who was losing her mind because she'd eaten the cabbage and *then* realized
that this particular selection was seasoned with
smoked turkey legs. Bianca had found it ironic
that sistah-girl had eaten the entire plate before
making this observation, demanding her money
back and threatening lawsuits. Not to mention
that she'd somehow missed reading the ingredi-
ents to the Chaka Khan Cabbage side dish clearly
listed on the menu. Bianca was furious, but had
too much work and too little time to argue. She'd
given the emoting customer a gift certificate for

two free dinners and a menu to take home so that she could study it before placing her next order. With a bright smile to hide her frustration, Bianca had asked Ms. I-Haven't-Eaten-Meat-In-Twenty-Years to pay particular attention to the items with a small *V* beside the name, identifying them as vegetarian dishes.

Eight hours ago, Bianca had linked arms with her husband and officially welcomed the guests to TOSTS' one-year anniversary. Tickets for the evening's event had been steep, six hundred and fifty dollars, but the price included an all-you-can-eat buffet, a champagne fountain (filled with the double-priced bubbly that had to be rush-ordered and Fed Ex'd to the event), and an intimate evening with the night's entertainment, John Legend. As if pleasing the palate and the auditory senses weren't enough, the tickets were also tax deductible, with part of the proceeds benefiting a soup kitchen. Following in the footsteps that the Taste of Soul founders, Marcus and Marietta Livingston, had set, the establishments Bianca managed did their part in making the communities around them a better place.

An hour ago, Bianca had kicked four-inch-high stilettos off her aching feet, slid a Mychael Knight designer original off her shoulders, separated herself from a Victoria's Secret thong, and eased into the master suite's dual-marble shower. Seconds later, Xavier joined her.

"*Mon bien-aimé de chocolat,*" Xavier murmured as he eased up behind Bianca and wrapped her in his arms. "You are the chocolate on the menu for which my heart beat all night long." He took the sponge from her hand and began soaping Bianca's body from head to toe.

"Umm, that feels good," Bianca said. She leaned back against her husband's wide, firm chest. Moments before, she'd been dog tired, but now her husband's ministrations were filling her with new, lusty energy. She wriggled her soapy body against his, and was immediately rewarded with a long, thick soldier coming quickly to attention. They made quick work of the cleaning process before Xavier lifted Bianca against the cool marble wall and joined them together in the age-old dance of love. The contrast of the cool marble, hot water, and even hotter desire swirled into a symphony with a melody known by Xavier and Bianca alone. This was their first time together in almost seventy-two hours. Ecstasy came quickly, and then they climbed into bed for an encore.

Five minutes ago, Bianca shouted out her second hallelujah, or more like an "uh uh uh oh oh oh yes yes yes . . . ahhh." Xavier, the quieter of the two lovers, had shifted rhythms from second to third gear, before picking up speed and heading for his own orgasmic home. He hissed, moaned, squeezed Bianca tightly, and went over the edge. Too spent to move, Bianca had kissed Xavier on the nose, turned herself to spoon up against him, and vowed to take a shower first thing in the morning. She smiled as Xavier kissed her on the neck. *That man knows how to rock my world,* she thought as she looked at the clock. It was 4:45.

At 4:50, a shadowy figure crouched along the

buildings on Los Angeles's west side. He stopped, looked both ways, and walked purposefully toward a door on the other side of the alley. It was the back door to TOSTS. In less than one hour, Bianca Livingston's world would get rocked again.